Amish
FRONT PORCH
Stories

18 Short Tales of Simple
Faith and Wisdom

WANDA E
BRUNSTETTER
JEAN BRUNSTETTER
RICHELLE BRUNSTETTER

SHILOH RUN PRESS
An Imprint of Barbour Publishing, Inc.

Print ISBN 978-1-64352-189-3

eBook Editions:
Adobe Digital Edition (.epub) 978-1-64352-191-6
Kindle and MobiPocket Edition (.prc) 978-1-64352-190-9

Cover Design: Greg Jackson, Thinkpen Design

Published by Shiloh Run Press, an imprint of Barbour Publishing, Inc., 1810 Barbour Drive, Uhrichsville, Ohio 44683, www.shilohrunpress.com

Our mission is to inspire the world with the life-changing message of the Bible.

 Member of the
Evangelical Christian
Publishers Association

Printed in United States of America.

Contents

But the fruit of the Spirit is love, joy, peace, longsuffering,
gentleness, goodness, faith, meekness,
temperance: against such there is no law.
GALATIANS 5:22–23

Love

SIMPLE ACTIONS

by Wanda E. Brunstetter

The tip of Anna Hostettler's pencil broke when she picked it up to write in her journal. She set it aside and grabbed another one. An ink pen would have worked better, but Anna preferred a pencil with an eraser. It gave her the freedom to delete anything she'd written or changed her mind about.

> *Like so many other days this past week, today has not been good. The temperature outside is soaring, and the humidity has become so thick I can barely breathe. While I was downstairs doing the laundry this morning, one of the cats got into the house and ate the bowl of cereal I'd left on the table. Then on the buggy ride home from the grocery store, my horse threw a shoe, and now I have a headache.*

Anna lifted her pencil from the page and reread the words she'd written. *Not a very positive journal entry.*

She quickly erased every one of her sentences. *I need to focus on something positive.* Anna tapped her pencil against her chin. *Let's see now. . . . What good things have happened in my life today?* Anna began writing again:

> *The whole-wheat bread I made this morning turned out nice and fluffy. When I went shopping after lunch, I saw my friend Margaret, and we had a nice talk. We decided to meet for lunch one day next week. I am certainly looking forward to that.*

Anna kept adding to the list of good things that had happened until a knock on the door interrupted her journaling.

Rising from her chair, she went to answer it and found her widowed English neighbor, Lucy Perkins, standing on the porch, wearing a dour expression.

"Good afternoon, Lucy." Anna smiled. "How are you doing today?"

"I'd be fine if your cats would quit coming into my yard." A vein in the elderly woman's forehead protruded. "They've been digging around in my flower beds again, and I'm tired of it."

"I'm sorry, Lucy, but our cats are free to roam outside or in the barn. They help to keep the mice population down."

Lucy's steel-blue eyes narrowed. "Can't ya keep 'em in the house?"

"My husband, Amos, has an allergy to cat hair, and he'd never stand for them being in the house all the time." Anna thought about the incident this morning when their calico cat had snuck in. It was a good thing Amos wasn't home at the time.

"*Humph!*" Lucy's pointy chin jutted out.

"Have the cats damaged your plants or flowers?"

"Well, no, but they could." Lucy's face tightened as she crossed her skinny arms. "And another thing. . . That noisy rooster of yours woke me up at the crack of dawn this morning with his boisterous cock-a-doodle-doing."

"I'm sorry, but it's normal for roosters to crow when the sun comes up." Anna shifted her weight, leaning against the doorjamb. *I should probably invite her in, but I'm not in the mood to listen to any more of her complaints.*

"Well, I can see that I'm not getting anywhere with you." Before Anna could respond, Lucy whirled around and stomped off the porch. As her neighbor strode out of the yard, Anna heard her mumble something about a barking dog, and that if people were going to have animals they should keep them under control. Surely she couldn't have meant their mixed-breed terrier. Little Trixie didn't bark that much—only when there was something to bark about—like the intrusion of an unwanted neighbor trying to ruin someone's day.

Now that Anna thought about it, Trixie, who'd been lying under the shade of the maple tree, hadn't even budged when Lucy came into the yard, much less done any barking.

Anna's skin tingled as perspiration formed on her upper lip. *Why are some people so difficult to deal with?* She'd often wondered why her finicky neighbor had chosen to live in the country if she didn't like farm animals and all of their noises. Sometimes, like now, Anna wished Lucy would sell her home and move somewhere else. If that time ever came, Anna's days would certainly be more peaceful.

"How did your day go?" Amos asked when he returned home from his job at Keim Lumber in the village of Charm.

"It was busy." Anna frowned. "And somewhat frustrating."

"In what way?" Amos placed his lunch box on the kitchen counter.

"I was in the middle of writing a journal entry when our neighbor Lucy Perkins showed up." Anna opened her husband's lunch box and took out his empty Thermos. "And she didn't come over for a friendly visit."

"Uh-oh. Don't tell me. . . . She came over to complain."

Anna nodded.

"What was it this time?"

She rinsed out the Thermos before responding. "Let's see now. . . . Lucy's first complaint was about our cats."

"What about them?" Amos pulled out a chair and took a seat at the table.

"They were in her flower bed, and she was worried they might do some damage to her plants."

"How did you respond?"

Anna dried her hands and joined him at the table. "I said they are outdoor cats and we can't keep them inside because of your allergies."

"Did Lucy accept that explanation?"

"Not really. She also grumbled about our rooster crowing. Said his crowing woke her up at the crack of dawn."

Amos smiled. "Roosters do tend to crow when the sun comes up."

"I told her that, but it didn't get me anywhere. When Lucy left the yard, she was mumbling something about a dog barking and said if people were going to have animals they should keep them under control." Anna heaved a sigh. "I think Lucy enjoys fault-finding."

"Unfortunately, some folks are like that. Guess all we can do is pray for our neighbor, because she's obviously not a happy person."

"I suppose." Anna made no mention that she'd been hoping and even praying that her neighbor would move. It wasn't right to feel that way, but she couldn't seem to help herself.

Feeling the need to find a different topic, Anna asked Amos what he would like to have for supper.

"You know, I was thinking about asking if you'd like to go out for our evening meal." Amos reached over and placed his hand on her arm. "You work hard all week, and I think you deserve a night off from cooking."

Anna smiled. "*Danki*, Amos, it's thoughtful of you. Did you have a specific restaurant in mind?"

"How about the Farmstead restaurant? Since it's just a few miles from here, it won't take us long to get there."

"That sounds good to me. I'll go change into a clean dress, and then I'll be ready to go."

"And I need to take a shower." Amos sniffed his shirtsleeve. "*Jah*, after working all day, I definitely need to clean up."

◆——◆——◆

Anna picked up a plate at the buffet station and was about to start down the line when she felt a nudge. She turned and was surprised to see her friend Katie behind her. "*Guder owed.* I didn't know you were going to be here tonight."

Katie smiled. "Good evening. I had no idea you'd be here either."

"Amos decided I should have a night off from cooking." Anna pointed at the table where her husband sat. "He ordered something from the menu, but I prefer to sample a few choices from the buffet."

Her friend chuckled. "Same here." She looked across the room. "Andrew's sitting with our little ones while I get my food, and when I return to the table it'll be his turn. We chose something from the menu that we know the *kinner* will eat."

Anna envied Katie and Andrew. They'd been married only four years and had been blessed with two children. Anna and Amos had been married five years and still had no children. She had miscarried twice and had come to accept the fact that they may never have any babies.

"Have you had a nice day?" Katie asked as they moved down the line and put food on their plates.

"For the most part it went well—at least till our persnickety neighbor came over to complain."

Katie tipped her head. "What was she unhappy about?"

Anna told her friend everything her neighbor had said, as well as her responses. Then she leaned closer to Katie and whispered, "It upsets me when Lucy complains like that, and I really wish she would move."

Katie opened her mouth as if she was going to say something, but instead she hurried along, putting chicken, mashed potatoes, gravy, and green beans on her plate. "I'd better head over to my table now, Anna. I don't want to keep Andrew and the kinner waiting. I'll talk to you again soon."

"Oh, of course." Anna stepped aside so Katie could pass her and get through the rest of the line quicker.

I hope Katie didn't think I was gossiping, Anna thought. *It just felt good to express my feelings about Lucy, and what I said was the truth, so how can that be gossip?*

◆――――◇――――◆

That night, before Anna got ready for bed, she went to the kitchen and took out her journal, prepared to write down a few things that had taken place during the remainder of her day.

"What are you doing?" Amos tapped her on the shoulder. "I thought we were going to read from the Bible, like we normally do before going to sleep."

"Oh yes. I didn't forget. Just wanted to write down a few more events of the day before I forgot what they were." Anna snickered. "I'm not getting any younger, you know."

"Jah, right. You're just an old lady of twenty-six years." Amos rolled his eyes. "I'll go get the *Biewel* now."

While her husband went to the living room to get his Bible, Anna scrawled a few things down in her journal:

> *Amos and I ate supper at the Farmstead restaurant this evening. I saw Katie and told her about Lucy coming over to see me today. I bet she's glad she doesn't have a neighbor who complains about everything.*

Anna set her pencil aside a few seconds before Amos returned to the kitchen. "I'm finished writing in my journal, so you can go ahead and read a passage of scripture if you'd like." She smiled up at him.

Amos pulled out a chair next to her and opened the Bible. "I'll be reading from Proverbs chapter 11 tonight."

Anna listened as he read the first twelve verses. When he came to verse 13, Anna's conscience pricked her. " 'A talebearer revealeth secrets: but he that is of a faithful spirit concealeth the matter.' "

The words Amos quoted about being a talebearer stuck with Anna, even as he read all the way to the end of the chapter. *Did he choose this particular passage to read because he suspected I was being a gossip this evening?*

When Amos closed the Bible and bowed his head, Anna did the same. At the restaurant, she had talked to Katie about her neighbor, which was gossiping, even though the things she had said were true.

Maybe that's why Katie didn't say much in response to what I told her. Quite likely she thought I was wrong for talking about my neighbor behind her back. I need to get control of my tongue, Anna told herself. *Lord, help me to remember not to gossip about Lucy anymore. From now on, I'll just try to ignore my cranky neighbor.*

She opened her eyes. *In fact, I'll do my best to avoid talking to her at all. If Lucy comes over to the house, it might be best if I don't open the door.*

The following day, while Anna was baking a batch of cookies, she looked out the window and saw Lucy out in her yard. From what Anna could tell, her neighbor seemed to be chasing something, as she ran about the yard, alternating between shaking her finger and clapping her hands.

I'll bet one of our katze *is in her yard and she's trying to get it out.* Anna rolled some ginger-spiced dough into a ball and placed it on a greased cookie sheet. *Think I'll go outside for a closer look.*

Anna placed the baking sheet in the oven, set the timer, and went out the back door. It shouldn't take long to find out what was going on in her neighbor's yard, so she ought to be back in the house in plenty of time to get the cookies out.

So as not to look obvious, Anna picked up the garden hose and began watering her tomato plants. This area of the vegetable garden was closest to the fence and gave her the best vantage into her neighbor's backyard.

"Out with you! Get out of my yard, you pesky cats!" Lucy hollered.

The sound of the elderly woman's clapping could be heard all the way into Anna's yard.

Anna cringed. They had to be her cats, because she saw no sign of them in her own yard. For that matter, Anna hadn't seen any cats in the barn when she'd gone there this morning to tell Amos that breakfast was ready.

Should I go over to Lucy's and see if it's our cats she's chasing, or just let it go? Anna bit the inside of her cheek. *If I go over there, Lucy will start complaining again. No, I'd better leave well enough alone. If she keeps hollering at the* katze, *they'll eventually come home.*

Anna felt something cold and damp. When she looked down she realized she'd been watering her foot instead of the tomato plants. *Guess that's what I get for being a nosy neighbor.*

Anna pointed the nozzle at the plants and stood there until they were good and soaked. She was about to turn off the hose when Lucy shouted from across the fence: "Okay, you mangy cats, now get out of my yard!"

Anna chose to ignore the outburst and didn't even look her neighbor's way. Instead, she turned off the hose and went back inside.

When she entered the kitchen, Anna smelled smoke. "*Ach*, my *kichlin!*" She grabbed a potholder and pulled open the oven door. Every one of her ginger cookies was burned to a crisp.

She glanced at the timer and saw right away that it had already gone off. How long ago, she couldn't be sure. But one thing was certain—this batch of cookies was ruined. They weren't even fit to feed the hogs.

"Guess that's what I get for going outside to spy on the neighbor," Anna muttered. "Well, at least the first two batches of cookies I made this morning turned out okay. At least I'll have some to give Amos when he gets home from helping his brother put a new roof on his house."

Anna turned off the oven and set the burned cookies on a rack until they were cool enough to throw in the garbage can. Then she glanced out the window and spotted two of their cats leaping over the fence and into the yard. She bit back a chuckle. "Guess they got tired of Lucy shouting at them. I wish she understood that cats like to roam and there's nothing I can really do to keep them here."

"How'd it go at your brother's place today?" Anna asked when Amos arrived home in time for supper.

"It went well, but I'm tired and hungry." He sniffed the air. "What's that good smell?"

"I made your favorite—fried chicken." She motioned to the stove. "Since I wasn't sure what time you'd get here, I put the chicken in the oven to stay warm."

"Yum." Amos smacked his lips as he took a seat. "And what's the plan for dessert?"

Anna dropped her gaze. "I baked some ginger cookies today, but lost an entire dozen when they burned."

"I'm surprised. It's not like you to burn anything you're cooking or baking."

"Well, I did today."

"What happened?"

Anna explained, frowning as she finished telling him about the incident with the hose while watching the neighbor chase after the cats.

Wearing a thoughtful expression, Amos stroked his beard. "If it happens again, I'll go over there and ask if the cats have done any damage to her property and offer to pay for it if they have."

Anna shrugged her shoulders. "It's up to you, but when I talked to Lucy the other day, she said none of her plants had been damaged. I think she's not satisfied unless she finds something to complain about." Anna rose from her chair. "Why don't you clean up while I get a vegetable cooking to go with the chicken? By the time you're done, supper should be ready."

"Okay, sounds good." Amos got up and came around the table to give her a kiss. "I can hardly wait to sink my teeth into that chicken."

◆——◇——◆

"There's such a difference in the weather today." Amos pointed out the front of their open buggy at the clear blue sky. "The temperature's mild compared to a few days ago, and there's hardly any humidity at all."

"Jah, it's a pleasant change. It'll make it a lot easier to sit through three hours of church today too." Anna fiddled with the ties of her outer bonnet, making sure they hadn't come loose. One time when they were traveling in their open buggy, the horse had decided to go faster than usual, and her bonnet had fallen off.

"Daniel Schrock's woodshop has good ventilation. I'm sure we'll all be comfortable."

"I hope so. Remember two weeks ago when Aaron Troyer fell asleep and almost fell off the wooden bench he sat upon?"

Amos smiled. "If his brother, Melvin, hadn't caught hold of his arm, poor Aaron likely would have hit the floor."

"If he had, I bet our bishop would have kept right on preaching."

Amos chuckled. "You could be right."

They rode along quietly for a while, until Daniel's place came into view. While Amos got the horse unhitched from the buggy, Anna went to visit some of the women who had gathered outside the woodshop. The first person she spotted was her friend Katie.

After greeting the other women there with a handshake, Anna turned to greet Katie in the same way. This was a common practice before their church service, with the men greeting the men, and the women welcoming the other women in attendance.

"How are things going with you and your neighbor?" Katie asked.

"Better now that I've decided to ignore her."

Katie's brows furrowed. "Do you think that's the best way to respond to Lucy's complaints?"

Anna bobbed her head. "I figure if I don't say anything back, she'll eventually quit coming over with all her complaints."

As more women arrived, Katie went to greet them. Anna had a feeling her friend didn't approve of the way she'd chosen to handle the situation with Lucy. Well, that was okay. Katie might think differently if she lived next door to someone like Lucy.

"The sermons delivered in church today were sure uplifting," Amos commented on their return trip home. "I especially enjoyed the one our bishop gave on the topic of love from 1 John 4:12. I liked how he mentioned that as Christians we should let Christ's love blossom and produce abundant fruit in our lives."

"Yes, it was a good message," Anna agreed. "In fact, it gave me an idea to begin writing in my journal the simple actions I take each day to show love to my friends and family."

Amos glanced over at Anna. "It's good to show love to our family and friends, but what about our neighbors?"

Heat flooded Anna's cheeks. Ignoring Lucy and gossiping about her were not loving things to do. The only problem was, if Lucy kept complaining, Anna wasn't sure she could act in a loving way toward her neighbor. It was something she needed to pray about.

As Anna did the dishes on Tuesday morning, a hummingbird caught her attention. It seemed more aggressive than most she'd seen at the feeder. Every time another hummer flew in to eat, the bossy one would chase it away.

"Don't be so selfish and unkind." Anna tapped on the window, which of course caused all the hummingbirds to fly away.

Anna finished washing the dishes and reached for the towel to begin drying them. When she looked outside again, rain was coming down. She watched several seconds to see if it would quit, but the drops became heavier.

Remembering the clothes she'd hung on the line after Amos left for work that morning, Anna set the dishcloth aside, grabbed the laundry basket, and hurried out the back door.

While removing the laundry from the line, Anna noticed two wide-open windows on the side of Lucy's house.

Maybe I should go over and tell her about the windows. She might have opened them for fresh air this morning and forgotten. In addition to the rain that is no doubt blowing into the house, one of our cats might decide to leap in through the open window. Then Lucy will really have something to complain about. Anna would want someone to let her know if she'd left windows open when it was raining. She felt obligated to alert her neighbor.

Anna quickly removed her clothes from the line, dropped them into the basket, and set it on the covered porch. When she returned from Lucy's house, she would hang the damp clothes in the basement.

❖ ❖ ❖

Holding an umbrella over her head, Anna hurried to the house next door. When she stepped onto the porch, she closed the umbrella and held it in one hand while she knocked on the door with the other. When Lucy didn't answer, Anna went around back and knocked on that door.

Still no answer.

Now that I think about it, I haven't seen Lucy for two or three days. I wonder if she went somewhere and forgot to close the windows before she left. Anna was about to leave but decided to see if the door might be open. Some people left their doors unlocked during the day, and Lucy might be one of them.

Anna turned the knob, and when the door opened, she stepped inside. "Lucy! Are you here? It's me, Anna Hostettler."

No response.

Anna called Lucy's name several more times, but all was quiet. *She must have gone somewhere. I'd better close those windows for her before going home.*

Anna stepped into the living room and closed the first window. Fortunately, no rain had blown inside—just a few drops on the windowsill. She went to the second window and closed it. Turning to go, Anna heard a low moan. It sounded like it had come from a room near the back of the house.

As she headed in that direction, Anna heard the moaning again. Upon entering the bedroom at the end of the hall, she was surprised to find Lucy lying in bed. The poor woman's cheeks were bright red, but the rest of her skin looked as pale as her bedsheets.

"Don't come any closer. I'm sick with the flu, and I don't wanna give it to you." Lucy lifted her head then fell back against the pillow with a groan. "My throat hurts, I ache all over, and my whole body feels hot."

Anna noticed the empty glass on the small table by Lucy's bed. "How long has it been since you've had anything to drink?"

"I–I had some water last night, but nothing to eat for a few days."

Anna picked up the glass. "I'll fill this with water and get you something to eat." Anna hurried from the room before Lucy had a chance to respond.

In the kitchen, she found a can of chicken broth, which she opened and poured into a kettle. While it was heating on the stove, Anna got a clean glass from the cupboard and filled it with water. She also located a box of crackers in the cupboard which she set on a small tray next to a bowl. Once the broth was heated sufficiently, Anna poured it into the bowl. Placing the glass on the tray, she carried it into Lucy's bedroom and placed it on her nightstand. She handed the glass of water to Lucy.

"Drink some of this first, and then you can try some of the broth."

"Why are you being so nice to me when all I've done is complain and say mean things about your animals since you and your husband moved in next door?"

Anna thought about a verse of scripture Amos had read last night during their devotions: *"Thou shalt love thy neighbour as thyself,"* *Mark 12:31.* She had tried to ignore God's commandment, thinking she could simply ignore her neighbor, but now Anna knew she'd been wrong.

"I forgive you, Lucy, and I apologize for not being as good a neighbor as I should be. I'll try to check on you more regularly, and please feel free to call on me or my husband whenever you have a problem."

Tears welled in Lucy's eyes. "Thank you, Anna. Your kindness today has made me feel loved."

When Anna returned to her home after telling Lucy she would be back later to check on her, she took out her journal. Picking up her pencil, she wrote: *A simple action is all that is needed to show God's love to a neighbor.*

If we love one another; God dwelleth in us,
and his love is perfected in us.
1 JOHN 4:12

LOVE ISN'T PAINLESS

by Richelle Brunstetter

"A*ch nee!*" One of the brackets screwed into the wall gave way and dropped to the hardwood floor. The new rod, including the dark-green shade, crashed to the floor shortly after. "I need to find some longer screws to make that work," Charles muttered, wiping his hands against his trousers. *This is pointless. I'll get it done later.*

He vacated his bedroom, closing the door behind him. Covering his mouth to suppress a yawn, Charles made his way to the living room. The chair he rested in most days squeaked as he flumped against the cushion.

"I wonder what Lorinda would be saying to me right now," Charles mumbled under his breath, raising his head to observe the multicolored quilt hanging on the wall. "Probably that I get too frustrated when things don't go as I'd planned."

The beautiful quilt on the wall was made by someone Charles loved with all of his being. That person was his wife, Lorinda, and Charles thought of her every time he looked at it. They'd been married for two years before Lorinda passed away when her appendix ruptured.

Lorinda mentioned she had abdominal pain, and although Charles was concerned for her, he told Lorinda not to worry about it. It wasn't until Lorinda spewed reddish-green bile that Charles finally took initiative and got help. But while Lorinda was having her appendix surgically removed, complications occurred, and she moved on from this world soon after.

Charles squeezed the arm of the chair. *When the pain in her stomach didn't let up, I should have insisted she see a doctor. If I had been more attentive to her, she'd still be here with me.*

After Lorinda died, Charles promised himself he would never find love again. But since the beginning of the year, he had bobbled back and forth on that promise. While he did blame himself for Lorinda's passing, he still wondered if he would be given another chance to love someone. Charles hoped he could be more heedful for whoever it might be.

A thumping on the front door resonated through the house, and he grimaced. *Can't I be left alone for the rest of my living days?* Charles couldn't deny that he needed to quit feeling bad, and there was only one person who usually brought him out of it. Getting up from his chair, Charles trudged out of the living room, dragging his socked feet along the floorboards. He shivered. The fireplace in the house was sometimes not enough to keep him warm during the cold months. And it was only a couple of weeks into January.

When he opened the door, the brisk weather greeted Charles fiercely. "Afternoon, Dianna."

"Hello, Charles." The young Amish woman at the door was bundled up in a black shawl, a violet scarf around her neck standing in sharp contrast.

Dianna King, Charles's childhood friend, had stuck by him for many years—even through his depression when Lorinda died. As a child, Charles had found Dianna to be somewhat overbearing. She had a habit of teasing him—probably because he refused to respond to her. Even after he'd delivered countless insults in an attempt to push Dianna away, she kept pursuing a friendship with him. Eventually, Charles had given in, and they'd been friends ever since. In a lot of ways, he was grateful for Dianna's diligence, as he needed her friendship now more than ever.

She had witnessed what Charles went through when Lorinda passed away. After the funeral, Dianna comforted him and prayed for him often during his time of grief. Those first few months had been the worst, but Dianna came by often to give him support. Even now, two years later, she dropped by regularly.

He shifted his stance to move out of the doorway. "Come on in."

"Whew. *Sehr kalt* out there, isn't it?" She tapped her boots on the porch before stepping inside.

"Yes, it's cold."

Dianna held out a platter covered in plastic wrap. "I brought over some goodies."

"That was nice of you."

As Charles held the platter, she pulled off her scarf and coat, hanging them on the rack by the door, and slipped off her boots and scooted them against the wall.

Charles returned the platter to her, and the two friends entered the kitchen. Although what was on the plate was obscured by the plastic wrap, Charles could tell what it was.

"Whoopie pies." He chuckled. "You know me so well."

Grinning, Dianna set the platter on the counter and unraveled the plastic covering. "Well, I have known you for a good many years."

"You didn't have to make these for me."

"What? Who says they're only for you?" Dianna plucked one from the pile of what seemed to be over a dozen treats and bit into it. With her mouth full, she spoke. "We're sharing these."

Charles snickered. "Manners, Dianna."

"Oh, sorry." Swallowing, she shoved the rest of the treat into her mouth.

He held up a pumpkin whoopie pie. "They're so pathetic."

"Hey, that isn't very nice. I worked hard on them."

"What I meant was they're tiny. Nothing to do with the taste."

She laughed. "They are miniature whoopie pies. I know I usually make them bigger, but I made them that way so we could eat more and not get too full."

Munching the sponge-textured treat, Charles finished the rest of it and smiled. "Are we playing Scrabble again?"

"You know it."

"I'll go get the box." He grabbed a second treat before leaving.

"Meet you out in the dining room."

He went out of the kitchen to the utility closet near the back of the house. The closet was filled to the brim with board games and cards. Most of them were older games, but there were a few newer ones too.

Charles finished the whoopie pie, brushing away the crumbs from his hand. He slid the game off one of the other boxes and brought it out to where Dianna was seated.

She waited, cleaning her glasses with a cloth. "Ready for me to win again?"

"You've always been a good speller. I remember when we were kids and you could spell the most complex words off the top of your head." Charles put the Scrabble box on the table and began taking out the board and the game pieces.

"Charles, you know how to spell those words too." Leaning back in the chair, Dianna slid her glasses back on. "It just takes you centuries to spell them out."

She helped Charles turn all the tiles upside down on the table. After that, the two of them swirled the pieces in different directions, mixing them up thoroughly. Before they began playing, Dianna mentioned how rich-tasting the whoopie pies were, so Charles headed into the kitchen to bring her a glass of water to drink. Once he came back, she was already scarfing down a couple more of them.

They drew their first letters, and Dianna placed her tiles on the board. She had a good lead for a while, which Charles expected. But as they continued playing, not to mention munching on the miniature treats, he completed more words on the board. It helped that he kept drawing blank tiles that could be used as any letter. The game finally came to an end when all the tiles were drawn from the pile.

"Wow, you won this time." Dianna leaned closer to inspect the board. "Good job, Charles."

"*Danki,*" he muttered.

"Want to play again?"

Charles hit his heel against the leg of the table to wake his leg up. "I have some new window shades to hang in my bedroom, so. . ."

"Is something on your mind?"

"Huh? Nothing, Dianna. Why do you ask?"

She gave a half shrug. "It seems like something's eating away at you." Dianna leaned forward in the chair. "Want to talk about it?"

"It's not that big of a deal." Charles fiddled with the Scrabble tiles to avoid her gaze, but she stared intently at him through her glasses.

"Big deal or not," she insisted, "we're going to talk about it."

If only he were better at masking his emotions, then Dianna never would've known something was up. Charles tapped a letter on the wooden surface of the table. "I know Lorinda has been gone for a couple of years, but. . ." He released his pent-up stress with a chuckle. "Here I am, thirty years old, yet I'm still moping like a child."

Dianna blinked her hazel eyes before she responded. "There's nothing wrong with feeling sad, you know."

"I don't know. Perhaps I'd be less sad if I found someone and moved on with my life."

"If you feel ready to ask someone out, then you should go for it." Dianna pursed her lips. "You deserve to be happy."

"I promised myself that I wouldn't fall in love again. I can't forgive myself for ignoring Lorinda when she was in pain."

"That wasn't your fault, Charles."

"It was. My actions proved that I'm not reliable." He rubbed around his eyebrows in an attempt to stifle his headache. His fingers were somewhat sticky from the remnant of whoopie pie filling. "Maybe someone like me isn't suitable for love."

Silence greeted his statement, and Charles stared at the table, waiting for Dianna to respond. When at last he looked up, her eyes stared blankly into the distance. It seemed as though Dianna had wandered somewhere else in her thoughts.

"Dianna?"

"It's getting late. I should probably head on home before the next snowstorm hits." She scooted from the table.

Charles stood. "Are you okay?"

"*Jah*. Of course." Dianna smiled. "It was fun playing Scrabble with you again. Same time tomorrow?"

Charles clasped his hands behind his back. "Sure. And if you're okay with it, we could play chess instead. You know, to mix things up."

"Chess sounds good." Dianna's laugh seemed fragile as she walked to the front door and slid into her boots. She took down her coat from the rack and draped the purple scarf over her shoulders.

"You sure you're okay?" He leaned against the wall next to the door frame.

"I'm all right." Dianna strolled over to the counter and lifted the empty platter. "I can't believe we ate all those whoopie pies." She returned to the front door, and turning to him and smiling once more, she said, "*Gut nacht*, Charles."

The crisp air outside stung Charles's face as Dianna opened the door and immediately closed it behind her. He stood with his back planted against the wall. Then he went in the dining room and sat down at the table where they'd been playing the game. Frustrated, he swept his arm against the table, sending Scrabble tiles across the room. "Maybe I shouldn't have expressed my innermost thoughts to Dianna. Things were going just fine before that." He grabbed the tile bag and went around the room, picking up the scattered pieces. He put the rest of the game together and carried it back to the closet.

Sighing, Charles straightened his spine with a stretch. "Guess I'd better hang those shades before falling asleep tonight."

He returned to the living room and turned off the battery-powered light. Standing in the dark, he peered out the window into the night as the snow fell like salt from a shaker. *I hope I can get over my fear of loving someone again.*

He went back to his room, observing the mess that was scattered next to the wall. Rather than continuing the project, Charles fell into his firm bed. Eventually, he reached for the comforter at the foot of the bed, enfolding himself in the fabric.

Dianna was never courted by anyone. She's probably lonelier than I am. Yet I vent to her about all of this. He pressed his palms against his temples. *I must be the world's biggest doofus. She deserves better.*

A month later, Charles paced around outside his home after he finished taking care of his horses. He'd planned to go out for supper later that evening with Dianna, but there was something on his mind that got him wondering about her. Before Charles met Lorinda, he had considered the idea that Dianna might have feelings for him. Why else would she have come around so often? Even after they'd finished school, Dianna stuck by him when she could've moved on. Of course once Charles began courting Lorinda, Dianna, although friendly, had not tried to come between them, and to him, that confirmed their relationship was strictly platonic.

But during the past few weeks, Charles had realized his feelings for Dianna seemed to be changing. At first he tried to deny what was happening, convincing himself the change was a natural result of their being friends for so long and that he was mistaking his friendship with her as romantic feelings. After many days of pondering the situation and seeing Dianna more often, Charles could no longer accept his rationalizations.

He brushed his ear with gloved fingers. *I want to take my chance to be closer to her. But what if she doesn't have those same feelings for me? I could ruin everything between us, and I won't have my best friend anymore.*

Striding through inches of fresh icy snow, Charles went into his home. He took off his gloves and jacket right away and was set on taking a nap before Dianna showed up. But his fatigue was outweighed by his nervousness.

When he went over to his chair, rather than sitting on the cushions, Charles dropped to his knees, clasping his hands together. *Heavenly Father, I don't know if I should be honest with Dianna about my feelings for her. If we're meant to be together as a couple, please give me the strength to be attentive to our relationship. I'm afraid I'll mess things up, and I don't want to hurt her in any way. I want to always be there for her if she'll have me.*

Charles couldn't fathom why he hadn't prayed in quite some time. It was no wonder he had a lingering feeling of misalignment in his life. But as anxious as he was, Charles certainly needed to be trusting the Lord.

Later that evening, Charles and Dianna were seated at the restaurant for what felt like hours. They both went for the buffet rather than ordering off the menu, so they had an abundant choice of food to consume.

Charles ate his last spoonful of mashed potatoes, then gulped down his soda. He picked up his napkin and patted his mouth. "How was your food, Dianna?"

"I would say my empty plate shows how my food was." She clanked the side of her fork on the middle of the dinner plate. "It's kind of nice not having to make my own meal, you know?"

"Jah. I get it. I do enjoy cooking and all, but there's all the cleanup afterward. Besides, it takes up too much time."

"And what precious time are you sacrificing by making a delicious meal?"

"Napping time."

Dianna's fingers grazed her chin as she snickered. "I guess that is very precious."

They continued talking until the waiter came to the table and handed them their check. Now that their supper was finished, Charles's nerves struck him like someone strumming the strings of a guitar. He still wasn't certain if confessing his feelings to Dianna was the right decision.

No need to stress over it, he thought while he opened the restaurant door for Dianna. *There's always the next time we see each other if I can't do it tonight.*

On the way to Dianna's house, wispy flakes descended from the gray hue of the winter evening sky. They had planned to play another board game after he took Dianna home, but if the snowfall increased before reaching her place, they might not be able to play after all.

"Hey, Dianna?" Charles stroked his throat. "When was the last time you fell in love with someone?"

"Wh—why are you asking me such a question all of a sudden?" She tugged the violet scarf to the tip of her nose.

His heartbeat accelerated. He could almost bet his face was the shade of a cardinal's feathers. "It's just that you've never been courted by anyone, and I was curious to know why."

Instead of being graced with a response, he was met with the sounds of his horse treading along through the snowflakes. *I can't believe I even asked her that. What was I thinking?* He was about to apologize for what had come out of his mouth, when Dianna gave his jacket sleeve a tug.

"I sometimes feel that people can hurry into marriage without giving it a second thought." Dianna's voice sounded muffled as she spoke through the scarf, until she hooked her finger on it to uncover her mouth. "While it does work out for some married couples, I never wanted to risk marrying someone unless I knew he was the right person for me."

Charles tightened his grip on the reins. "So you've been asked out before?"

"More than one occasion."

"But you never dated any of them. I would remember if you had."

A visible puff of air escaped from her nose. "I knew God would bring me the right person and I would know who it was when the time was right."

"What if. . ." He moistened his dry mouth, giving himself a moment of reprieve from his nerves before speaking again. "What if who you are meant to be with was someone you've known for a long time?" Charles looked over at Dianna, although he couldn't see her expression in the darkened buggy. "Someone who has been there for you even when times were tough. Someone who motivates you to do things you wouldn't normally do on your own willpower."

She remained quiet.

"Dianna?" Charles heard her mumble something, so he lifted his hand and pulled the scarf down. She was giggling, and Charles felt his body heat rising. "What's so funny?"

"I wondered how long it'd be for you to admit your feelings."

Sputtering, Charles jerked his head back. "You knew?"

"Of course I knew. Like I've told you before. . .I'm good at knowing when something's up."

"Wait, so does that mean you have feelings for me as well?" Charles noticed his voice went up in pitch. He must sound hysterical to Dianna right now.

She slid off her glasses, pressing a palm against her eye. "Yes, I do."

Charles barked out a laugh. "How long?"

"For a while, Charles."

"Why didn't you say anything before?"

"I wanted to wait for you to come to terms with your feelings." Dianna put her glasses back on. "You were dealing with a lot of self-doubt."

"Still kinda am." He pushed against the seatback.

"Charles." She stretched her hand on the seat and inched closer to him. "Are you willing to give this a chance? I am aware of your concerns, but I'm willing to try to make this work if you are."

Dianna's reassurance was exactly what Charles needed to know this relationship was meant to be. His prayer had been answered, and there was no way he would let his opportunity pass by. He placed the reins in one hand and placed his other hand on hers.

"I–I'm willing to make things work." Charles savored the feelings of belonging that filled him.

Dianna rested her head on his shoulder as they traveled along the side of the road. Deep inside, Charles knew this was what God had meant for him. He did worry things would be awkward for a while, since they'd be more intimate with each other now, but he shook away those thoughts and enjoyed the moment of being cozy together in the buggy as the snow continued to fall.

"Charles, you know what's pleasant about all this?" Dianna asked.

"About what?"

"About us. None of this feels uncomfortable." She lifted her coat from the back of the seat. "Yet we've been officially together for a few weeks."

"I suppose knowing each other for years kind of prepared us, huh?"

"It doesn't feel strange. I've never been courted before, and I figured if I were to be, it would be nerve-racking. But not with you."

"I'm glad." An electric jolt traveled up his body. *I bet you're happy for us, Lorinda.*

For the most part, everything between them was like it always had been. Dianna still came over to his house to play board games, and they'd been going to the same restaurant almost every week. They went out again that evening, and when they left the restaurant, the sun was setting on the streets and buildings of the town.

Before they headed back home, they were going to walk around for a bit and pick up some things from a couple of the stores. The crosswalk sign flashed, indicating it was time for them to cross.

Dianna stepped off the sidewalk. "I'm very thankful to have you, Charles. I want—"

Thunk!

The sound resonated in his eardrums. A blaring horn made him cover his ears. The vehicle hightailed it out of there, and it took a few grueling seconds for Charles to realize what he had witnessed.

"Dianna!" The streetlights obscured Charles's sight as his knees collided with the asphalt. He gripped Dianna's shoulder, turning her over as carefully as he could. "No, please. This isn't. . . It can't be." Charles cradled her head.

Dianna's heart-shaped *kapp* wasn't covering her bun anymore, but he didn't bother to look for it. Her eyes were closed, and her body was as limp as the faceless doll from childhood.

"Is she okay?"

With his heartbeat pounding in his ears, Charles barely heard the voice behind him. He whipped his head around. "She got hit! She needs an ambulance!"

In a panic, the elderly Englisher dug into his pants pocket. "I'll call 911."

"Stay with me, Dianna." Charles looked back at her. His face sweltered as he suppressed the urge to sob. *This is my fault.* He pressed his teeth together. A cold bead of sweat trailed down the bridge of his nose. *I should have been paying attention. I could have stopped her from crossing.*

Not knowing whether Dianna's injuries were critical, Charles felt anxiety sweep over him at the possibility of losing someone he loved once more—all because he was not being as attentive as he should've been.

The suspense made Charles seek any form of comfort in the waiting room, so he resorted to pinching the brim of his hat between the pads of his thumbs. Many scenarios ran through his mind concerning the way this situation could play out. Initially, because of the shock of what he'd witnessed, he had almost forgotten the EMT's request to notify her next of kin about the accident. But as soon as he'd arrived in the emergency room, Charles had used one of the phones at the office to leave a voice message for Dianna's parents, although he wasn't sure how long it would take for them to visit their phone shack and get his report. He was the only one Dianna had for the time being.

A handful of people sat in the room with Charles. Some were alone, and others gathered with their spouses or children. One of the kids, who was playing with a stuffed animal, stopped and stared at Charles for a while. He paid no mind to it though, since he was used to having curious eyes gawking at him.

He still couldn't believe what had happened to Dianna. Charles was upset with the person who hit her, especially because the driver hadn't bothered to stop. There was no ice on the road to cause the vehicle to lose traction, so the driver had run a red light either because they weren't paying attention or because they were just too impatient to hit the brakes and wait. Charles was amazed at how insensitive people could be.

Dianna should've looked both ways before stepping off the sidewalk. But he understood why she hadn't. Drivers were supposed to yield for pedestrians at crosswalks.

When the ambulance and police arrived, an officer asked Charles to describe the vehicle. Regrettably, Charles didn't recall what model the car was, and the fading light hadn't helped him see the color of it or get a good look at the license plate. All he could remember was that it was a smaller car, not a truck.

After some time had passed, the front desk called his name. *Please let this be good news.* He got up from his seat and went over to the person who had called him over.

"Charles Smucker. A friend of Dianna's, correct?" the receptionist asked while reading the paper attached to her clipboard.

"Yes, we've been friends for many years."

"If her injuries were fatal, then we'd only permit family members into her room at this time."

"So that means she's all right?"

"Your friend was left with minor injuries. Bruising, some cuts, and a minor concussion. We'll be watching her for the night, but she can return home sometime tomorrow."

The receptionist called one of the other workers to lead Charles to Dianna's room. The room was divided with a curtain hanging in the middle of the space. The nurse peeked behind the curtain. "She's resting." The nurse looked back at him. "There's a chair by the bed you can use."

"Thank you."

After the nurse left, he went over and sat in the chair.

Dianna opened her eyes. "Charles. . ."

"I'm so thankful you're going to be okay. I called and left your folks a message to let them know you were in an accident and that you're at the hospital."

"Thank you, Charles. I know they'll be coming here as soon as they can."

He took hold of her hand. "How do you feel?"

"I am pretty sore." She touched the tube of the IV lodged in her arm. "Especially from this. It's probably going to leave a bruise."

Charles entwined his fingers with hers. *Is she lying to me to keep me at ease?* he wondered. "You also have a concussion, but it could have been much worse. I could've prevented you from crossing. If only I had responded faster. . ." His chest tightened. "I was so afraid of losing you."

"You can't blame yourself. It wasn't your fault. As for who hit me, I've already forgiven them. Hard times are unavoidable, and there will be times in life when a person we care about may be hurt or taken from this world." Dianna squeezed his fingers. "I understand why you're scared, Charles, but I'm going to be fine. There's nothing to be afraid of."

At that moment, Charles fully understood why he had fallen in love with Dianna. She always offered encouragement and a positive focus.

"Charles, I promise to stay by your side for the rest of my living days."

From all the pent-up frustration he'd been holding inside, Charles let his tears fall, lifting her hand and kissing it gently. "I love you, Dianna."

"I love you too." Tears trickled down her cheeks, but her smile was as tender as ever.

Charles was thankful that Dianna only suffered some scrapes and bruises. He had learned a lot from the way God had worked through her, and he knew she'd continue to remind him of the importance of devotion and faith. He wanted nothing more than to give his worries to God from now on.

There is no fear in love; but perfect love casteth out fear:
because fear hath torment. He that feareth is not made perfect in love.
1 JOHN 4:18

Joy

CARDINAL AT THE WINDOW

by Wanda E. Brunstetter

Weighed down by a lack of motivation, Esther Stutzman lay on her bed, drowning in her sorrows while staring up at the ceiling. After several hours of nonstop crying, her three-month-old twin boys had finally fallen asleep. If it were possible, Esther would spend the rest of the day right here in her room—away from the responsibility of taking care of her and Abe's seven children. The babies, Jerod and John, were her second set of twins. The first set, Barbara and Becky, had turned three a month ago. They were napping in the room across the hall. Emma, age six; Thomas, age eight; and Mark, age ten, were in school. But today was their last day of the session and then they would be home until the end of August, so Esther would soon have to deal with all seven of them.

She rolled onto her side, staring vacantly across the room. *I'm so depressed. How am I going to get through this without losing my mind?*

Esther wished they could hire a young woman to come in to help out, but finances were tight and there was no money for anything but the essentials. During the first few weeks after the babies were born, some of the women from church had come during the day to help out. But they all had homes and families of their own, so they couldn't come over indefinitely.

If Mama hadn't died from a brain aneurism last year, she'd still be living with us, and I'd have all the help I needed.

Esther's cheeks burned, and she pressed her palms against them as a sense of guilt overtook her. It wasn't only her mother's help she missed; it was her companionship. When Esther's father had died three years ago in a hunting accident, Esther's mother had moved in with them. Not only had Mama assisted with the children, household chores, and gardening, but she and Esther had also spent many hours laughing, visiting, and simply enjoying each other's company. Esther's husband helped out when he could, but he worked long hours in his buggy shop, so caring for the children fell on Esther's shoulders. It had been wonderful having Mama there not only to help with the children's care, but to fill Esther's lonely hours.

"*Mammi*. Mammi." The door to Esther's bedroom, which she'd left ajar, opened all the way, and Becky rushed in. "*Daschdich.*" She pointed to her mouth. "*Hungerich.*" Becky touched her stomach.

Frowning, Esther sat up on the bed. "How can you be thirsty and hungry when we just had lunch?" she asked in Pennsylvania Dutch.

Becky giggled.

Esther clenched her teeth to keep from shouting, *Go back to bed!* Instead, she patted the mattress beside her. "Come lie down here beside me. We can take our naps together."

Becky's bottom lip protruded. "*Ich lei net gem.*"

"I know you don't like to nap, but you need one."

The stubborn girl, her arms folded defiantly, would not move.

Esther's gaze flicked upward. *Lord, please help me.* She didn't want to lose her temper, but she couldn't give in and let Becky have her own way.

Esther stepped down from the bed, strode across the room, and lifted the child in her arms. "You and I are going to take a nap," she said firmly, placing Becky in the middle of the bed.

The little girl looked up at Esther and blinked several times. Esther figured tears were forthcoming.

"I'll be right here beside you, so close your eyes now and go to sleep." Esther lay down on her back and took hold of her daughter's hand.

It didn't take long before she heard Becky's even breathing. The little girl didn't stir, so Esther felt certain she was asleep. At last Esther's eyelids closed as she relaxed against the pillow. *Maybe now I can finally get some much-needed rest.*

Waa! Waa! Waa!

Esther sat up with a start. She'd been sleeping so soundly, it was hard to wake up. "Oh no. . . . Are the *bopplin* awake already?" She looked at the spot where Becky had been sleeping and saw that she was gone. *Now where did that little* schtinker *go? I hope she's not the cause of her brothers being awake.*

Esther glanced at the battery-operated clock on the table beside her bed. It was a quarter to three. She'd slept longer than she thought, and the other children would be arriving home from school soon.

She clambered out of bed and stumbled from her room. First things first. She had to get the babes diapered and fed, then find out what the girls were up to.

Half an hour later, Esther picked up one of her satisfied boys and headed for the living room. When she got there, her mouth gaped open. "What in the world has happened in here?" She stared at the muddy paw prints on the floor and grimaced when she saw a filthy animal lying on her husband's chair.

Esther turned and carried John back to her bedroom. *Here I thought I was gaining some ground, but I was wrong. Now I've got a big mess to clean up.* She placed John in his crib next to Jerod.

Esther's hands became fists as she burst into tears and flopped onto her and Abe's bed. *My husband isn't going to be happy that he won't be sitting in his favorite chair this evening after working all day.* She sniffed deeply. *It'll be wet from being cleaned and scrubbed—if I can even get all the dirt washed off, that is.*

Esther's crying eased, and she sat up on the bed and looked over at Jerod and John, who were also crying. "I'm sorry, sweet boys. Mommy's day just got extra busy. When I get the living room in better shape, I'll come back and get you both."

Esther collected herself as best as she could and headed back to the living room. There was no sign of the other children, but the dog was still on the chair. "Okay, Rover—outside you go."

Esther took the dog gently by its collar and led him out the front door. When she went to grab the mop and the bucket, the girls showed up. She frowned. "Who brought the dog into the house?"

The girls pointed at each other.

Esther's frown deepened. "You're gonna help me with some cleaning. We'll grab a couple of the old bath towels in the linen closet, and as I mop, you two can dry the wet floor.

They both nodded.

Esther dunked the mop into the soapy water and wrung it out. Then she started cleaning the dog's muddy prints. As she and the girls worked together, the floor began looking better. She paused and cleared her throat. "I'm going to take a break and go check on your siblings."

She left them alone, went to her room, and found the infants asleep. Esther carried them to the living room and placed them in the wooden cradles their father had made.

She looked at her girls still wiping the floor. "When you're done, I want you both to go to your room and think about what you did."

"Okay, Mammi." Their chins quivered. They finished their task and tearfully fled the room.

Esther looked at the soiled chair. Some of the mud was beginning to dry. It would take some effort to get it cleaned.

She went into the kitchen and pulled out several supplies, then headed back to the living room. Using a small whisk broom, Esther brushed as much of the caked-on mud as she could into a dustpan. After that, she scrubbed with a towel, using soap and water. Most of it came off, which was good, but no one would be sitting there the rest of the day unless they wanted a wet seat. Esther scrubbed a bit more, until she couldn't get any more dirt out of the material. Now it just had to sit and air dry.

She stepped over to look at the babies; they were both wide awake, but at least they weren't crying.

Esther went back to the kitchen, put away all the cleaning supplies, and washed her hands. Then she returned to the living room and picked up Jerod. She took a seat in the rocker and got it moving. *Finally, a moment of peace. Thank You, Lord.*

A few minutes later, Esther noticed John squirming and starting to make noise, so she put Jerod down. She checked baby John's diaper, but it was fine. "You just want to be loved too."

Esther picked John up and went back to the rocker. It was still dark and rainy outside. She looked over at Abe's chair and shook her head. "I'd like to be better at running this household, but I just don't see how."

As she rocked the baby, Esther looked at the clock. *What a day. Abe will be home shortly, and I haven't even thought about what to fix for supper.* She closed her eyes and tried to calm her nerves. It wasn't easy when she felt depressed and defeated. It seemed as though nothing was right in her life anymore. The joy she'd once felt was completely gone.

Esther had just put water on the stove to heat for a cup of tea when Thomas and Mark came in through the back door. Emma limped in behind them, sobbing and rubbing her knee.

Esther rushed forward. "What happened?"

"I–I tripped on a rock and fell down." Tears trickled down Emma's reddened cheeks.

"Oh, quit your bawlin', Emma," Mark said. "I've fallen harder than you did just now, so it can't hurt that bad."

"*Jah*, Sister, you're actin' like a big *boppli*," Thomas put in. "And ya ain't got nothin' to cry about."

Leaning against one of the lower cupboard doors, Emma cried even harder.

Esther shook her finger at the boys. "Shame on you for making your sister feel worse. Now say you're sorry and get on up to your room and change your clothes while I tend to Emma's wounds."

Mark stepped forward and touched his sister's arm. "Sorry, Emma."

Thomas remained where he stood. "I'm sorry too."

Emma dropped her gaze to the floor and whimpered. "I bet neither one of you is sorry. You only said that 'cause Mama told you to."

Mark looked at Esther and shrugged his shoulders. Thomas, in his usual copycat fashion, did the same.

Esther pointed to the kitchen door. "Go on upstairs now."

Without a word of protest, the boys turned and hurried from the room.

"Okay now, Emma, please take a seat at the table." Esther pulled out a chair. "I'll clean up your knee and then put medicine and a bandage on it."

Emma did as she was told. As Esther started down the hall, she heard the babies crying.

Esther's jaw clenched. *They'll have to wait until I take care of Emma's knee. There's only one of me.*

That evening, when Abe came in the door, he took one look at Esther and knew something was wrong. She sat at the kitchen table with her forehead resting on the wooden surface. For a minute he thought she might be asleep, but then she lifted her head and looked at him with a dazed expression.

"Was is letz do?" He touched her shoulder.

"I'll tell you what's wrong here—just about everything, and we can start with that." Esther's tight voice pierced the air as she pointed toward the living room.

Abe stepped into the living room and came right back in. "Did something happen in there? The boys are asleep in their cradles, and I didn't see anything out of the ordinary."

"You would have if you'd sat in your chair."

His forehead creased. "What do you mean?"

"Barbara and Becky let the dog in, and he made a muddy mess on your chair. They did it while I was sleeping. I cleaned it the best I could, but now, of course, it's all wet." Esther sighed. "Jerod and John have been fussy today, and after I got them and the girls to sleep I went to my room to lie down for a while."

"I'm guessing you didn't get enough sleep, because you look *mied*."

"I am tired and also discouraged."

"What are you discouraged about?" he asked, taking a seat beside her.

She lifted her hands. "Everything. Emma fell on the way home from school, and Thomas and Mark said she was acting like a baby because she cried when she hurt her knee."

Abe frowned. "I hope you didn't let them get away with it."

"No, I made them apologize to their sister, and then after they changed their clothes, I sent them out to the barn to do some extra chores."

"It sounds like you handled things well." Abe smiled. "You're a *gscheit* woman."

"Not wise enough it seems. If I were smart, I would have dead-bolted the front door, and they couldn't have let the dog in."

"Well, you can't think of everything or be everywhere all of the time."

Esther made little circles on her forehead with her fingertips. "Beginning tomorrow, things are going to get even crazier around here."

"How come?"

"Emma, Thomas, and Mark are out of school for the summer, remember?"

"Oh, that's right. But that's a good thing, because you'll have the older kids' help."

"I'm not sure how much help they're going to be." She released another heavy sigh. "It'll just mean more work for me."

"You know what I think, Esther?"

She shook her head.

"You need to quit working so hard and find some fun things to do. A little joy in your life, jah, that's what you need."

Esther sat, continuing to slowly shake her head. "It's hard to think about doing anything fun when there's so much work to be done." She rose from her chair. "Speaking of which. . .I need to start supper."

Inhaling deeply through his nose, Abe pushed up his sleeves. *If Esther won't listen to me, then I'll get someone else to talk to her.*

The next day, after Abe left to run some errands in town, Esther stood at the kitchen window watching raindrops pound the ground. The dismal weather matched her sullen mood.

"Mama, there's nothin' for me to do." Thomas came up behind Esther and tugged on her apron.

Esther turned to look at him. "Did you and Mark finish cleaning your room like I asked you to do after breakfast?"

He bobbed his head. "Been done a while already. We wanna go outside and play, but the rain won't stop." His brows puckered. "How come God makes it rain anyways?"

"God sends the rain so the trees, plants, and flowers will grow. I thought you knew that already."

He scuffed his bare toe against the wooden floor. "Jah, guess I did, but it shouldn't be raining the first day we have off of school."

It looks like I'm not the only one feeling depressed today, Esther thought. *I wish I could say something to cheer my boy up, but this wet weather we're having is pulling me down too.*

"If you and Mark have finished cleaning your room, then what is he up to?" she asked.

Thomas shrugged. "He's lying on the bed, reading a *buch*."

"Maybe you ought to find a book to read too."

Thomas shook his head. "Naw, I do enough book reading in school. Guess I'll go out to the barn and see what the *katze* are up to."

"Good idea, and while you're there, make sure the cats have food and water."

"Okay, Mama." Thomas grabbed his jacket and raced out the back door.

Esther heard Jerod and John crying in the next room. She was about to head for the living room when Barbara and Becky ran into the kitchen.

"The *bopplin* are cryin'," Barbara announced.

"The bopplin are cryin'," her twin sister repeated.

"Jah, I hear them. I'll go take care of them right now." Esther did a quick glance around the kitchen to make sure there was nothing for the girls to get into while she was gone. At least the marking pens had been put away and were no longer within easy reach.

Why do I feel so depressed all the time? Esther asked herself as she headed for the living room. *I feel like crawling back into bed and pulling the covers over my head. If only there was something to smile or laugh about.*

Abe pulled his rig into Bishop Henry's yard, got out, and secured his horse to the hitching rail. He paused beside the buggy and rubbed his forehead. *If Esther knew I was here, she'd be upset. Sure hope this is the right thing to do.*

"What's the matter, Abe? You got a *koppweh*?"

Abe jumped at the sound of Henry's voice.

"Uh, no headache. I was just thinking, is all. Didn't see anyone when I pulled in, so you kinda took me by surprise."

"Sorry about that. I was in the barn, and when I heard the horse and buggy pull in, I came out to see who it was." Henry shook Abe's hand. "What can I do for you today, friend?"

Abe reached under his straw hat and scratched his head. "Actually, I was hoping I could talk to your *fraa*. Is she home?"

"Jah, Ruth is in the house, doing some baking this morning." Henry put his hand on Abe's shoulder. "I'll walk in with you. Maybe she'll offer us some *kaffi* and *kichlin*."

"Cookies and coffee would be nice, but I wasn't planning to stay very long. Just need to talk to Ruth about something."

"Oh, okay. Come on then and follow me up to the house."

When Abe entered the kitchen with Henry, he saw the bishop's wife taking a tray of cookies from the oven.

"Look who's here, Ruth," Henry announced. "It's the buggy maker, and he came to talk to you."

She set the cookie sheet on an oversized potholder and turned to face Abe. "I hope you know we're not in need of a new buggy, and our old one doesn't need any repairs either."

Abe shook his head. "I'm not here about a buggy. Came to talk to you about my fraa."

Ruth pinched the skin at her throat. "Is Esther all right? She's not sick or hurt, I hope."

"Not physically. She's *verleed*."

"What is she depressed about?" Henry asked.

Abe shrugged. "I'm not sure, but she's been this way since our twin boys were born, and it's continued to get worse."

Ruth gestured for them to take a seat. "It could be postpartum depression, but since the birth of the twins was three months ago, it might be something else."

"Would you be willing to talk to Esther—find out what she's depressed about?"

"Of course. I might have some suggestions to help Esther deal with her depression and find some joy in life again."

Abe sagged against his chair. "*Danki*, Ruth. If anyone can help her, it'll be you."

Esther had put Jerod, John, Barbara, and Becky down for their naps and was about to go see what her other three children were doing, when she heard a horse and buggy pull into the yard. Thinking it must be Abe returning from his errands, Esther didn't bother to look out. Besides, she didn't want to be reminded that it was still raining.

Esther started up the stairs to see what Emma, Thomas, and Mark were up to. The boys had spent much of the morning in the barn. But after lunch they'd gone to their room. After Emma swept the kitchen floor and helped Esther do the dishes, she'd gone to her room as well.

Esther opened Emma's door first and found her lying on the bed with a book. She closed the door and headed down the hall to the boys' room. Esther was about to open their door when she heard a knock on the front door.

That can't be Abe. I'd better hurry downstairs. I don't want the knocking to wake the bopplin.

Esther made her way to the front door. When she opened it, she was surprised to see their bishop's wife on the porch.

Ruth offered her a rosy-cheeked smile. "Hello, Esther. If you're not too busy, is it all right if I come in?"

"Yes, of course." Esther didn't feel like visiting with anyone today, but she didn't want to be rude. "The little ones are sleeping in their rooms down the hall, so let's go to the *kich*."

Ruth left her umbrella on the porch and followed Esther into the kitchen.

"Please, take a seat."

Ruth pulled out a chair at the end of the table.

"Would you like a cup of tea?" Esther asked. "I have hot water in the teakettle on the stove."

"Danki, that would be nice."

Esther fixed them both tea, handing one cup to Ruth, and took a seat across from her. "I'm surprised to see you out on this rainy day. It's never fun to drive around in nasty weather in our open buggies."

"Oh, a little rain doesn't bother me. I stay fairly dry under my big umbrella." Ruth blew on her tea and took a sip.

"The rain bothers me. I don't even like to look at it," Esther admitted.

Ruth set her cup on the table and cleared her throat. "I came by to see how you're doing."

"I'm fine and so are the *kinner*. None of us got the flu bug that was going around a few weeks ago."

"I'm glad you're fine physically, but how about spiritually or emotionally?"

Esther bristled. She didn't want to talk about her emotional or spiritual life. Both were on rocky ground and she couldn't seem to control her melancholy feelings or negative attitude. Esther kept telling herself she would feel better, but every day when she woke up she felt the same.

"Did you hear my question?" Ruth asked.

"Jah, and I'm fine." Esther dropped her gaze, unable to look at the bishop's wife directly.

"Your husband believes you are suffering from depression. He asked me to speak with you and offer some encouragement."

Esther's fingers curled around the handle of her cup until her knuckles whitened. "Abe had no right to say anything to you about the way I've been feeling." Her pulse quickened. "I wonder how many other people he's told."

"I don't know if he's spoken to anyone else, but when he mentioned your depression, I felt concern. He said it's been going on since your twin boys were born."

Tears welled in Esther's eyes. She couldn't deny it.

"Have you told the doctor about it? Could your depression be a hormonal thing?"

"I had a checkup a few weeks ago, and the doctor said I was fine." Esther dabbed at her eyes. "I'm so tired, and I've lost the pleasure in all the things I used to enjoy doing. Not that there would be time to do any of those things, even if I wanted to."

"You need to make time for fun as well as for relaxing."

"That's hard to do when you have seven kinner demanding your attention."

"I understand. Henry and I raised ten children, and although it was a challenge some days, I always made a little time for myself each day." Ruth leaned slightly forward. "Would you like me to give you some practical suggestions?"

"I guess so." Truthfully, Esther didn't think anything Ruth had to say would make a difference in the way she felt.

Ruth got up and sat in the chair closest to Esther. "Well, first of all, you'll need to make an effort to change your thoughts whenever you're feeling down in the dumps. You should focus on things like the beauty of nature and the humorous things your children do." Ruth placed her hand on Esther's arm. "You might try going outside and breathing in some fresh air. Of course, you also ought to take care of yourself by eating regular meals, drinking plenty of water, and getting enough sleep. You may also want to write down some of the things you are grateful for, or a list of things that went well during the day. Gratitude helps a person direct their attention away from negative thoughts and onto positive feelings."

"Sometimes it's hard to do any of those things when the kinner are fussy."

"I understand. And here's an idea for whenever you feel over-whelmed."

"These days, that's most of the time."

"This has always worked for me whenever I've felt overwhelmed or depressed." Ruth pointed one finger in the air. "Even if the kinner are demanding your attention, go to your room and lie down a few minutes. Keep your arms by your sides, resting them as loosely as you can." She gave Esther's arm a few pats. "But the most important thing you can do to bring joy back into your life is to think about and quote some Bible verses out loud. I like quoting Isaiah 61:10—'I will greatly rejoice in the Lord, my soul shall be joyful in my God; for he hath clothed me with the garments of salvation.' Of course, there are many other helpful verses, like Psalm 51:12 and Nehemiah 8:10."

"I suppose I could try to do some of those things." Esther gave a weak smile. She couldn't believe how much wisdom Ruth had. But then, she was the bishop's wife and often spoke to women in their community who were facing some kind of a problem. "Danki for caring enough to come here and talk to me," Esther said.

"You're welcome. Oh, and if you need a break from the kinner, please don't hesitate to ask. In addition to myself, there are other women in our community who would gladly come to help out with the children so you could have a few hours to do whatever you wanted."

Esther wasn't sure if any of the things Ruth had suggested would remove the cloud of depression that hung over her, but she was willing to at least give some of the ideas a try.

For the next several days, Esther tried to put some of Ruth's suggestions into practice, but it seemed like an impossible task. Between household chores, yard work, and child care, there was no time for rest. She hadn't taken the time to write out the things she was grateful for, as the bishop's wife had told her to do. Esther wanted to think positive, joyful thoughts, but negative things kept happening, pulling her further into depression. She had let her physical appearance go and hadn't been eating well. Esther didn't get enough sleep and couldn't find joy in the things she used to. It was difficult to talk about her feelings with others, but she felt thankful she'd been able to open up when Ruth came over.

If only something good would happen, I might find something to laugh or smile about, Esther told herself as she scrubbed the kitchen floor where Barbara had spilled a jar of maple syrup that morning. The children—even the babies—had a knack for making at least one mess during the day.

"There I go again, thinking negative thoughts." Esther tapped the side of her head. "How can I break this negative habit?"

"What's a habit, Mama?" Emma asked, skipping into the kitchen.

"It's when a person does something over and over."

"Oh, you mean like when the bopplin cry all the time?"

A smile came to Esther's lips, as though of its own accord. "Not quite, Emma. Your little brothers cry when they're hungry, need their *windele* changed, or just want to be held. Someday when they're older, they won't cry so much."

Emma moved closer to Esther, looking up at her with big brown eyes. "But you cry, Mama. I hear you sometimes."

"That's true. Everyone cries when they're sad or hurt, but it's not the same thing as a habit." Esther placed her hand on the top of her daughter's head. "Did you come into the kitchen because you wanted to ask me a question, or do you need something?"

Emma shook her head. "Came to tell you about the red *voggel* at the *fenschder*."

"What bird? What window?"

"The one in there." Emma pointed toward the door leading to the living room, and then she tugged on Esther's dress. "Come see, Mama. It's so *schee*."

"All right then, please show me the pretty red bird."

When they entered the living room, Thomas, Mark, and even Barbara and Becky were gathered around the big window.

"Look, Mama. . .just like I said, there's the schee voggel." Emma's eyes sparkled as she pointed at the pretty bird eating from the feeder Abe had built and secured to the windowsill.

The other children were also pointing, as well as giggling and talking about the bird's pretty red color.

"It's a cardinal," Esther said. "Isn't it a remarkable bird?"

"What's *markable* mean?" Thomas questioned.

"The correct word is *remarkable*, and it means 'amazing,' " Esther explained. "All birds are nice, but this bird's color is amazing."

" 'Mazing," Barbara and Becky said.

Everyone laughed, including Esther. Ruth had been right—focusing on things found in nature, such as the pretty bird eating from their feeder, had given her something to feel joyous about.

As the day progressed, Esther decided she would look for things to smile about—the babies' cute antics, her three girls' excitement as they pranced around the yard chasing butterflies. She even found pleasure in watching Mark and Thomas play fetch with their dog. These were all things Esther had barely taken notice of these past few months. She was eager to see Abe when he got home from work today and share with him all that she'd learned about being joyous.

While supper cooked in the oven, Esther took a seat at the kitchen table and made a list of all the things that had made her smile. After she'd written it all down, she opened her Bible and looked for the word *joy* in the concordance. Several passages of scripture were listed under the heading. She looked up several and wrote them down, including the one Ruth had mentioned from the book of Isaiah.

After Esther closed the Bible, she bowed her head and prayed. *Heavenly Father, help me to be more observant of the things You have created for my enjoyment—including my special children. Even when I'm having a rough day or things don't go the way I'd planned, help me to have a joyful heart. Instead of fretting over every little thing, I want to enjoy the time I have to raise my children. And please help me to spread Your joy to everyone around me. Amen.*

I will greatly rejoice in the LORD,
my soul shall be joyful in my God.
ISAIAH 61:10

UNEXPECTED JOY

by Wanda E. Brunstetter

Hopkinsville, Kentucky

Susanna Riehl leaned on her husband for support as she watched her parents' coffins being lowered into the ground. It didn't seem possible that their lives had been snuffed out in a buggy accident four days ago. *Poor Mom and Dad—they never even had a chance.* Susanna could not help feeling the suffering from all of this. Would the void inside her ever be filled with joy again? She struggled just standing here watching the actions that represented the finality of her parents' lives on this earth.

She lifted her gaze to the darkening sky. *Why would You take them, Lord? Don't You care how much my mamm and daed meant to me?*

Leon pressed his shoulder against hers. No doubt he too felt a great loss. Susanna's parents had lived in the *daadihaus* next to their home for the past five years, and Leon had become very close to her dad.

Susanna closed her eyes, remembering how Leon and Dad used to sit on the porch together, discussing the weather, talking about the crops growing in the fields across the road, and sharing stories from their past. They'd also gone fishing together a good many times and always enjoyed a friendly game of horseshoes or checkers.

Susanna and her mother had spent many hours together too— gardening, baking, quilting, and visiting over a warm cup of herbal tea. Mom's favorite kind was spearmint, made from the spearmint leaves she grew in the small garden behind the grandparents' house. These would all be nothing but memories for Susanna now, and somehow she would have to work through her loss.

Her attention returned to the pallbearers as they continued to cover the caskets with the shrinking pile of dirt. The sound of the shoveling seemed hard to endure, and she wiped at escaped tears repeatedly. Her swollen eyes closed for a moment while she released Leon's arm.

Susanna placed both hands on her bulging stomach. The baby she carried in her womb would be born in two months, and Susanna's heart broke as she realized the child would never have the opportunity to know his or her maternal grandparents.

She pictured her parents' faces and remembered them holding Jerry as an infant. *If only they were still here.*

Susanna heard a child talking and opened her eyes. She tried not to stare at Frieda while she whispered to her son as he stood between her and his grandparents. It was tough seeing her good friend have the support of her parents that Susanna used to have and now craved so much.

Susanna glanced at her and Leon's three children: Ervin, age seven; Lydia, who was five; and Jerry, who'd recently turned three. They would all miss their grandparents and had been cheated out of the years ahead when they should have had more time to spend with them.

As the last shovelful of dirt was placed on the coffins, the mourners repeated the Lord's Prayer silently, and the graveside service concluded.

Susanna remained in place as she looked at the solemn faces of her four grieving brothers. Although they too would miss Mom and Dad, they lived in a different county in the state of Kentucky and didn't get to see their parents on a regular basis—not like Susanna and Leon, who had seen her folks every day.

Leon took Lydia's and Jerry's hands, while Ervin looked up with a quivering chin. "I miss *Grossdaadi* and *Grossmammi.*"

Leon knelt down and released the hands of the two youngest. "I know, Son. Come here."

Ervin stepped over and leaned into his father's embrace. Leon looked up at Susanna with sadness as Lydia and Jerry joined in the hug.

A sense of bitterness rose in Susanna's chest as she reflected on the senseless act that had killed her parents. *If the driver of the pickup truck had been paying attention to the road instead of talking on his phone, Mom and Dad would still be alive.*

"Why are you sitting here in the dark?" Leon asked when he entered the living room, where Susanna sat on the couch. Before she had a chance to respond, he lit the lamp overhead.

She released a heavy sigh. "I've just been sitting here thinking about my mamm and daed, and wondering if I'm ever going to get over the hurt of losing them."

Leon took a seat beside her. "It will be an adjustment—there's no doubt about it." He took hold of Susanna's hand. "But we'll get through this together."

Susanna appreciated her husband's support, but his words did nothing to alleviate the emptiness she felt. She wondered if it would ever get any better.

Sometimes during the day the children's needs diverted her thoughts for brief moments. Like this morning when Jerry had a missing sock that he couldn't find. Susanna had looked around the house until she'd found it on a kitchen chair. And yesterday Lydia spilled chocolate milk on her favorite stuffed toy and wanted it cleaned. Susanna sprayed stain remover on the area and worked on it until it came clean. Lydia had smiled and hugged her for fixing it. But those moments didn't last long, and the empty feeling always resurfaced.

Susanna's thoughts went back to her parents' vacant place.

"What about the daadihaus?" Susanna wiped the tears that escaped through her lashes. "Do we leave it sitting empty, or should we rent it out to someone?"

"Those are questions that don't need answers right now. We should take our time in making a decision about what to do with your parents' home."

Susanna slowly moved her head up and down. "I suppose you're right. Tomorrow morning, though, I'm going next door to do some cleaning. Mom never liked a dirty or cluttered house."

"Do as you wish, but I don't want you working too hard." Leon placed his hand on Susanna's stomach. "You need to take care of yourself and get plenty of rest. We don't want this *boppli* to come early, like Lydia did."

"Don't worry. I won't overdo. And when Jerry goes down for a nap tomorrow, I'll see if Lydia will take one." Susanna placed her hand over Leon's. "While the little ones are napping, I'll rest too."

"What about Ervin? What's he going to do while the three of you are resting? I'm sure you won't talk him into taking a nap."

"No, he's too big for naps. Or at least he thinks he is." Susanna pointed at one of her son's books, lying on the coffee table. "I'm sure Ervin will be more than willing to lie on the hammock outside and read."

"Glad to hear it." Leon rose from the couch. "The *kinner* have all been asleep for a couple of hours now. Don't you think it's time we also go to bed?"

"You go ahead, Leon. I have a few things I need to do in the kitchen, and then I'll be in."

"Okay." He leaned over and kissed her forehead. "If I'm already in bed and snoring away, just give me a nudge."

Susanna smiled in spite of her melancholy mood. When her husband got to snoring, it took a lot more than one little nudge to make him stop.

After Leon left the room, she turned off the gas lamp and made her way to the kitchen with the aid of a flashlight. The lamp above the table was still lit, so she sat there to make out her grocery list. Even though a lot of food had been brought in from women in their Amish community, they were running low on a few items. She would ask Leon to stop at the grocery store on his way home from work tomorrow afternoon. That way, Susanna wouldn't have to go anywhere, leaving her free to concentrate on cleaning Mom and Dad's house, as well as taking care of her children's needs.

Tears stung Susanna's eyes, nearly blinding her vision. She wasn't sure she could even enter the daadihaus. So many memories awaited her there. Susanna almost choked on the sob rising in her throat. *If only Mom and Dad hadn't gone to town the day of their accident, they'd be in their cozy little house right now.*

The following morning, while the children colored pictures in the kitchen, Susanna sat in the living room, holding a Bible in her lap. She'd read a few verses and was meditating on them when she heard a buggy pull in.

A short time later a knock sounded at the door. Susanna was surprised to see her friend Frieda on the porch.

"I brought you two loaves of banana bread and a dozen chocolate cupcakes." Frieda handed the plastic containers to her.

Susanna already had a pantry full of goodies that other people had brought over, but she smiled and said, "*Danki*, Frieda."

"I have a few hours before I need to be home," Frieda said. "Is there anything you need help with?"

"Actually, there is. Would you be willing to stay here with the kinner long enough for me to go over to the daadihaus and do some cleaning?"

"I wouldn't mind doing that, but is it really necessary for you to clean your parents' house today?" Frieda placed her hand on Susanna's arm. "You look *mied*, and you've been through a lot these last few days. Don't you think you ought to rest up?"

"I have to admit I am tired, but cleaning the daadihaus is something I feel compelled to do."

"All right then, I'll stay and watch the children, but please don't overdo."

"I won't. I promised Leon last night that I'd take it easy." Susanna gave her belly a pat. "He's worried the boppli might come too early."

"Your husband has a right to be concerned. I've known you since we were teenagers, and you've always been a worker. But you do tend to push yourself too hard at times." Frieda rested both hands on her hips. "It might be better if you stay here and rest and let me do the cleaning."

Susanna shook her head briskly. "I appreciate the offer, but it's my place to do it."

"Okay, but if you're not back in two hours, I'll come and get you." Her friend gave a small laugh. "I don't mean to sound bossy, but I can't help but worry."

"I'll be fine." Susanna poked her head into the living room, where the children were playing. "I'm going over to the daadihaus, but Frieda is here and she'll be staying with you till I get back."

"Okay, Mama." Ervin looked up from the book he was reading. Jerry and Lydia said nothing, so engrossed were they with their toys.

Susanna returned to the kitchen and stepped up to Frieda. "If the kinner don't cooperate with you, tell them they won't get to eat any of those delicious-looking cupcakes you brought over."

Frieda shook her head. "I'm sure they'll be fine."

Susanna slipped on her everyday work apron and went out the back door.

The minute Susanna entered the daadihaus, a cold chill swept over her body. Dad's favorite over-stuffed chair sat empty, as did her mother's rocking chair.

Susanna's throat felt so swollen she could barely swallow as she lowered herself into Mom's chair and pushed her feet against the floor to get the rocker moving. She leaned her head back and closed her eyes. *Oh Mama, I miss you so much. I doubt that the ache in my heart will ever go away.*

Susanna continued to rock, visualizing her parents here in this cozy room, drinking coffee and talking about their day. *Are they doing something similar in heaven today?* she wondered.

Susanna hadn't thought much about heaven until someone she knew passed away. While some people believed their good works would get them to heaven, her church district taught that only those who accepted Christ as their Savior would go to heaven when they died. Susanna's parents had professed to be Christians, putting their whole faith and trust in God's Son and acknowledging Him as their Lord and Savior. She had every confidence that Mom and Dad were in heaven right now. Susanna just wished her parents could be here instead, so she could tell them how much she loved them. Her heart longed for them to be alive and to be here for many more years to come. She had never dreamed her parents' lives would end so early.

All alone in their living room, Susanna clutched her work apron and cried. *I feel so burdened with sorrow, Lord. Life is too short. Please give me joy again.* Her eyes remained closed as she wiped at the tears. The realization that Mom and Dad would never be coming back was a heavy burden for Susanna's broken heart to bear.

The grandfather clock chimed, and Susanna opened her eyes. She'd come here to do some cleaning, and if she didn't get busy, it would soon be time to head back to her house. She couldn't expect her friend to stay and watch the children all day. Frieda had her own things to care for at home.

Susanna stopped rocking and stood. She would start with the kitchen.

Sunday morning, Susanna woke up to the sound of noisy children running down the hall. No doubt they were eager for breakfast.

Groaning, she pulled herself out of bed. Fixing the morning meal seemed like drudgery today, but the thought of going to church was even worse. Susanna would have to either put on a fake smile or deal with people asking how she was doing and offering sympathies for her loss. It might seem odd, but too much sympathy made her feel worse. Even talking about her parents' death was painful.

I wish it wasn't Sunday. I'd like to skip the service and just stay home today. Susanna rubbed the sleep from her eyes. *But I need to set a positive example as a Christian to my family and friends, like my folks did for so many years.*

After slipping into her robe and slippers, Susanna made her way to the kitchen. When she stepped inside, she was greeted by four eager faces.

"Can we have *pannekuche* for breakfast?" Ervin asked.

"Sorry, Son, but I don't have time to make pancakes this morning. You can have your choice of cold cereal, and there's some banana bread left."

Ervin heaved a sigh. "Okay."

"Okay," the other children repeated.

Susanna glanced out the kitchen window and saw Leon heading for the house. His horse, Barney, was already hitched to the buggy and waiting at the hitching rail.

Susanna opened a cupboard door and took out two boxes of cereal. She placed them on the table, along with a bottle of milk. She'd begun to put slices of banana bread on a plate when Leon came into the house.

"How's everyone doing this morning?" He went around the table and patted each of the children's heads.

"Good, *Daadi*." Lydia looked up at him and grinned.

"Good, Daadi," Jerry and Ervin repeated.

Leon looked over at Susanna. "You look mied. Are you feeling okay?"

"I'm fine." Susanna turned away to get the bowls and silverware.

No way would she mention in the children's presence anything about the dream she'd had last night that had left her feeling drained. In the dream she'd gone next door to the daadihaus and found it completely empty. Nothing remained to remind Susanna that her parents had ever lived close by, not even a teaspoon.

"I'll go wash up, and then we should eat and get changed into our church clothes," Leon said.

Church was the last place Susanna wanted to be today, but she would force herself to go.

By the time church was halfway over, Susanna's back had begun to hurt. Since Lydia had whispered that she needed to use the restroom, Susanna took the child's hand and slipped quietly out of Deacon Beiler's barn.

When they entered the house, she was relieved to see that no one was lined up outside the bathroom door. While Lydia stepped inside, Susanna went to the kitchen for a drink of water.

After taking a paper cup from the stack on the counter, she turned on the faucet and filled it with cold water. Susanna was glad most of the Amish homes in their area had indoor plumbing. A trip to the outhouse would not be fun—especially during the cold winter months.

She'd finished her drink and was about to check on Lydia when Frieda entered the kitchen. "How are you doing this morning?" her friend asked.

"A little sore from sitting on the hard bench." Susanna reached around and rubbed the small of her back. "Guess I should have brought a cushion to sit on this morning."

"I'm sure there are a few throw pillows on the sofa in the living room. I don't think Sally would mind if you borrowed one to sit on during the remainder of church."

"I'll be okay."

Frieda reached out and touched Susanna's arm. "Did you look in the mirror this morning?"

"Of course. I had to make sure my hair was put up okay and that my head covering was on straight."

Frieda pursed her lips. "There are dark circles under your eyes. I suspect you're not sleeping well. Is the *boppli* kicking, or is your grief keeping you awake at night?"

"I'm still grieving." Susanna shook her head. "Don't see how I'm supposed to move on with my life as if nothing's changed."

"Nobody expects you to pretend you didn't lose your parents. But you shouldn't dwell on it, Susanna. Your family needs you—more than ever right now—and you ought to look for some things to feel joyful about."

Susanna crossed her arms over her chest. *Frieda has no right to be saying such things to me. She hasn't lost a parent, so she doesn't understand.*

Susanna felt relief when Lydia came out of the bathroom. "I'm ready to go back to church now." The child looked up at Susanna and smiled.

"*Jah*, we need to return." Susanna clasped her daughter's hand and headed out the door.

When they entered the barn, scripture reading was over and Bishop Zook had begun preaching. Susanna took a seat, and the minute she sat down, she regretted not having brought out a pillow. Well, she wasn't going back in for one, so she'd just have to endure.

The bishop's sermon was taken from Psalm 126. When he read the fifth verse, about sowing in tears and reaping in joy, Susanna thought about her mother and how she'd enjoyed tending her garden. But because Susanna's parents had died before planting season, this year there would be no garden behind the daadihaus.

Maybe I should plant their garden, she told herself. *I bet if Mom was here, she would like that. Who knows—maybe she'll look down from heaven and see her nice garden.*

The following evening, after Leon got home from work, Susanna asked if he would till the small patch of ground where her mother had previously planted her vegetable garden. Leon graciously agreed and got to work on it right away.

Susanna spread a blanket on the grass so she and the children could sit and watch the proceedings. After only a few minutes, Jerry and Lydia jumped up and ran off to play in a different area of the yard.

"How come Daed's diggin' up the dirt by Grandpa and Grandma's house?" Ervin asked, scooching closer to Susanna.

"He's preparing it for the garden to be planted," she responded.

The boy's brows furrowed. "If Grandma and Grandpa are up in heaven, how they gonna plant a *gaarde*?"

"They won't be planting this garden, Son. I'll be planting the seeds and taking care of it in honor of them."

"What do you mean?"

"Well, it would be my small way of showing respect for my parents." Her tone softened. "I've loved and admired them for setting a good Christian example for all of us."

Ervin nodded and rested his hands upon the blanket. "Can I help?"

"Of course." Susanna glanced across the yard where her two younger children were playing. "Lydia and Jerry can also help, if they want to."

Ervin tipped his head to one side. "How are they gonna help? They're too little to plant a gaarde."

"Once the rows are ready for planting, I'll let them drop in some of the seeds." She patted his shoulder. "You can help me with most of the work though."

Her son's eyes brightened. "When can we start?"

"If your daed finishes all the tilling today and gets the dirt raked smoothly, we should be able to make our rows and start planting tomorrow morning."

"Okay, this is gonna be fun! I'd better go tell Jerry and Lydia about the plans we've made." Grinning widely, he skipped off in the direction of his siblings.

Susanna was pleased with his eagerness to help. As Ervin grew older, he might not always think planting a garden was fun.

The next morning, after Leon left for work, Susanna hurried to do the dishes and get her laundry hung outside. Once that was done, she called for the children to come join her behind the daadihaus.

"This morning I am going to plant seeds in Grandma and Grandpa's garden," she explained. "Ervin has said he would like to help. How about you, Lydia? Do you want to plant seeds that will grow into Grandpa and Grandma's favorite vegetables?"

Lydia bobbed her head. "Can Jerry help too?"

"Certainly." Susanna held up a plastic bag filled with several packets of seeds. She opened the sack and held it in front of Jerry. "Reach inside and pull out a packet of seeds. It will be the one you can help me plant."

Jerry reached in and pulled out a package of seeds. Pointing to the picture of corn on the front, he grinned up at Susanna and said, *"Welschkann."*

She nodded. "Jah. They are corn seeds."

Jerry held on to his packet while Lydia chose one from the bag. *"Baahn!"*

"Right. The seeds in the package you chose are beans."

Next, Ervin reached into the plastic sack. He squinted at the packet and wrinkled his nose. *"Reddiche.* They make me *garbse."*

"Some radishes can be a bit strong, but these are mild ones, so I don't think they will make you burp."

Lydia giggled and pointed at Ervin. "You sound funny when you garbse."

"Do not." He pointed a finger back at her. "You smack your lips when you eat."

"Uh-uh." Lydia shook her head vigorously.

Susanna held up her hand. "Okay, you two, that's enough. If you want to help plant Grandma and Grandpa's garden, then you need to learn to get along."

"Sorry." Ervin looked at Lydia.

"Me too," she responded.

"All right now, I want all of you to watch as I get this garden ready for planting." Susanna took the hoe and mounded up the dirt to make the first row. Then she took the tip of her hand shovel and pulled it along the dirt to make a small trench. While Susanna looked back at the finished row, she remembered her parents working on this plot of ground. Dad, in his tattered straw hat, was bent over raking out any rocks he could find. Mom, wearing one of her stained frocks and in her black garden clogs she liked to wear, would be right with him, raking too, and they'd be chatting or joking with each other while they worked.

Smiling, Susanna looked over at her children. *I don't want to take things for granted in this life.* She stepped up to her son. "We'll let Jerry go first." She took the packet of corn seeds from him and tore off the end. Then Susanna poured a few seeds in Jerry's little hand and put some in her own hand as well. "Watch what I do, Son, and then you do the same with the seeds I gave you." She dropped corn seeds into the trench she'd made, making sure to space them several inches apart.

"Now it's your turn, Jerry." She guided her young son as he dropped his seeds in the places she pointed to. They kept going until the whole row had been planted and covered lightly with the loose garden soil. When they finished, Susanna told Lydia it was time to do the bean seeds.

Susanna helped her daughter through the process, and then it was Ervin's turn. He'd apparently been watching how his siblings had done it, for he zipped down the row, dropping radish seeds into the dirt like a pro. He even covered them with just the right amount of dirt.

Susanna wished her parents could be here to watch their grandchildren's enthusiasm about the garden. She was sure they would have been quite pleased.

Unexpected tears began to flow, dribbling down Susanna's cheeks. Remembering the Bible verse about sowing in tears, Susanna wondered if she would ever reap anything that would bring her joy again.

Susanna reached up high to water the hanging basket of red fuchsias. She'd bought it to put out on the front porch of the daadihaus. Her mother had liked them and seemed content in having the pretty flowers every year. Dad usually was the one who would buy her the fuchsias. They enjoyed sitting on their glider and watching the hummingbirds come feed on the sugar water from the feeders.

More memories came to mind, overwhelming Susanna, until she heard the thudding of feet on the steps behind her. Drying her eyes, she opened her arms to her children.

◇———◇———◇

"Mama, come see. Come see!" Ervin gave Susanna's apron a tug.

Susanna set her mending aside. "What do you want me to see?"

"The reddiche are growing. Come out to the garden and see for yourself."

They headed around the back of the daadihaus to the big patch of dirt. It had been twelve days since she and Ervin planted the radish seeds, so it was about the right time for the radish leaves to pop out of the ground. Susanna never expected him to get so excited over a root vegetable he didn't even like that well. But Ervin's eagerness propelled her forward.

Ervin got there quicker than Susanna, though, because he ran all the way. "See, Mama. See right there." He pointed to the green leaves poking out of the ground. "Them is my reddiche, jah?"

"Yes, Son, they surely are. It won't be long till we can pull them out of the dirt and bring them in the house to wash and eat."

Ervin knelt down by the row and almost touched one. "How long?"

"About a month, I'd say, depending on how well we feed and water them."

Ervin wrinkled his nose, but then his expression changed as he leaned close to one of the tiny green-leafed plants. "I get to eat the first reddich we pick, okay?" He spoke in a bubbly tone.

Susanna nodded. "I'm fine with it."

He clapped his hands, hopped up and down, then turned and started to walk away.

"Where are you going?" she called out to him.

Ervin stopped walking and turned to face her. "To get the hose. I'm gonna water my reddich plants."

"That's fine, but don't give them too much water. Just sprinkle lightly. We don't want the other seeds in the garden to wash up out of the soil before they have a chance to germinate."

"I'll be careful, and I'm gonna water the rest of the garden too, so Lydia and Jerry's seeds will grow."

Susanna chuckled. She'd never imagined her son would be so excited about growing radishes. She could hardly wait to see Lydia's and Jerry's reactions once their seeds turned into plants.

Susanna felt the baby kick, and she placed her hands on her stomach. A sense of joy flooded her soul as she thought about the new life that would join her family soon. Although she still missed her parents, and always would, Susanna found comfort in knowing God had blessed her and Leon with their special children.

Ervin slid the hose over near the fringe of the garden and ran back to turn on the water. The nozzle squirted with pressure and sent some soil flying. The stream didn't mess up any of their plantings however.

Susanna remained silent nearby, just to oversee things while her son got busy with his task.

Ervin picked up the hose and began to gently spray over the area, making the soil darken with the needed moisture.

She smiled as she continued to watch. *From this moment on, I'm going to focus on the joy my kinner and husband bring to me and look to the future, just as Mom and Dad would want me to do.*

They that sow in tears shall reap in joy.
PSALM 126:5

Peace

NINA'S STRUGGLE

by Richelle Brunstetter

Millersburg, Ohio

Before the sun had risen, Nina Miller awoke with her skin damp from the waist up. She lifted her hands, brushing the tips of her fingers along her eyelashes. "Only a dream—or was it a nightmare?" Fragments of the dream were somewhat obscured, but Nina had an idea of what it'd been about.

Nina grew up without a father. He passed away when she was three years old, and she had no memory of him. Since she didn't know how he died, Nina's subconscious formed its own scenarios from time to time. Sometimes the uncertainty of how accurate those dreams were frightened her.

Nina's mother never explained how he passed away. In fact, Nina knew very little about her father. Throughout the years, she would ask about him, but couldn't muster the courage to pursue the matter after her mother's mental breakdown years back. As she got older, Nina perceived her mother's despondency in a different light and discovered she had been taking antidepressant supplements to ease her mental issues. Most days, Mom would be all right, but sometimes Nina returned home from work to the sounds of her mother's sobs from the living room.

Because of her mother's fragile mental health, it was easier for Nina to pretend she didn't wonder about her father. But now that she was twenty, she was more than old enough to know the truth. If Nina wasn't going to get answers from Mom, she needed to take the initiative and find the answers for herself.

Nina stood from the side of her bed. The bedroom door beckoned her—she wasn't going to hesitate this time. She crept from her room, guided by the light of a battery-powered lantern. One of the floorboards creaked when too much pressure was applied. *I need to be quiet. Mamm could wake up at any moment.*

Nina peered into the hallway, then tiptoed to the staircase leading to the attic. She'd rummaged through some things up there before, but always gave up in fear of her mother catching her.

She relaxed her shoulders when she reached the top. With ease, she quietly opened the sticky old door, yet turned around to make sure she was in the clear. Nina pressed the button on the lantern, and bright light illuminated the walls and the memorabilia stacked up around her. Chairs, drawers, and other furniture pieces were piled in disarray. Nina took in a deep breath. *Right now, my quest is for answers.* Sheer nervousness shot through her, however, given that her mom slept in the room right below her feet.

Nina placed the lantern in the middle of the attic floor, contemplating where to look. She went over to a large wooden box and grasped the lid. Nina wavered before lifting it, since a few old dresses were piled on top. Her mother came off as being disorganized, but she had a knack for knowing when something was out of place. That gave Nina another reason to be careful about searching through the drawers and boxes. She gently set down the lid and peered into the box.

"Oh." Nina tilted her head. "There's an old birdcage in here."

The cage was difficult to see in the dim light, so she held it up to get a closer look. Nina observed the bars of the cage, which were somewhat rusted. She questioned why she'd never seen it before.

Placing the cage on the floor, Nina squinted as she looked in the box again, noticing something else. She leaned farther in and pulled it out to view in the light. A chill trailed down her spine. "Why is there a photograph in here?"

The photo was of a young man who stood near a tree, wearing a wide grin. He had light-brown hair, similar to hers, and was dressed in a collared shirt, jeans, and loafers.

Why would we have a photo of an Englisher in our attic? She held it closer to her eyes. *Is he someone who knew my parents? Or is he a relative who isn't Amish?*

Nina flipped the picture over. There was something legible on the back of the photo.

My beloved, Tanner Miller. 03/09/1975

She rose to her feet. "No, this isn't—it can't be." Turning the photo back over, Nina observed the facial features of the young man in the image, then went over to an old mirror leaning against the wall. She tapped her fingernail on his crooked nose, then looked at her face in the reflection and raised her hand to her nose. Misshaped, precisely like his. "I resemble him."

Tanner wasn't a common first name for Amish, though it was more common for children nowadays to have a name that wasn't traditional. But the person in the picture was in his early twenties in the seventies.

Nina stepped away from the mirror, but her vision blurred as her body flew off the floor and twisted in midair. The next thing Nina knew, she was lying on her side with her head throbbing.

She lifted her head and rubbed her hip, since it took the brunt of the impact when she fell. *I must've tripped on the birdcage.*

"Nina!" a voice called from downstairs.

Nina clambered up and grabbed the photo and birdcage from the floor. Her face heated, and the warmth traveled through the rest of her body. *I have to put everything back.*

Placing the cage in the wooden box, Nina hovered with the photo over the box until she noticed her mother, who stood near the entryway of the attic.

"What are you doing up here? And what was that thump I heard above my head?"

Nina draped the picture to her side, praying her mother hadn't noticed it. "Nothing, *Mamm.* Just looking for a spare blanket up here and then happened to trip."

"We have blankets in the closet downstairs. You have no reason to be up here." The wrinkles around Mom's eyes deepened as she stomped over to the light. Mom lowered her gaze to Nina's level; her blue eyes pierced through Nina as she wrenched the photo from her grasp. "What are you doing with this?"

"I. . .I was—"

"I raised you better than to snoop in other people's belongings." Her mother flicked the picture at her. "Now go downstairs and take care of your chores before work."

Nina watched as her mother concealed the photo in the sleeve of her dress. Swallowing to moisten her mouth, Nina spoke up. "That's my father, isn't it? He has our last name."

"We're finished, Nina." Mom had a low rasp to her voice, but her eyes were pooling over. "Have you no respect for people's privacy, especially your own mother's?"

Nina almost backpedaled from the conversation, prepared to apologize for bringing it up again. But something urged her to push further. "I have every right to know who he was and how he died. Why can't you just tell me?"

"Enough! You're not allowed up here again. If I catch you, you'll be in a lot of trouble. Understand?"

Nina bit her tongue. The problem with addressing issues between parent and child was the issue of authority. Although Nina was an adult, Mom still looked at her as though she were a child.

She hurried past her mother to go downstairs. She couldn't process all the new information she'd found. Her father, whom Nina had wondered about all her life, may not even be the person she had depicted him to be. Was Nina's father an Englisher? Did her mother give birth out of wedlock? Was that the reason Mom never talked about him for all these years?

◆――――◆――――◆

The workday was usual, except for Nina's distraction over what took place that morning. It was also unfortunate her job was waitressing, because keeping track of customers' orders and getting the food served required plenty of focus. Nina miswrote some of the orders, irritating some customers, and she had come close to toppling a tray with empty dishes.

"Hey, Nina." Maggie, a friend and coworker of Nina's, prodded her shoulder. "You doing okay? You seem out of it."

Nina grew somewhat anxious as the line continued to gradually increase from the entrance of the restaurant. This wasn't the time or place to talk about what was distracting her. "I have a lot on my mind. That's all I can say for now."

Maggie nodded, then pivoted in the direction of the tables. "We should hang out after work. If you want to talk about it, I'm all ears."

"*Jah*. Sounds like a good idea."

From there, Nina's nerves calmed somewhat as she proceeded to wait on tables throughout the day. She was thankful to have friends who were genuinely concerned about her.

When it was time to head home, Nina hung up her work apron and gathered her belongings. It turned out that Maggie had an errand to run first, so Nina would have to wait to go over to her house. She wasn't looking forward to going back home and seeing her mother, but she needed answers. *I can't let this go. There was a purpose to my finding that photo, and I'm not going to give up so easily.*

It wasn't a far trek from the restaurant to home, and Nina wished her horse didn't have such a rapid pace to his stride. She wanted more time to collect her thoughts and approach the situation properly. She tightened her grip on the reins, taking in the early summer air as her horse's hooves clinked against the pavement. *I can't keep going on like this. Neither of us can.*

When she arrived home, Nina took her time hitching her horse to the post. She jittered her foot against the gravel, and her heart thumped erratically. Nina clasped her hands and prayed before heading to the front door. *Heavenly Father, this entire ordeal has been stressful for me for years. But I know it's been stressful for my mother also.* She kneaded her palms together. *Please help the two of us find peace and release us from this in Your time. In Your name, amen.*

Nina opened the front door and dropped her belongings near the entryway. "Mamm?" She hurried over to the living room, where her mother was crocheting a colorful square, which Nina assumed to be a potholder.

"*Hallo*, Nina." Mom tightened a stitch before placing the potholder and crochet needle on her lap. "How was it at Der Dutchman today?"

"Busy and stressful. It would've been smoother if I didn't have so much on my mind." Nina went over to the arm of the couch and stood at a comfortable distance from her mother.

"What exactly is on your mind?"

Nina flinched. "What went on this morning, Mamm. Remember? When I found the photo?"

It was a temperate summer day, yet the air in the room caused chills to run through Nina as she watched her mother's expression switch from a pleasing smile to a straight line. Nina's gaze trailed upward, and she saw the anger in Mom's ocean-blue irises, making her regret bringing up the subject.

"Don't make me upset." Mom crossed her arms. "None of this is necessary."

Nina lifted her hands, then let them fall. "It is necessary. I don't understand why you can't be honest with me."

"Because I don't need to be."

"You do. You're not the only one who is in pain. Imagine going through life not knowing anything about your family." Nina desired nothing more than to scream. Her mother was still treating her like a child, and Nina was fed up with it. However, she held in her frustration and kept speaking with composure. "I need to know, so please. . . Was he an Englisher? Did you have me out of wedlock? Is that why you don't talk about him?"

Mom craned her neck. "How can you make such broad assumptions?"

"I wouldn't be making assumptions if you spoke the truth."

"I beg of you, Nina. Stop asking me."

But Nina couldn't stop. "At least you knew who he was, but I know little about him. All because you refuse to tell me anything. Can't you at least tell me what happened to my *daed*? Is it really too much to ask?"

"Am I not good enough for you, Daughter?" her mother faintly whispered.

"That has nothing to do with it."

"Then what else would it be?" Mom's low voice cracked as she lowered her head. "Why else would you bring him up?"

Nina faltered for a moment, questioning whether she was in the wrong for making Mom feel worthless. Maybe Nina didn't value everything her mother had done for her. Why else would she be fixated on knowing who her father was? Or perhaps it was Mom's method to make Nina feel guilty, in an attempt to divert her from the discussion. Nina gripped the arm of the couch and responded firmly. "I've had enough of this. I need to leave."

Nina walked out of the living room, not looking back at her mother. Why had she thought that talking things out would help?

"Where do you think you're going?" Mom called from the other room.

"What you're doing is selfish. I don't care that you're clinically depressed, because keeping me in the dark is not right. Regardless of the reason." Nina collected her things from the floor and grasped the doorknob. "I'm going to Maggie's place. Was planning to anyways."

As she walked out of the house, Nina kicked some gravel into the lawn before heading to her buggy. She threw her belongings on the back seat, scrutinizing herself while unhitching her horse from the post. *I can't believe I said all of that to Mamm.* Nina pressed her palm against her cheek. *Is she really selfish for not wanting to bring up her unpleasant memories?*

"Nina, I can't take this silent treatment anymore." Mom squished the damp wash rag against the counter.

Nina's fingers tightened around the handle of the broom as she swept it along the floor of the kitchen. It had been almost a day since she had refused to speak with her mother, knowing the conversation wasn't going to go anywhere unless Mom were to speak willingly.

"What you're doing is childish, Nina."

But yesterday Maggie advised her to do as much as she could to get her mother to open up. If she needed guidance for how to do so, then the best course of action was to ask God for it. All Nina could do was continue to pray that Mom would be honest with her at some point.

Leaning the broom against the wall, Nina huffed a breath. "I can't take you withholding secrets from me." She observed the freshly swept floor, mostly to avoid eye contact. "If I were to be honest, Mamm, it feels like you don't trust me."

"Sit down."

Nina looked up at her mother and blinked. She had anticipated more resistance from her, but instead Mom was pulling out a stool from the island. Without thinking twice, Nina sat. The stool creaked as she shifted her weight.

"I know why you're eager to know about him. Your daed loved us very much. All the times we shared, and when you were first born, everything was going right for all of us. I didn't have anyone else when I moved to Millersburg, and I knew it would be difficult being on my own. But your father made it more bearable."

Her mother spoke the truth when it came to how lonesome it was to have no family around. From what Mom had told her growing up, she left her community in Pennsylvania. Mom didn't give any details as to why, but with the photo Nina found in the attic, several speculations formed in her mind.

Mom was quiet for a few minutes. Nina pulled at a loose thread from the string of her *kapp*. Then she slid off the stool, no longer willing to bear the silence. "You won't tell me anything else about him? Not even about his family? They don't live around here?"

"I told you all you need to know."

Nina didn't agree. She still didn't even know whether her father was English or not. Not only that, but there was still the question of whether Nina was born out of wedlock. But at least she had more hope now that her mom had said he was a good person. *Perhaps she'll say more about him when the time comes.* Nina believed it would be soon.

Pushing the stool under the island, Nina went to the front door and leaned over to slip on her battered shoes that she used when she fed the animals in the barn. "Well, I was planning to head to town to hang out with some friends. So I guess I should get my chores done before heading out."

"Okay, Nina."

"Mamm?" Nina said as she slipped on her left shoe. "Thank you." Her mother pursed her lips. "For what?"

"For opening up."

A month had passed, and Nina wished she could go back to any situation other than what she now faced.

Nina sat in the waiting room of the hospital, tapping her flip-flop against the floor. Her mother had been hospitalized for two weeks because of kidney failure. The doctors had explained that the cause was acute renal failure and that her mother probably would not recover from it. During those two weeks, Nina visited her mother after finishing with work at the restaurant. She'd shared with her boss and coworkers what her mother was going through. Her employer was sympathetic, offering some days off, and Maggie had offered to work extra time so that Nina could leave early and go up to the hospital to be with her mother.

When she was permitted to enter Mom's room, Nina's legs trembled as she went in. It was astonishing how the color of her mother's skin blended into the white bedsheets like a blanket of snow. She took a seat in the chair next to her mother's bed near the window, fumbling with her fingers while waiting for a response.

"Nina, I'm sorry." Mom stroked her throat and grimaced. "I never should've kept you from knowing who your father was. I was. . . selfish." Curling her blanched lips, her mother spoke again. "I need to tell you, before I leave."

"Don't say that." Nina dropped her head.

"Your father, before he passed on, wrote a letter to you that I have. I kept it hidden all these years."

Nina looked up at her mom. While she was stunned to learn about the letter, she wasn't surprised that her mom hadn't shared it with her.

Mom's eyes moistened. "I resented God for taking your father away from me, and I didn't want to be reminded of the good times we had shared. And I had to raise you all on my own, hoping I would be enough for you." She turned her head to gaze directly at Nina. "But you were right. What I did to you was wrong."

Nina could only nod in response as she stared intently at her mother.

"I. . .I'm sorry for everything I put you through, Nina. I hope you can find it in yourself to forgive me."

This was all too much for Nina to comprehend. Here her mother was at the brink of moving on from this life, and all Nina could think about was the letter. A letter that she should have read already but hadn't because of Mom. Part of Nina didn't want to forgive what her mother had done. If Mom had been honest and given her the letter, they wouldn't have argued in the first place.

"Th–the letter. . .is s–some. . . ," her mother choked out.

Nina was on the verge of demanding to know where the letter was kept. But soon her mother would no longer be part of this world. As resentful as she felt toward her mother's actions, Nina loved her with all her soul. She deserved to be at peace.

Her hands trembled as she clasped Mom's hand. Swallowing against the burning sensation in her throat, Nina rubbed her mother's hand in an attempt to warm it up. She knew what she needed to say. "I. . .I forgive you," Nina whispered. "I love you, Mamm."

Mom's eyelids fluttered shut as she mouthed, "*Danki.* I love you too." Her grip loosened around Nina's hand.

Goodbye, Mom. She brought Mom's hand to her cheek and blinked rapidly.

A couple of nights alone at home had become too much for Nina to bear. She awoke from another vivid dream, reliving her mother's passing.

Nina rubbed her moist eyes with the edge of the sheets, then turned her gaze to the ceiling. Mom's funeral would be in a few days, and most of the people attending wouldn't know her very well since she kept to herself so much. Her mother conversed with some of the same people during Sunday services, but other than that, she spent most of her time in solitude. Nina supposed Mom had been content with that.

Unraveling the warm bedsheets from her body, she rolled over onto her stomach. The back of her throat burned. Nina was exhausted, yet restless. She wanted to wait awhile before falling back to sleep, having learned through experience that her dreams were more likely to continue from where they left off if she went back to sleep too soon.

Nina yawned and stumbled from her room with lantern in hand, leading herself down the hallway to the kitchen. She poured herself a glass of cold water and quenched her thirst with a few gulps, then placed the glass in the sink with the rest of the dirty dishes. Nina kept reminding herself she needed to wash them, but so far she had ignored those reminders.

She walked into the living room, all alone in the home where she had roamed for over twenty years. She remembered sitting in the middle of the braided oval throw rug with all of her toys scattered around, her mother watching her from her chair, humming with a bemused expression.

"Mamm." Nina's voice quavered. She went over to her mother's chair. Lying on the cushion was the colorful potholder she had started a month ago. There it was, all finished and neat, well-made with her frail hands. Skimming her fingers underneath the potholder, Nina brought it close and nuzzled it beneath her chin. Her eyes stung, and she gasped for breath.

Swabbing her face with the sleeve of her nightgown, she laid the knitted piece back down on Mom's chair. Nina went back down the hallway to return to her room. But catching a glimpse of the stairway to the attic, Nina went there instead.

How surreal to think that it was only a little over a month ago that she and Mom had talked about the photo she found in the box. She crept over to it and lifted the lid, no longer caring about the pile of dresses on top. They dropped inelegantly to the floor, and the lid struck the side of the box. Impulsively, she picked up the first thing she saw, which was the top of the birdcage, and gave it a toss. It clanked against the floor, rolling until it bumped the wall on the other side of the attic.

Sinking to the floor, Nina bent her knees and brought her feet together. She wrapped her arms around her legs, but that didn't prevent the cold from cutting through her body. Her heart thudded dully in her chest. *I am truly alone in this world. I have no living family, and my friends aren't enough for me to feel content.* She pressed her face to her knees and sobbed.

Nina stayed in the same spot for what seemed like hours. Since there were no windows, she wasn't sure whether the sun had come up yet or not. Surprisingly, she dozed off once or twice while seated on the floor. Perhaps it was time for her to crawl back into bed, unless it was so late she had to get ready for work. Rising from the floor, Nina brushed her nightgown and glanced toward the birdcage on the other side of the room. *I should probably put it back where it belongs.*

As she approached the cage, she noticed something on the bottom. Nina shuffled closer, picking it up and taking a closer look. There was definitely something peculiar about the birdcage.

"Is that a latch?" Nina questioned, unhinging the fastener. When it opened, a folded-up piece of paper landed on the floor. As she paused to examine it, her heart started to race. Nina briskly grabbed and unfolded it:

> *Dear Nina,*
>
> *I never thought that this would happen. I figured I would be raising you and seeing you grow up. I had hoped to spend as much time with you as I possibly could. But everything happens for a reason, and I trust in the Lord all the time. Even though I won't be around to tell you what went on in my life, I have been given the time to write it down for you to read later.*
>
> *I was originally from Pennsylvania. Grew up there ever since I was born. But even though I was from Pennsylvania, I wasn't from a populated Amish area. I was born and raised in Philadelphia, with my parents and my brother and sister.*

"Philadelphia." Nina rubbed her clammy forehead. "So he was an

Englisher." She kept reading the letter.

> *Later in my life, your grandmother told me how our ancestors were in fact Amish. They branched off at some point, and then generations later, I was brought into this world.*
>
> *Before graduating high school, I was accepted to a university within the state. I wanted to attend mostly to get out of the city and see more of the farmlands. Though I wasn't ambitious enough to enroll in any colleges that were too far away from where I lived, I'm glad that wasn't the case. Otherwise I never would've met your mom.*
>
> *Funny thing is, when I first met her, I was with a group of friends who knew a few of your mom's friends. What I didn't know until later was that your mother was on rumspringa, and that sure caught me off guard.*
>
> *But as fate would have it, your mother and I grew fond of one another. The issue was, I was almost finished with school while your mother was wanting to join the church. At the time, it seemed like we were both set on continuing with our plans and going our separate ways. But your mother, she changed me in many ways. And I fell in love with the simple life more than I ever thought I would. So I dedicated myself to converting to the Amish way of life, and your mom and I joined the church. Though we didn't join the one in your mother's community. Our families didn't approve of us being together, and although it was a tough choice to pursue, we both left our families behind for the sake of living happily together.*

"Mamm leaving her community wasn't from having me out of

wedlock." Nina lowered the letter, feeling a sense of reprieve. She brought the paper back up to her face and continued reading.

One of the reasons your mother's family wasn't fond of me was due to my addiction. I was a smoker since high school, and they disapproved of her being with someone who would be a negative influence on her. But even though your mother allowed me to smoke for the couple of years we were dating, she was able to inspire me to quit.

Years later, we were blessed with a baby we named Nina. The cutest baby I've ever seen. You must be wondering why this letter was put in a birdcage. It was my profession. Not only did I make birdcages, but I made other metal objects that I sold in my store.

Nina sat next to the birdcage, wrapping her finger around one of the rusted bars. "That's why I didn't recognize it. Mamm must've taken it down sometime after Daed passed away." She continued to read the letter:

Even if I may not be around as you grow up, I will be watching over you. The years of smoking caused me to have lung cancer, and although I was able to move about fine for a while, it worsened over time.

Your mother blames herself for what I'm dealing with now, saying she should've stopped me sooner and then none of this would've happened. Which is silly of her to think, since she had absolutely no part in my condition. That was all on me. But she has always struggled with depression and tends to put herself at fault for things she can't control. Still, she has always cared for you and loved you, and I know she'll continue to do so.

In that moment, Nina realized she had never genuinely appreciated her mother's sacrifices or what she endured when her husband passed away. Nina regretted ever assuming Mom had given birth out of wedlock, especially when her parents cared for her so much.

> *I hope you two will look out for each other, and I hope*
> *to see you both someday. I'll miss you and your mother. I*
> *love you, Nina.*
>
> > *With love always,*
> > *Daed*

Nina embraced the letter, shutting her eyes and bowing her head. *Thank You, Lord, for providing me with the answers I've been searching for. All I can ask for now is a sense of peacefulness about all the things my parents did for me.*

When she finished praying, her body tingled with overwhelming emotions. Now that she knew she had family in Pennsylvania, she hoped she would be able to visit them someday and that they would accept her with open arms. For the first time in her twenty years, Nina felt a deep sense of peace.

> *And let the peace of God rule in your hearts, to the which*
> *also ye are called in one body; and be ye thankful.*
> COLOSSIANS 3:15

TRANQUILITY

by Wanda E. Brunstetter

"M ammi, my *schuck* came untied again."

"Can't I have a moment's peace?" Ruby Weaver spoke through her teeth with forced restraint. She was tired of someone always needing her for something. After the many times she'd shown her five-year-old daughter, Sharon, how to tie her shoes, she should have gotten it by now.

"Mammi, did you hear what I said?" Sharon looked up at Ruby with wide eyes.

"*Jah*, I heard. If you'll take a seat on the folding stool, I'll be right with you." Ruby lifted her hands from the soapy dishwater, and by the time her daughter was seated on the stool, Ruby had dried her hands.

"Pay close attention, Sharon. I'm going to show you once more how to tie your shoe."

Ruby stood next to the stool and leaned over. Grasping the laces on Sharon's sneaker, she said, "Now watch and listen carefully, Daughter." Ruby went through the process of making the ties look like bunny ears and showed Sharon how to form them so they made an X.

"That part's easy, Mama." Sharon frowned. "I can't remember what to do next."

"Watch closely." Ruby looped one bunny ear over and through the top of the other bunny ear. "Then we pull the bunny ears out to the side away from the shoe. This will make a knot that won't come undone easily." Ruby pointed to Sharon's other shoe. "Now put your other foot on the top step of the stool and make your bunny ears the way I did."

With forehead wrinkled and the tip of her tongue sticking out of her mouth, Sharon fumbled with her shoelaces. It took several tries, but she finally got it.

Ruby was tempted to untie the first shoe and have Sharon try to tie it, but she had dishes to finish and baking to do, so she let it go.

"Why don't you go get Stephen and find something to play with?" Ruby suggested. "And be careful not to wake your baby sister. Marian was fussy last night, and neither of us got much sleep."

"Okay, Mama." Sharon hopped down and scampered out of the kitchen.

Ruby turned back to the sink. As much as she loved her three little ones, she'd be glad when they could attend school with their four older siblings. Maybe once they were all in school, she'd finally have some time to herself.

By noon, Ruby was so tired all she wanted to do was lie down and take a nap. The chaise lounge on the back porch looked so inviting, but there was no time for that now.

Ruby opened the refrigerator and took out a package of lunch meat along with mayonnaise and pickles. She wished Sharon and Stephen were old enough to fix their own lunches, but if she turned them loose in the kitchen, there was no telling what would happen.

Ruby remembered the last time she'd given Sharon a jar of peanut butter and a piece of bread when she'd asked if she could make herself and her brother a sandwich. The end result was two children with more peanut butter on their faces and hands than on the bread—not to mention what had been smeared all over the kitchen table. So until Sharon and Stephen were old enough to fend for themselves without making a mess, Ruby would continue to fix all of their meals. She had enough work to do without cleaning up the youngsters' messes.

Ruby took out a loaf of bread and placed it on the table. She'd taken out four slices and put them on paper plates when she heard baby Marian howling. No doubt her precious one-year-old would cry until she'd been fed, so Ruby hurried from the room to tend to the baby's needs.

Once Marian was diapered and fed, Ruby headed back to the kitchen to finish making lunch. When she entered the room, the sight before Ruby caused her to holler, *"Was is letz do?"*

"Nothin's going on here, Mammi. Stephen and me are just makin' our sandwiches," Sharon responded.

Ruby rubbed her forehead as she stared at the mess on the table. In addition to bread crumbs everywhere, including the floor, the jar of mayonnaise lay on its side, with the contents smeared all over the place. As if that wasn't enough, her three-year-old son had taken a bite out of each piece of lunchmeat, which lay on the table in a heap. Ruby knew he had done it, because a hunk of meat hung out of his mouth. The worst part, though, was the pickle juice from the jar that had also been tipped over, running off the table and onto the floor.

Ruby spent the next fifteen minutes cleaning up after the children and putting everything away as Sharon and Stephen ate their soggy-looking sandwiches.

When they finished eating, the children went to their rooms to play. Ruby, with her nerves on edge, went straight to her room and shut the door. Taking a seat on the bed, she took a few deep breaths and closed her eyes. *Dear Lord, please help me. I feel like I'm coming apart at the seams, and if something doesn't happen to change things soon, I may cave in.*

Ruby's prayer came to an end when the baby started crying again. She wished she could ignore the sound and lie down for a nap. But like a dutiful mother, she got up, dried her eyes, and went out of the room.

❖——◆——❖

"How was your day?" Ruby's husband, Elam, asked when he came home from work that afternoon.

She grimaced. "It was busy and hectic. How was yours?"

"Things went well at the cabinet shop. I had several new customers today."

"That's good." Ruby gestured to the stack of mail on the roll-top desk in the kitchen. "There's the mail. I haven't had time to go through it."

"Okay, I'll take a look." He picked up the letters and took a seat at the table.

While Elam went through the mail, Ruby began peeling potatoes. "There's chicken baking in the oven, and I'll make mashed potatoes just the way you like them."

"Sounds good, Ruby." Elam smacked his lips. "Oh, there's a letter here from your friend Esta. Should I slice the envelope open so you can read it now?"

"No, that's okay. I'll read it later. I need to get supper going so we can eat."

"Okay, I'll put her letter back on the desk and you can read it when you have some free time."

Free time? Ruby's fingers tightened around the potato peeler. *When will I ever have any free time?*

When supper was over and the dishes were done, Elam suggested Ruby join him on the porch to enjoy the setting sun.

"That sounds nice, but I have to bathe the baby, and then there's some mending to do, and after that. . ."

"Can't it wait?" Elam's shoulders drooped. "Seems like all you ever do is work, work, work."

"That's because there's so much that needs to be done." Holding her hands behind her back, Ruby gripped her wrists. "The work of a *mudder* with seven *kinner* is never done, and this house is never quiet and peaceful."

Elam's forehead wrinkled. "Do you resent our children?"

"No, it's not that." She shook her head vigorously. "I just never get any time to myself, except when I'm sleeping, and even then the *boppli* often wakes me." Ruby tipped her head and pointed to the door leading to their living room. "Hear that? Our baby daughter is at it again."

Ruby hurried out of the kitchen. Elam didn't understand. The only way she could keep up with all her chores and meet everyone's expectations was to work hard and keep moving. Maybe someday when the children were grown, she'd have a minute to herself and things would be peaceful.

The following morning, Ruby hurried to gather up all the things she would need to take to the quilting party that would take place at Hannah Yoder's house. The quilt the ladies were working on was for the Haiti benefit auction next month. Since Ruby's older children were in school, Ruby figured she could manage the three younger ones. Sharon and Stephen would probably play with Hannah's two small children, and little Marian would hopefully take a nap while Ruby worked on the quilt with the other women. She had promised to go and didn't want to be late. She'd also gotten up early this morning and made two dozen chocolate cupcakes, which she'd put in a plastic container and left sitting on the table.

"Stephen! Sharon! I'm ready to go," Ruby called as she carried her basket of sewing supplies down the hall.

When Ruby stepped into the kitchen, she halted and her mouth dropped open. The lid was off the plastic container, and both children stood there looking at her with chocolate all over their faces. The evidence of what they had done lay on the floor—crumbs and torn cupcake papers. To worsen the situation, an empty bottle of milk sat on the table. From the appearance of the floor, it looked like a good deal of the milk had been spilled.

Blowing out a breath that rattled her lips, Ruby shook her finger at the children. "Did either of you ask if you could have one of those *bissel kuche* or *millich*?"

"No, Mammi." Sharon's chin trembled, and Stephen's eyes filled with tears.

"The little cakes were to take to the quilting party, and the milk you drank was the last bottle. Now I'll have to stop at the store on the way home today and get more."

"S–sorry, Mama. I thought the little cakes were for us to eat." Sharon's tone sounded sincere.

Ruby pointed a finger. "You must always ask first, understand?"

"Jah." Sharon bobbed her head. Stephen did the same.

Ruby handed each of the children a sponge. "Now, clean up the milk while I sweep the crumbs and papers off the floor."

Stephen and Sharon got down on their knees to sponge up the milk, and Ruby went to the utility room to get the broom and dustpan. They'd be late for sure now, but there was nothing she could do about it.

"Another day with no peace or tranquility," she muttered.

"Mammi, how come you're makin' the horse go so fast?" Sharon asked from the back seat of Ruby's buggy.

"Because we're running late, thanks to you two making a mess in the kitchen this morning."

"S–sorry, Mammi," Stephen said with a whimper.

"Well, what's done is done." Ruby eased up on the reins a bit. There was no point in making her horse pay for their tardiness. Hopefully they wouldn't be too late to the quilting party.

When they entered the yard where the event was taking place, Ruby guided her horse to the hitching rail. She was about to get out when Stephen began hiccupping.

"*Hic. . .hic. . .*Mammi, it won't. . .*hic. . .*stop."

"Should I *kitzle* him or *schmatz* him on the back?" Sharon asked.

"No tickling or smacking on the back." Ruby looked over her shoulder. "Stephen, keep breathing while you cup your hands over your nose and mouth."

He did as she asked, but the hiccups continued.

"Here, try this." She handed him a bottle of water. "I'm going to count to ten, and each time I say a number, you need to take a sip of water."

Stephen held the bottle up to his lips and drank as Ruby counted. "One. . .two. . .three. . .four. . ." By the time she reached five, his hiccups had subsided.

"Whew, that's a relief. Now, you two stay in the buggy until I get the horse secured at the rail." Ruby opened her side door, stepped down, and glanced up at the house. *I bet everyone thinks I'm not coming.*

◆———————◆———————◆

As Ruby sat with the other women who had come to work on the quilt, she had trouble keeping her mind on this special project they'd taken on. There were so many things she needed to do at home, but she'd promised to help with the quilt, and she wouldn't back out. When Ruby agreed to do something, she followed through unless she had an emergency.

"Your little one is sure growing," Karen Stoltzfus commented, looking at Marian happily playing across the room with her siblings and two other young children.

"Jah, she's outgrowing many of her clothes, and now that Marian has started walking, she's become a handful."

Doreen, one of the older women present, clicked her tongue. "My kinner are grown and married, but now I have grandchildren to enjoy and watch grow."

Someone mentioned the weather and how quickly the lawns and

gardens were growing. This discussion caused Ruby to think about all the yard work at home that needed to be done. One more reason she should have stayed home today.

"Mamm, how come you've been so grouchy lately?" eleven-year-old Arianna asked when she came into the utility room where Ruby was washing clothes Saturday morning.

Wiping a hand across her damp forehead, Ruby sighed. "I'm just tired is all. Seems like I never have any time to myself." She wasn't about to admit to her daughter that her nerves were on edge, and even the baby's crying made her muscles twitch. It wouldn't be right to burden her daughter with that information or tell Arianna that all she wanted was a little peace and quiet. She might think Ruby resented her children.

"I'm sorry you don't get much time to yourself." Arianna stroked Ruby's arm. "Want me to finish the laundry so you can go rest?"

Ruby shook her head. "No, that's okay. I'll have it done soon, and then it'll be time to start lunch. Just keep an eye on your baby sister for now. And don't take Marian out of the playpen unless you plan to be with her every second. Now that's she's walking, she gets into everything if left unattended."

"No problem, Mamm. I won't let the boppli out of my sight." Arianna gave Ruby a hug before leaving the room.

She's such a helpful child, Ruby told herself. *I should be more appreciative. I don't really have time, but I think I'll make her favorite dessert tonight.*

"I keep forgetting to ask—what did your friend Esta have to say in the letter she wrote you a week ago?" Elam asked as he helped Ruby feed the chickens Saturday morning.

She pinched the bridge of her nose. "Oh, that's right. You did mention there was a letter that had come from her. I've been so busy I forgot all about it." Ruby threw more feed out to the squawking chickens. "Where did you put the letter, Elam?"

"Left it on the desk, along with the rest of the mail. Surely you must have seen it when you went through the other mail that day." He reached down and stroked a rooster's head. It was one he called Mighty Mike, and the silly chicken often followed Elam around like it was his pet.

"Think I'll go inside and look for that letter."

"Good idea. Let me know if you need help looking for it."

"I will. Thanks." Ruby tossed the remainder of the food on the ground and headed for the house.

As soon as Ruby entered the kitchen, she went straight to the roll-top desk. Yesterday's mail was still there, but nothing older than that.

Ruby's brows pulled in as she tapped her finger against her chin. *I wonder where Esta's letter could be. I hope it didn't get thrown out. She's probably waiting for a reply from me, but since I haven't read her letter, I have no idea how to respond.*

Ruby went to the living room where Arianna sat holding her baby sister. "Have you seen a letter from my friend Esta anywhere here in the house?"

Arianna shook her head. "When did she send it?"

"I don't know when Esta mailed the letter, but it arrived here a little over a week ago." Ruby sighed. "It was on the desk in the kitchen, but it's not there now, and I have no idea where to look." *Just add that to my list of things to do.*

Arianna looked down at the baby. "Well, Marian sure couldn't have taken it, but maybe Stephen, Sharon, Jay, or Noah knows where it is. Want me to go around and ask them?"

"Jah, I'd appreciate that." Ruby leaned down and scooped Marian into her arms. "I'll put her in the playpen while I do some more searching."

For the next hour Ruby looked around the house for her friend's letter. Elam and the older children searched too. The longer Ruby looked, the more frustrated she became. She was about to give up, thinking the letter must have gotten thrown out with the trash, when Elam walked into the living room, where Ruby stood with her arms folded.

"I found what you've been looking for." He handed her the envelope.

"Where did you find it?" she asked.

"In your sewing room. A corner of it was sticking out from under a bolt of material."

Ruby rubbed her chin. "I wonder how it got there."

Elam shrugged. "I'm guessing you may have put it there. I don't believe it was any of the kinner, since they don't usually go into your sewing room unless you're fitting them for new clothes."

Holding the letter in her hand, Ruby lowered herself to the couch. She sat a few seconds with her eyes closed, then opened them and blinked. "Now that I think about it, I do vaguely remember picking up Esta's letter the day you brought it into the house. So I must have taken it into my sewing room and set it down when I went to get something." Her gaze flicked upward. "Oh Elam, I'm only thirty-five and getting so forgetful."

He took a seat beside her and clasped her free hand. "You're just preoccupied because you are working so hard all the time."

"Maybe." She sighed. "I hope that's all it is."

"I've told you before—you need to relax more and take some time out for yourself. And you can do that right now by taking the time to read your friend's letter." Elam rose from his chair. "I'll leave you alone so you can read in peace." He left the room before Ruby could protest.

She really didn't have time to read the letter right now, but if she set it aside she might never get around to reading it.

Ruby opened the envelope and pulled out the pretty stationery with a bluebird in one corner and a red rose in the other. What really caught Ruby's eye, though, were the bold letters at the top of the page: *If your day is hemmed with prayer, it's less likely to unravel.*

She contemplated those words. *How much time do I spend in prayer? Seems like I'm always too busy to read my Bible and pray. I wonder what else my friend has to say.*

Ruby silently read Esta's letter.

> *Dear Ruby,*
>
> *I hope this finds you and your family well. You've been on my mind lately, and I wanted you to know that I've been praying for you.*
>
> *I found this stationery when I was out shopping the other day, and the words written across the top spoke to me. I thought maybe you would appreciate them too.*
>
> *So often I get caught up in the busyness of life and forget to take time out to relax, do some things just for fun, and most of all spend time in God's presence, for that is where we truly find a sense of peace and tranquility.*
>
> *I look forward to hearing from you soon. I'm eager to know how you're doing.*
>
> *Love and blessings,*
> *Your friend Esta*

Ruby placed the letter in her lap and closed her eyes. *Lord, forgive me for not taking time out to spend with You. Help me to remember to slow down and spend more time enjoying my husband and children. Please fill my soul with a sense of peace. Amen.*

Resolved to set her chores aside for the next half hour or so, Ruby asked Arianna to keep an eye on the younger children. Then she picked up her Bible and went out to the back porch.

Taking a seat in a wicker chair, Ruby opened her Bible and read a passage of scripture from Isaiah. It was just the reminder she needed in order to experience perfect peace. All she had to do when things became hectic was keep her thoughts on God.

Ruby bowed her head once again. *Heavenly Father, thank You for all Your many blessings. Please fill my heart with peace, and help me remember to keep my thoughts on You, even during the most stressful, hectic days.*

When Ruby's prayer ended, she heard a buzzing sound and looked up. Five hummingbirds, flitting back and forth, were busy at the feeder hanging on a shepherd's hook near the porch. She sat for several minutes, watching and enjoying the scene. For the first time in many weeks, Ruby felt a sense of peace and tranquility. She determined that whenever possible she would do her devotions outside, or at least near a window, so she could enjoy the beauty of God's creation.

Thou wilt keep him in perfect peace, whose mind is stayed on thee: because he trusteth in thee.
ISAIAH 26:3

Longsuffering

MIRIAM'S CARE

by Jean Brunstetter

I s that smoke I'm smelling?" Miriam stopped in the middle of clean-ing off the front porch with a hose. She swung open the screen door and dashed through the smoke into the *daadihaus* kitchen.

"Oh no!" A saucepan smoked furiously on top of the stove. Miriam grabbed potholders and dumped it in the sink, then doused it with water. She looked for Mom and found her in the bedroom. "Mama, what are you doing?" She watched her pull some clothes from the dresser.

She smiled up at Miriam. "I'm organizing my sock drawer."

"Mama, did you try to make something on the stove?"

She stood there for a moment. "Some soup. Why?"

"Well, the pan you used is ruined and most of the house stinks of smoke."

"Oh, I'm sorry." She rested a hand to her mouth.

"I'll make you something to eat, but please, next time just let me know if you want something to eat."

Her mother nodded and stepped back over to the dresser, then pulled out some more garments. The puzzled look upon her mother's face wasn't anything new these days. Miriam stood watching her mom but didn't say anything.

Mama turned and smiled. "Is your sister coming to visit us soon?"

I mentioned yesterday and this morning that I didn't know anything so far. "I've called Doris, but I haven't heard back from her yet." *It would be nice if Doris came to visit. Then we both could give our* mamm *the extra attention she needs and deserves.*

For the past two years, Mama had lived with Miriam and her hus-band, John, in the daadihaus attached to their quaint little farmhouse.

She had been diagnosed with Alzheimer's disease, and the news had devastated the family. Miriam counted herself blessed to have a husband who continued to be supportive.

Her sister, Doris, was another matter. While she had told Miriam she would try to come out to visit as often as she could, those visits were few and far between. Miriam resented Doris for not helping out with the heavy care she and John routinely gave. When she did visit, she constantly fussed over Miriam's less-than-perfect housekeeping skills. She tried to ignore the comments. Mama didn't fuss over how things were kept, so why should Doris? Usually Miriam would just bite her tongue and try to survive the visit without creating conflict.

After she'd cleaned up the kitchen and aired out the house some, Miriam made soup for Mamm. When she finished, she left her mother to read while she went outdoors to the phone shed to check messages. On the way, she shut off the gas to the daadihaus. She sighed. *It's frustrating to see this happening to Mom.*

As Miriam headed down the driveway, a buggy pulled in. It wasn't unusual for friends or family to come calling. In fact, it was nice to catch up on what was going on.

"Hi, Miriam. How's it going this morning?" Mama's friend smiled.

"Hello, Cindy. It's been busy. Mamm's in her room with a book, but I'm sure she'd enjoy your company. Also, the house might still smell of burnt soup."

"Uh-oh, what happened?"

"Mama tried to cook and left the food on high."

"I'm sorry, Miriam. But with what you are facing, you're doing a good job."

"*Danki.*"

"Did I tell you that we sold our open buggy?"

"No."

"Well, of all things, an English couple wanted it."

"Really, what for?"

"They just thought it was quaint and had to have it." Cindy let out a laugh. "The extra money will be nice to put in the bank."

"Yes, that'll be nice for sure." *Yesterday, Martha came by with her sister to visit with Mama, and they also complimented me on taking good care of her. But they don't realize the challenges I face. Sometimes I don't feel like I'm doing enough for Mama.* Miriam's thoughts were brought back by Cindy's loud sneeze.

She looked up at her. "Bless you."

"Danki. I won't be staying too long—I've got more errands yet. What are you up to?"

"I'm heading to the phone shed to check the messages."

"All right then. I know my way around your home."

Miriam smiled and went on her way. *I'm glad Cindy came by to visit with Mama. I wish the visits from friends would help Mama with her memory.* She opened the door and took a seat. Miriam went through the calls until she'd found her sister's, and played it. "Hi, John and Miriam. It's Doris. I'm planning to come out to visit you all in a couple of weeks. I'll call back again to let you know the details as soon as I can arrange it. Take care and we love you. Also, please tell Mom we miss her and love her. Goodbye."

Miriam sat there with blurred vision. *I'm looking forward to seeing my sister, but she'll no doubt make me feel bad about not keeping things perfect.*

Miriam entered Mama's small kitchen and heard her visiting with Cindy. Her mother even laughed about something that made the day brighter. Miriam liked hearing her mom's laughter. She had water heating for tea for herself and went to see if the ladies would like a cup too.

Miriam stepped into the bedroom. "Would either of you like a cup of tea?"

"That would be nice, Daughter." Mama patted her friend's hand. "Cindy, would you like some?"

"Sure, maybe a quick cup would be good." She reached into her tote bag and pulled out a box. "I got you this when I was out shopping."

Miriam stayed in the room to see what the gift was. Mama unwrapped it to reveal a nice box of chocolates.

Her mother smiled widely. "Thank you, Cindy, for thinking about me. These are my favorite."

"I know they are, and when I saw them at the shop I thought of you and couldn't resist getting them."

"I'll go get the tea started and be back soon." Miriam left them.

Returning to the main kitchen, she prepared the hot beverages and took them to the women. By the time she got back to the kitchen for her own cup of tea, her husband, John, had come in from working.

"Hello, how's things going? It looks like your mom has a guest."

"Hi. Things are going pretty well. Cindy is with Mama right now, and they're having some tea."

"That sounds good. I stopped in at the phone shed, and it appears that we had a couple of messages." He shook his head. "I liked the ad for needing to inspect our dryer vent. You know—the one that if it's clogged it could cause a fire. We're Amish—we don't have an electric clothes dryer."

Miriam smiled. "Yes, I know. I was out there before you and listened to the two messages. The other one was from Doris about coming here to visit us. When she gets the details figured out, she'll let us know."

"That'll be nice. A visit from your sister is long overdue, and she'll be able to help you with Mamm."

"I agree. You're probably *hungerich* and would like some lunch."

"Yep, I am hungry, and I'm sure we can come up with something tasty to eat." He grabbed his commuter mug and rinsed it out at the sink.

Cindy came into the room. "I've told your mama goodbye already, and I wanted to say the same to you." She walked over and hugged Miriam.

"Thank you for coming by this morning and bringing Mamm those chocolates."

"She's a dear, and so are you. I'll try to come by next week to see her." Cindy smiled at them and left out the kitchen door.

As Miriam watched Cindy head to her buggy, she told John about what Mama had done earlier. "I shut off the gas to the daadihaus so it won't happen again."

John shook his head. "I'm glad only a pan was burned and nothing else."

"I agree." She tapped her chin. "Why did my sister have to move so far away? This all would be much easier if she were also living here in Millersburg."

He looked at Miriam. "I'm kind of in the same boat as Doris. My brother and family live in a different state. But there's a lot more people there to help out with my parents. And they know all about what we have going on here with your mamm."

"Yes." She smiled. "I'm sorry for feeling like I do."

John stepped over to the refrigerator and gave the handle a pull. "It's okay. Some days are hard. I wouldn't mind a corned beef sandwich. Do we have any of that *sauergraut* left?"

"If we do, the sauerkraut would be down on the second shelf."

"Yep, we have some left." John grinned and pulled out the container.

"Miriam." Mama's voice trailed into the kitchen.

John quickly grabbed the bread and condiments for the sandwiches. "I'll go check on her."

Miriam smiled and watched him leave. *I'm so glad I have John to lean on with Mamm needing a lot of care.* She went ahead and started putting the sandwiches together. A few minutes later, John and her mama emerged. She was using her cane today to steady herself.

"I got lonesome and was wondering when we were going to eat supper."

Miriam looked over at John and frowned. "We are preparing to have our lunch, Mamm. I fixed you some soup, remember?"

"I'm sorry, dear. I have a hard time remembering things." She shook her head.

John got down chips and a box of crackers and set them on the table. "It's okay. We're here to help you."

"He's right, Mama. We'll try to be here for you the best we can." *If only I had more help, especially from my sister. How long can John and I endure this suffering?*

A couple of days passed, and Miriam weeded the flower bed while her mother worked on a needlepoint project on the porch. It was a beautiful warm day, and the postman had come along to deliver the mail. Miriam pulled off her gloves and laid them down in the grass. "I'll go see what he's dropped off for us in the box."

She strode away and retrieved the stack that was there and began to go through the mail. Most of it was junk, but she found a letter from a dear old friend, Katie Miller. They'd gone to school together, but seven years ago, Katie had moved away to Illinois. They'd kept in contact through letters but had only been able to see each other twice since the move. *I'll take these into the house. I can't wait to read her letter and see how things are going.*

After taking in the mail, Miriam went back outside to finish weeding the flower bed. Mama began to hum the song "He Lives." The cheerful tune drew Miriam in, and she hummed along with her mother. Even though Mama hummed the tune repeatedly, it was still enjoyable and actually made Miriam's weeding fun.

Soon Mama asked when they'd be having lunch. It had been a while since their breakfast and Miriam's middle actually felt empty.

"Let me go inside and check on the time."

"That would be good, Daughter."

She went inside, and sure enough, it was time for lunch. Miriam got out the beef and vegetable stew from the refrigerator. She poured it into a small pot and began heating it on the stove. Using her cane, her mother came into the kitchen and took a seat at the table. *"Halwer zwelf uhr."*

"You're right. The hour is eleven thirty." Miriam continued to get their lunch ready.

"What are we having?"

"The stew from yesterday."

"I'll get the bowls."

"Thank you, Mama. This stew should taste even better than the first night since it's had a chance for all the ingredients to blend together."

Mama scratched the side of her head as a strange expression crossed her face. "Look at the calendar. I've got a dentist appointment coming up."

"Of course, we made the appointment weeks ago."

Mama gave a brief laugh, but her humor faded quickly. "Oh dear, listen to me. Why can't I remember things?"

"It's okay, Mamm, we all slip up at times." Miriam hugged her and went back to getting the food ready.

Mama went to the counter and opened the cupboard doors. She stood there staring at the vast assortment of plates, bowls, and glassware. She'd reached for one of the dishes, then stopped. "Will we be needing a small plate for our meal?"

"I think we could use them for the chips and crackers, plus we'll need a couple of bowls."

"Okay, now I'm good." She smiled.

Miriam stirred the warming stew and finished setting the table. Her gaze went to the pile of mail on the counter. She figured it would be nice to read the letter from Katie while eating, so she set the envelope by her glass. Soon the stew was steaming, and Miriam dished up their hot food.

Her mother took a seat and waited for Miriam, then they prayed silently. As they ate, Miriam picked up the letter and opened it.

"Who's that from?"

"It's from Katie."

"Katie who?"

"Katie Miller. You remember her."

"Oh *jah*." She blew on a hot spoonful of stew.

"Be careful, Mama. Don't burn your mouth."

"I'll give it a few stirs and add in some crackers to help it."

"Sounds *gut*." Miriam opened her letter and began to read it to herself. "This is good news. Katie is moving back to our community and will be staying here soon with their family."

"That is good news. I'm glad for her and the family."

"Me too. I can't wait to tell John about this."

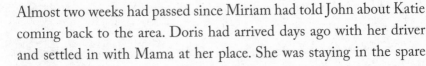

Almost two weeks had passed since Miriam had told John about Katie coming back to the area. Doris had arrived days ago with her driver and settled in with Mama at her place. She was staying in the spare room nearest their mom. Miriam felt better having someone else in the house with Mama at all times. At least for a couple of weeks until Doris needed to get back to her family in Pennsylvania. Miriam was enjoying the opportunity to relax with John in the living room.

"Your mamm seems happier with Doris staying here these past few days." John sat down in his chair.

"Doris took Mama out for a jaunt to visit with Mary Yoder. She's been down with a bad back for a week and a half. I'd mentioned to my sister that I was planning to take Mom out to see Mary, but Doris told me to relax today and let her take care of it. She said that you and I really have our hands full with Mama."

"We do, but that's normal under the circumstances we're dealing with."

"I agree." Miriam frowned. "One thing that I've noticed already is that Doris is really taking over the cleaning. It's like my clean isn't good enough for her and she's been reorganizing things here and there. It reminds me of the way things were when I was young."

"Oh, I hadn't noticed that, but then again, I'm out working during the day."

"Yes, I've been trying not to react to Doris's way of doing things and to her not wanting to live near Mamm to help out. It's not easy to be a good Christian at times, so I need to keep praying."

Patting her shoulder, John replied, "I think the way you are handling things with your sister right now is the best way. Your patience will pay off in the long run for yourself and everyone else in your life."

"Thank you, Husband. I'm going to take my sister's advice for now and relax today."

"I see nothing wrong with that." John glanced at the clock hanging on the wall. "It's about lunchtime. How about you and I go for a bite to eat in town?"

"It would be nice to have some time alone with you. I'll get ready."

"While you're doing that, I'll be outside getting the horse and buggy prepared."

"Okay, I shouldn't be long." She watched her husband slip on his hat and head out the door.

It would be a treat for them to go do something on a whim. Miriam loved her family tremendously, and Mama was very important to them. *Since Doris arrived, things are easier around the house, but I can't help feeling like I'm trying to pass the white glove test.* Miriam groaned. *I swept and dusted Mamm's area just a day ago. Yet my sister still dusted the same room over again because she noticed a cobweb in the bookcase.* Miriam shook her head and slipped down the hall to get changed. She went to her dresser and checked her face in the mirror.

While repinning her hair, Miriam reflected on how they'd canned peaches the day before. It was just like old times. John moved the big box of ripened fruit from the closed-in porch into the kitchen before he left for work. Their mother brought over the peaches she'd chosen from the box. Then Miriam and her sister prepared the fruit for the jars for steaming. She was thrilled with how much they'd gotten done, and Doris seemed happy about being able to take home some canned peaches for her family.

While daydreaming in front of her mirror, Miriam was bought out of her musings by her husband's voice. "Are you about ready to leave? The buggy is prepared to go."

"I'm set. I'll follow you out."

Miriam couldn't wait to have a nice meal out with just the two of them. She wouldn't expect this again for a while, but that was fine. *I love my sister, but when she goes behind me and redoes things I've already taken care of, it's hard not to snap. And knowing that she'll be leaving me with all this responsibility soon doesn't help either. I hope I don't go and say the wrong thing to her.*

◆———◆———◆

Miriam rubbed at the kink in her back and hoped it would loosen up. She couldn't believe how much her mom's memory had declined in the months since the doctor had diagnosed her. This morning her mother told them she'd woken up with a sore throat and was feeling tired, so Miriam and Doris were tending to her needs.

"I wonder who gave Mamm that virus. She doesn't need this right now."

"It's hard to say who passed the cold around, but we'll deal with it." Miriam took a seat next to Mom on her bed. Then she reached out and gave her a big hug. "I love you, Mama, and we'll take good care of you."

"Thank you, Miriam." Her voice sounded a bit raspy and strained. She took out a red disk from its wrapper. "I've got a cherry-flavored lozenge for you to take for your sore throat."

She nodded and popped it into her mouth.

Doris felt Mom's forehead. "She does feel pretty warm."

"Okay, can you get her a glass of cool water and a cup of applesauce?"

"Sure, and I'll bring the thermometer to check her temperature." Doris left the room.

Miriam took Mom's hand and held on to it. She wanted to give her some comfort right now. *If I were Mama, I'd want some attention from a loved one.* "Mamm, would you like me to read from your Bible?"

"Yes, I'd like that." She smiled.

Miriam let go of her mother's hand and got the Bible to read. She thumbed through to where a ribbon marked one of the pages. Miriam read some verses from the book of Mark. Doris stepped into the room with the drink and snack for Mama and placed them on the nightstand. "Here's your cool water, Mamm."

"Thank you." She took a sip and set it aside. "Please keep reading, Miriam."

Doris left the room as Miriam continued reading the rest of the verses and finished with a prayer. *Lord, help our mamm to get better. I'm asking for a miracle, that You would restore her mind to what it was, Lord, but Your will be done for Mama. Amen.*

Miriam set down the Bible and gave Mom her applesauce to eat. Then she stepped out of the room and looked for her sister. Doris sat on the couch holding her knitting. She looked up and grimaced. "I'll be going home in a couple of days. I dislike leaving you this way. Will you be okay when I'm gone? I hope Mamm will be feeling better so you won't have so much to do."

"Things will go back to what they were before you came to visit. I can hope things will get better. But the truth is, Mama will most likely keep declining with time."

"It breaks my heart to see her going through this."

"You needn't worry about our mamm. That's why John and I are here. The Lord knows what each of us can handle, and He has chosen us to take care of her. You along with your family can always come and visit Mama anytime."

"I appreciate that." Her eyes filled with tears. "I need to confess something to you."

"You do?"

"Yes. When I first moved away from here, it was easy for me because it was like an adventure. But through the years it's been rough not living close to my family."

"Really? You've never said anything to me about this, but I'm glad you've opened up about how you've felt." Miriam reached out and gave Doris a hug.

"It's my turn." She sniffed. "I've got a confession of my own about you and me." Miriam looked at Doris through watery eyes.

"You do, Sister? What is it?"

"You've always been good at keeping a clean and organized home. I know I can never measure up to your standards. I've struggled with this since we shared a bedroom as kids."

Doris hugged her sister. "I'm sorry for making you feel that way. I'll try to be more thoughtful of your feelings from now on."

The girls sat and visited in the kitchen for a while, planning the remainder of the meals during Doris's stay.

"Miriam," Mother called from the living room.

She got up and went to her. "What do you need?"

"I'd like some tea."

"I'll heat you some." She looked around. "Where's your cane? I don't see it. You shouldn't walk without it, Mamm. If you fall, you could get hurt."

"Okay."

Miriam went to find the walking stick and found it by Mama's bedroom closet.

Doris popped into the room. "I've started heating the water for tea.

I heard you two talking, so that's done."

"Thank you." Miriam picked up the cane. "I wish Mama would grab this to walk with, because sometimes she wobbles and reaches out for balance."

"That would be a good habit for her to get used to," Doris agreed.

"We should probably change Mamm's bedding and open up the window for some fresh air."

"I'll go get some new sheets and strip the bed if that's okay."

"Sure, and after I get Mama's tea, I'll help you with making her bed." Miriam left her sister.

With the two of them working together, the job was done quickly. Normally John would be filling in, but with Miriam having Doris to help out, John was freed up earlier in the morning to go do his job shoeing horses, which was nice for a change.

Miriam assisted Mama as she got back into bed. She could hear Doris scrubbing the porcelain in the bathroom and humming while working. Miriam looked around the bedroom and picked up the dirty clothes from the hamper. "I'm going to do the laundry, Doris."

"Okay."

Mom smiled. "I'd like to help you, Daughter, but I need to rest."

"That's all right, Mama. You just take it easy." Miriam slipped out of the room and gathered a few more things from her own room to add with Mother's clothes. After she'd put all the clothes in the washer, Miriam stood there rubbing her lower back. *I hope I can put up with my stiffness and pain through the day. Lord, please give me relief and the strength that I need to help out with Mamm. Thank You. Amen.*

A week had passed since Doris left for home. Miriam went over to her mama's kitchen to look for some oatmeal in the cupboard. Her back felt better after she'd gone to the chiropractor a day before Doris had left, and she hoped the treatment would hold for a while.

She debated on boiling eggs and having mush ready for Mom. But Mama did like her eggs sunny side up with a couple pieces of toast. Miriam figured she'd wait and see what her Mom would like first. She was glad her mama had gotten over her cold and could get around better. They'd be attending church this morning, and Miriam had eaten a couple of doughnuts earlier with John at their place next door.

Mama came into the room. "Good morning, Doris."

"Good morning to you. But I'm Miriam, Mama."

"Oh yes, I'm sorry, Daughter. I do miss your sister."

"I understand, Mamm. We all miss her for many reasons. Are you hungry?"

She nodded. "What did you have to eat?"

"John and I had a couple of doughnuts."

"Hmm. . .I think I'd like some toast with eggs."

"I'll heat up the pan to get your breakfast started."

"Do we have any *kaffi* this morning?"

"But Mama, you don't like coffee, remember?"

Mom stared off for a moment and sighed. "I think that is right. I'm not a coffee drinker at all."

"Would you enjoy some hot tea or cranberry juice?"

"Either one is fine with me. I'll sit here at the table while you do that."

Miriam got her some juice and plopped an egg cooked sunny-side up on top of a slice of toast. She left the kitchen and headed for her mother's bedroom, where she made the bed and laid out Mom's church clothes.

After Miriam's mom had finished her food, she headed for her bedroom. Miriam was just coming out of there and smiled at her mom. "You'll need to get ready to go."

Mama stepped into the bedroom. "Miriam," she called a moment later.

"Yes, I'm here."

"Why are my church clothes out?"

"Because today is Sunday. Go look at your calendar on the wall." Miriam pointed toward it.

"Okay, I'll take a look at it." She stepped over and glanced for a second. "You're right. Today is Sunday. I'd best get ready to go."

After church, Miriam visited with Katie Miller, who was staying at her parents' place. Her best friend's youngest son, Wayne, was with her as well, but her husband hadn't joined them yet. Miriam enjoyed chatting and invited Katie and Wayne over for supper later.

Once home, Miriam helped her mother change out of her church clothes and into another dress and then went next door. She planned on fixing an easy meal of a vegetable casserole, salad, and marinated chicken. John didn't mind barbecuing, and she would put together all the other food needed for their supper.

Mama came over from her place with her cane and sat in the kitchen. "Who's coming over later?"

"Just Katie Miller and her son Wayne. Katie's folks had other plans."

"Oh, I see. What's John doing outside?"

"He's probably cleaning off the grill for the chicken we'll be having for supper."

She nodded.

"I'm washing off some vegetables to use in the casserole."

"Would you like some help?"

John came into the kitchen from outside. "I need to buy a new grill scrubber. The one I have isn't working the best. But I'll make do for now."

"Write it down on the grocery list on the refrigerator. We can pick one up next week."

"That would be a good idea."

Mom's eyes appeared watery. "Your *daed* liked to cook outside on the grill. I sure do miss him."

"I know you do, Mama, and I miss him too."

John turned to her. "He was a good man. And a well-respected minister of our community."

Mom set her cane aside. "If I can work at the table, maybe I can help you with something."

"I never turn down a helping hand. In fact, here's a cutting board if you wouldn't mind chopping up some broccoli."

"Okay. That sounds easy enough."

Miriam gave her the washed and drained vegetables and watched as Mama began to cut up the broccoli. She appreciated her mother's assistance, as well as John's. Family was a necessity in her life, and she liked being a part of it.

After dinner they all were in the living room. Mother sat working on her needlepoint and John visited with Wayne while Miriam and Katie talked.

"I'm glad to be back in our community. We've found a nice house that will work for us. It belonged to an English family, so we'll have to convert things over to gas."

"I can't wait to see it."

"How about tomorrow? That would be fun. I could come by and get you both."

"That sounds great. Let's plan for it."

Mama seemed to be listening while working on her project. Miriam hoped that was the case.

At that moment Mom looked up from her work and commented, "Sounds like fun going to see your home."

"We haven't purchased it yet, but we are praying that the Lord will help us to get it."

Mama smiled and went back to her needlepoint.

"It'll be wonderful to have my best friend back in Millersburg," Miriam said. "It will be like old times."

"I agree, and I'll be here to help you with things when you need it." Katie patted her arm. Miriam had to admit she felt overwhelmed at times, but she knew others were watching her. She thought it best to try to keep moving forward, hoping to encourage someone else.

Today Miriam felt a heavy weight lift away from her shoulders. *I am truly blessed the Lord has answered my prayer.*

"Maybe it would be good to have dessert." John stood up and stretched.

Miriam smiled up at her husband. "I think that's a nice idea."

"How about I help you get things ready?" Katie looked over at her.

Miriam stood. "Thank you. I'll go ahead and get the pies out."

In the kitchen she pulled out the desserts from the refrigerator and set them on the table. Katie helped gather the utensils and dishes. Miriam then checked on the coffee and got the hot water going. She closed her eyes. *Thank You, Lord, for my family and for bringing back my best friend and her family. With the help You provide, I can stay the course with longsuffering. Thank You, heavenly Father. Amen.*

With all lowliness and meekness, with longsuffering,
forbearing one another in love.
Ephesians 4:2

LAURA'S CHOICE

by Wanda E. Brunstetter

Hey, miss, can you help me over here?"

Laura Herschberger turned away from the table where she'd been looking through some bolts of material to see who had called out to her. She didn't recognize the middle-aged English woman with frizzy red hair, but the lady kept an eye on Laura and gestured for her to come over to where she stood by the front counter.

This is strange. I wonder what she wants. Laura set the material aside and joined the woman. "Did you have a question for me?"

The woman pointed to the battery-operated candles that had been placed on one end of the counter. "What is the price of those?"

"I'm not sure." Laura's brow creased. "Isn't there a price sticker on them?"

"No, but I figured since you work in this store, you'd know what they cost."

A warm flush crept across Laura's cheeks. "Oh no, I don't work here. The owner is in the back room looking for something."

Just then, Phoebe Miller showed up with two bolts of material in different shades of green. "Would one of these be what you want, Laura?"

"*Jah*, this one is perfect." Laura gestured to the blue-green material. "Once I get the dress made, I'll make a matching shirt for David. We'll use them in two months for the wedding of my youngest sister, Doretta."

"How is your husband? Is he still farming, or has he found some other kind of work to do?"

Laura was about to respond when the red-haired woman stepped between them. "Excuse me, but are you the owner of this store?" she asked, looking at Phoebe.

"Yes, I am."

"Then can you please tell me how much these candles are?"

"They are ten dollars a pair."

"Okay, I'll take two sets."

Phoebe smiled. "I'll be with you as soon as I ring up my other customer's material." She motioned to Laura.

Deep wrinkles formed on the other woman's forehead. "I realize she was here first, but I have someplace I need to go, so I'm in a hurry."

"It's all right, Phoebe," Laura was quick to say. "I'll leave the material here on the counter and look around some more." She set the bolt down and stepped away.

The red-haired woman turned to face Laura and smiled. "Thank you."

"You're welcome." Laura headed down the aisle where the sewing notions were kept but paused along the way. She couldn't help looking at the sewing books. One in particular stood out. It was identical to the book she'd purchased some time ago that was at home in her sewing room. Laura sighed. *I've bought some nice material from this store to make an adorable baby nightgown, but what for?* She shook her head and moved away from the books. *I'll probably never become a mother.* This kind of inner talk was negative, but Laura couldn't seem to control her thoughts.

After picking out a few spools of thread, she turned down the next aisle and stopped in front of some baby clothes and other items specifically for infants.

Her heart clenched as she picked up a pair of baby booties. Laura wanted nothing more than to be a mother, but after four years of marriage, she'd begun to think it would never happen. According to the doctor, there was no physical reason she and David couldn't have children. But Laura was convinced there must be something wrong with one or both of them. Her family and friends had told her to be patient and stop fretting, but as the months went by, she'd grown more impatient. It was difficult to keep a positive attitude when her prayers went unanswered. Lately David seemed to be spending more time than usual in the fields, and she wondered if her negative attitude had affected their marriage.

Tears gathered in the corners of Laura's eyes as she held the booties against her chest. *Have I done something wrong to be made to suffer so long? Can I ever feel complete if I have no children?*

When Laura arrived home that afternoon, she put the horse and buggy away and carried her purchases up to the house. As she stepped onto the porch, she almost tripped on their cat, Sassy, lying beside two of her kittens. It might be ridiculous to compare herself to a mama cat, but Laura couldn't help feeling jealous because the pretty gray-and-white feline had babies. In fact, it was Sassy's second litter.

Laura stepped around the sleeping cats and entered the house. Her first stop was the sewing room, where she placed the material and notions she'd purchased in town. Within her little room, the walls and shelves were decorated with a few inspirational sayings and Bible verses, along with some keepsakes. Laura enjoyed the way the room looked, and she always tried to keep it organized. She also had several bins, shelves, and cabinets to store all her sewing notions and material. Laura felt this room was the best in the house for her to escape and be creative.

She pulled the sewing notions from the brown paper bag and put them away. Laura wasn't in good spirits at this time, thinking about her present situation. She plopped into her seat at the sewing table and handled the material she'd bought. Her mood darkened as she glided her hand across the fabric. *If I had time to work on this now, it might lift my spirits and take my mind off my situation.*

Laura glanced across the room at a simple plaque that read PRAY. She paused and reflected on the word. Even though praying wouldn't hurt, she pushed the idea aside. She hadn't seen an answer to her most important prayer.

Laura was tempted to cut out the pattern for her new dress right now, but it would have to wait until sometime next week. Laura had other, more important things to do, for tomorrow she and David would be having a yard sale, and some items hadn't been priced yet—not to mention the tables that needed to be set up.

Maybe I should wait until David comes in from the fields so we can work together on things for the sale. Laura fingered the bolt of material longingly. *I'm really not in the mood to price the rest of our yard sale items right now.*

Laura went to the cabinet where she kept her sewing supplies and took out the pattern she used to make her dresses and capes. Then she placed a cutting board on the sewing table and spread the fabric on it. Next she placed the pattern pieces over the material and pinned each one in place. Laura clamped her teeth together. *If I'd chosen another color of material, then there'd be two new dresses for me to wear. I should have thought about that when I was at the store.* She kept busy trimming along each pattern piece with her sharp sewing scissors. Some women in their community found sewing to be a bother and would rather cook or clean house. But not Laura. Once she got going, it was hard for her to quit. She couldn't wait for the new dress to be finished and hanging in her bedroom closet.

Time slipped away as the natural light dimmed in the room. Laura kept her fingers busy until she glanced at the small clock on the work-table and realized she'd been working for a while. But she didn't mind because her nerves had finally relaxed.

Laura had finished cutting all the pieces when she heard David come in the back door. She set everything aside and went to greet him.

"You're here earlier than I expected," she said, joining him in the entryway.

He nodded and took off his tattered straw hat. "I knew we still had more yard sale items to price, so I decided to quit work a little sooner today."

"Would you like to do it now or wait till after supper?"

"Now's fine—unless you're busy with something else."

"It's nothing that can't wait."

"Okay, then let me get a glass of cold water and we can head on out to the barn."

When Laura entered the barn, she and David went off in different directions. Her focus was to clean out some boxes and see if there was anything else they could sell at the yard sale. She discovered some old milk cans and glass canning jars. *I wonder if we could get much for these.*

Laura looked around the area a bit more before she moved back to where she'd seen David go when they'd first entered the barn. She found him kneeling next to a wooden box filled with old tools he'd replaced with newer ones last year. "How was your day?" he asked before putting a sticker on the side of the box beside him.

"It was okay." Laura heaved a sigh. She wanted to tell David how she'd felt when she held the baby booties, but it was best not to say anything. They'd already had too many discussions about her inability to get pregnant, so there was no point in bringing up the subject. Although David had said he would like to have children, he didn't seem to care as much about it as she did. If he did care, he would have been more verbal about it. So Laura had decided the best thing to do was avoid the subject and try to keep her mind off of it by keeping busy.

"I was looking at some old canning jars and milk cans along the side of the barn." Laura pointed in that direction. "Should we get rid of those we don't want?"

He nodded. "Sure. They're only taking up space anyway."

"It'll be good to dispose of some things we don't need, and the cash will be nice too."

"That's for sure. We can always use some extra money to help with expenses."

They talked about other things until all the items had been priced. Then Laura said she needed to go up to the house and get supper started.

"Okay, no problem." David smiled up at her. "I'll get the tables set up in the yard while you're doing that."

Laura left the barn and started for the house. *I hope our sale does well so we can earn some extra money. It would be nice if we could buy my sister something special for her upcoming wedding.*

At seven o'clock Saturday morning, eager-looking people hoping to get a good bargain had already flooded Laura and David's yard. The sale wasn't supposed to begin until eight, but they had everything set out, so there was no point in turning people away.

An English woman, who appeared to be six or seven months pregnant, stepped up to Laura. "Do you have any baby furniture for sale?"

This was not a question Laura wanted to answer. She didn't even want to think about baby furniture, and if she did have any, it would be in use, not for sale. Barely able to find her voice, Laura replied, "No, sorry, we don't have any baby furniture, because my husband and I have no children."

With a wrinkled forehead, the lady pushed a lock of brown hair out of her face. "It's my understanding that most Amish couples have several children, so I just thought. . ." Her voice trailed off. "Sorry, I shouldn't have said anything."

"It's okay." Laura bit the inside of her cheek. *I hope no one else comes to the yard sale asking for baby items today,* she thought as the woman walked away.

Laura was surprised to see her cousin arrive. As far as she knew,

Mattie didn't care much for yard sales. Maybe she'd changed her mind and decided they weren't so bad after all.

"*Guder mariye,*" Laura said as her cousin approached.

"*Jah,* it certainly is a good morning." Mattie's face radiated with joy. "I came by to see how things are going with your sale, and to tell you my good news."

"Well, we've barely gotten started, but a few things have sold already." Laura moved closer to Mattie. "What's your good news?"

Mattie placed both hands against her stomach. "In about seven months, James and I are going to become parents."

Laura swallowed hard and forced herself to smile and give her cousin a hug. "Congratulations, Mattie." It didn't seem fair that her cousin was going to have a baby. She'd only been married six months. *Why are some people blessed with children while others, like me, are not? I'm running out of patience.*

———◆————◆————◆———

"How would you like to take a ride with me out to the garden center on the other side of town?" David asked as he and Laura sat at the breakfast table the following Saturday morning. "I heard they're having a sale today. And since we have some extra money from our yard sale, we may as well spend some of it today."

Laura fingered the edge of her cereal bowl. "I don't really need any plants right now."

"I thought you might like to replace the azalea bush that froze over the winter months and shows no sign of life." David set his coffee cup down and looked directly at Laura.

She shook her head. "I really don't care about that." Truth was, she didn't care about much of anything these days other than wanting a baby.

"What do you care about, Laura?"

Her husband's tone was so serious, she was taken aback. "Do you want to know the truth?"

"Of course I do."

She drew a deep breath and let it out in a rush. "I care about us, and I want a *boppli*." Tears sprang to Laura's eyes, despite her resolve. "I don't think God's going to answer my prayers, and apparently He doesn't care how long I've been waiting and suffering."

David's forehead wrinkled. "You're not the only one suffering, Laura. And you should know that a bitter, angry attitude is not going to change things. Remember, this situation involves both of us, not just you."

"You're right. I don't mean to be so self-centered and agitated." She wiped her eyes with the corner of a napkin.

He reached over and clasped her hand. "Do you want to adopt a baby?"

Laura shrugged her shoulders. "I. . .I'm not sure. Is that what you want?"

"I want whatever is best for our marriage." David rubbed the back of his neck. "If a baby means so much to you, then I think adoption should be a consideration."

She gave a slow nod. "I'll give it some thought."

"We need to pray about it too."

"Jah." Laura stared at her half-eaten cereal. *I wonder if praying will do any good. So far it sure hasn't.*

"So how about it, *Fraa*? Should we take a ride out to the greenhouse after the dishes are done?"

Laura didn't want to disappoint her husband, so she forced a smile and said, "Okay."

David grinned at her. "How about this. . .I'll wash and you can dry?"

"That sounds fair. *Danki*, David."

"I'm happy to help out." He finished eating breakfast, grabbed his dishes, and jumped up from the table. "I'll get started on them now."

David was obviously happy that she'd decided to go with him, but her heart really wasn't in it. For his sake though, she would go and pretend to enjoy herself. She might even find a few more things to plant in her vegetable garden.

The local greenhouse parking lot was almost full, and people were still pulling in, looking for a spot to park their vehicles. David carefully maneuvered their horse and buggy over to a spot available for the Amish. "This place is crazy busy today."

Laura nodded. "Maybe we should have stayed home."

"Naw. We'll be fine once we get inside and start looking for things."

She climbed down from their rig and secured the horse to the rail after David set the brake. As Laura walked along with David, she noticed signs posted in several places, identifying the sale items. She couldn't believe how busy the garden center was. Apparently everyone here was looking for a good bargain today.

"I'm going over to look at the azaleas." David pointed in that direction. "Are you coming with me?"

"You go ahead. Think I'll check out some of the tomato plants."

He smiled. "Okay. We can meet at the cash register when we're done."

Laura hurried off toward the vegetable plants and found three different varieties of tomato plants she wanted to buy. She put them in one of the small wagons that were left. Laura had begun pulling the wagon toward the checkout counter when she saw a young English woman pushing a baby girl in a stroller. The child was so adorable, Laura had to stop and say something to the mother.

"What a cute baby! How old is she?"

"Heather turned nine months a week ago." The woman patted her daughter's head. "She's our third child. The other two are home with their daddy today." She gestured to Laura. "Do you have any children?"

Laura stared down at her tomato plants as she slowly shook her head. "I'd like some though."

"Children are a lot of work, but oh, what a blessing."

Laura blinked rapidly, hoping the tears pricking the backs of her eyes didn't let go. *Maybe David and I should consider adoption.*

When Laura and David arrived home from their visit to the greenhouse, she was glad to be away from the rush of people. Her head throbbed from the shopping, and especially the long wait to pay for things. *It seems like lately all I do is wait and suffer.* Laura leaned against the buggy, rubbing her forehead for a moment. Finally she turned and reached inside the rig to pull out some of the items they'd bought. From there, even though her head still hurt, she went straight to the garden to plant her tomatoes. It would be better to get it done now than to wait till Monday.

"Where would you like the azalea planted?" David asked.

She shrugged. "It doesn't matter to me."

"Guess I'll put it in the same place as the other one that died." He started in that direction.

As Laura plunged her shovel into the ground, she thought about the cute baby she'd seen at the greenhouse. *How fortunate the boppli's mother is to have three children.* She drew in her bottom lip. *I want a baby so bad.*

When Laura finished with the tomato plants, she hurried over to David. The azalea had been planted, and now he was on his knees in front of the flower bed, pulling weeds.

"I've been thinking more about your suggestion to adopt," she said, going down on her knees beside him.

He turned his head toward her. "Have you made a decision?"

"Jah. I think we should check into it."

"That's fine, but can it wait a few more weeks? I'm really busy in the fields right now, and the application to adopt may take up too much of my time."

"Sure, that's fine." Laura's wait had gone on so long, what difference did another few weeks matter? Besides, once they applied, it would probably take some time before an adoption could take place.

Laura rose from the ground. "Guess I'll head to the house and make our lunch."

"Okay, I'll be there soon. Just want to pull a few more weeds before they take over the whole flower bed."

"I should be used to waiting for things," Laura mumbled as she entered the house. "But that doesn't make it any easier."

Three weeks later, as Laura was hanging out her laundry, she spotted her grandmother's horse and buggy coming up the lane. Grandma had a way of showing up at a time when it was least expected but most needed. Today was certainly one of those days, as Laura had been struggling with a negative attitude ever since she'd gotten out of bed. She'd dreamed that she'd been holding a baby. She didn't know if it was a boy or a girl. The only thing she knew for sure was that the baby was hers. Laura wished she could have kept on dreaming, but when the alarm went off, she'd been jolted out of bed and back into reality.

When Grandma pulled her horse up to the hitching rail, Laura ran over and secured the gentle mare named Bessie.

"Morning, Granddaughter." Grandma stepped down from the buggy and gave Laura a hug. "Need a hand hanging your laundry?"

"I'm almost done. Why don't you go on up to the porch and take a seat on the swing? I'll join you there shortly."

Grandma glanced at the clothesline. "If I helped you hang the rest of the laundry, we'd get the job done quicker."

There was no point in protesting, so Laura nodded. She and her grandmother walked side by side over to the clothesline. Laura leaned down and picked up a towel. After giving it a good shake, she clipped it to the line. Grandma grabbed one of David's shirts and hung it on the line. They worked quietly together until all the laundry had been hung. Then Laura picked up the basket, and they headed for the house.

"Go ahead and take a seat." Laura gestured to the porch swing. "I'll take the laundry basket inside and get some iced tea and *kichlin*."

"I don't need any cookies, but a glass of cold tea would be nice." Grandma lowered herself onto the swing.

Laura went inside and returned with two glasses of iced tea. She handed one to her grandmother and took a seat on the swing beside her.

"Can I ask you a question, Grandma?"

"Of course. What would you like to know?"

"How long were you and Grandpa married before your first baby was born?"

"Quite a while, actually." Grandma took a sip of iced tea and blotted her mouth with her hand. "It was almost five years, in fact."

Laura blinked several times. "Really? But you had ten *kinner*. I just assumed your oldest must have been born within a year or so after you got married."

Grandma shook her head. "And I must admit, I became very impatient, waiting for what I didn't know would ever occur. I even had moments when I was angry with God for not answering my prayers about becoming pregnant." She chuckled. "Little did I know that once your uncle Thomas was born, I'd have nine more kinner during the next fifteen years."

"The Bible says we should be longsuffering, but I'm not good at waiting for things—especially things I may never get," Laura responded.

"I wasn't patient either, and sometimes I complained about my situation. But one day I realized that my negative attitude and self-pity were not pleasing to God. So I began to focus on other things and put a smile on my face. I came to realize that if it was God's will for me and your grandpa to have children, it would happen in His time."

"David and I have considered adoption, and last week we contacted an adoption agency and filled out paperwork." She sighed. "We are hoping it won't be a long process." Laura clasped her grandmother's hand. "Danki for sharing your story with me. From this moment on, I'm going to try to relax while I enjoy time spent with all the wonderful people in my life." A lump formed in her throat. "And even if David and I never become parents, I'll try to accept it as God's will and make every effort to be content."

A week later, as Laura sat on the front porch shelling peas, she saw her husband's horse and buggy pull into the yard. She watched as he got out of the buggy, unhitched his horse, and walked the gelding into the barn. He was there longer than usual, and Laura had finished the peas by the time David emerged from the barn. When he stepped onto the porch, she knew from his somber expression that something was wrong.

"What is it, David? You look *umgerrent*."

"I am upset, and you will be too when I tell you about the phone call I received this afternoon while I was at work."

"Who called you, David, and what did they say?" Laura's heart began to pound. She hoped it wasn't bad news.

Groaning, he lowered himself into the chair beside her. "The adoption agency called to let us know that they'd received our application, and. . ." He paused and swiped a hand across his damp forehead. "Apparently there's a long waiting list, and it could be a year or even two before our names come up to be considered as adoptive parents."

Laura sagged against her chair. "I am *schlecht gebasst*."

He reached for her hand and gave her fingers a tender squeeze. "I understand, for I'm very disappointed too."

She sniffed and struggled to hold back tears. "Maybe it's not meant for us to have children. Maybe God doesn't think we'd make good parents."

David shook his head. "I don't believe that's it at all. I just think we need to be patient."

"You mean longsuffering, don't you?"

"Jah, that might be one way of putting it. Perhaps it's a testing of our faith."

Laura was at a loss for words. She felt powerless over the present or her future. If children were not in her and David's future, she must learn to accept it and stop complaining, as she had previously promised herself she would.

"Are you ready to go to the store with me?" David asked Laura one Saturday morning.

"I don't feel up to it today," she murmured, holding both hands against her queasy stomach.

With raised brows, he looked up from where he sat at the dining-room table. "What's wrong? Do you have a *bauchweh*?"

She shook her head. "I don't have a stomachache, but I feel nauseated."

"Sorry to hear that. Do you think you're coming down with the flu?"

"I don't believe so. The only symptom I have is an upset stomach—no fever, muscle aches, or fatigue." Laura touched her stomach again. "I just feel sick to my stomach, so I'm wondering if it might be something I ate last night."

"That's possible. Maybe you should drink some peppermint tea and go lie down," David suggested. "I can go to the store by myself."

"Okay. Danki for understanding." Laura turned toward the hallway. "I don't feel like drinking any tea right now, but I believe I will lie down for a while." As another pang of nausea hit her, Laura hurried out of the room.

Another week went by, and Laura still felt nauseated a good portion of each morning. At David's prompting, she'd finally made an appointment to see the doctor and now sat in the examining room, waiting to get test results.

"Do I have some kind of a virus?" Laura asked when the doctor returned.

He shook his head. "No virus. You're pregnant."

Laura sat silently for several seconds, letting his words sink in. It didn't seem possible that after all this time, she could actually be expecting a baby. "Are. . .are you sure about this?" she stammered.

"Absolutely."

"Oh my. After waiting and hoping for so long, I can hardly believe it." Laura had a feeling of lightness in her chest. She couldn't wait to go home and tell her husband the exciting news.

When Laura arrived home that afternoon, she spotted David in the field behind their house. No doubt he would be out there for several more hours. *Guess I'll have to wait until he comes in for supper to tell him about my doctor's appointment.*

Laura entered the house and put her purse away. She wanted to come up with an original way to tell her husband she was expecting a baby.

An idea popped into Laura's head and she went straight for her sewing room.

By the time she'd finished her project, she heard David calling out to her. "Laura, I'm done working for the day! Is *nachtesse* ready?"

With her hands behind her back, Laura stepped out of the sewing room. "Sorry, but I haven't started our supper yet."

"How come? Are you feeling sick to your stomach again?"

"No, but I went to see the doctor today, and. . ."

David's eyebrows pulled together as he took off his straw hat. "Are you okay?"

"I will be soon."

"What's that supposed to mean?" He moved toward her. "What did the doctor say is wrong with you, Laura?"

"This is why I've been feeling so queasy." Laura pulled her hands out from behind her back and held up the little nightgown she'd made.

David pulled his fingers through the ends of his thick hair. "Is that a *nachthemm* for a boppli?"

She gave an eager nod. "Jah, it's a nightgown for our baby. The doctor confirmed that I am pregnant."

"That is the best news!" David tossed his hat aside and pulled Laura into his arms.

Laura brought a shaky hand up to her cheek to wipe the tears that had fallen. She felt thankful for the lesson she'd learned about practicing longsuffering and waiting for God's perfect timing, and she could hardly wait to tell her parents and siblings about her and David's great news. Maybe she would wait until after her sister's wedding to make the announcement. There was no point in taking anything away from Doretta's special day.

I waited patiently for the LORD;
and he inclined unto me, and heard my cry.
PSALM 40:1

Gentleness

A CHANGE OF HEART

by Wanda E. Brunstetter

Y ou want to move where?" Salome Yoder's arms dropped to her sides.

"Rexford, Montana," her husband, Stephen, repeated. "I've heard there's great hunting and fishing there, and I think it would be good to begin a new life in the *wildemis*."

Salome blew out a series of short breaths to gain control of her emotions. She had no desire to live in the wilderness, away from her friends and family.

He gave her arm a gentle shake. "Well, say something. If I can find a job, are you willing to move there?"

Curling her fingers into her palms, Salome gave a slow nod. She felt that she had no choice but to move with her husband to the isolated community of Rexford. Hopefully after they got there, Stephen would see how unhappy she was and move back to Kalona. Better yet, maybe he would become dissatisfied and be the one to suggest returning to the only home they'd ever known.

Salome turned away from her husband and stared out the living-room window at the darkening sky. Would it be wrong to pray that Stephen couldn't find a job there?

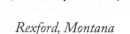

Rexford, Montana

Salome wandered around the yard, looking at all the trees surrounding their log-cabin home. What a difference from the two-story home they'd left behind in Kalona. Fortunately, they had only been renting a house there, but if they returned home, it would probably be unavailable.

They'd only been married a year, but it seemed like the honeymoon was over. *Stephen is perfectly happy here, but doesn't he care about me and my needs? I don't know anyone here, and this community is so small. There's just nothing interesting or exciting to do.*

Salome scrunched up her face. *I'm never going to adjust to living here, no matter how long Stephen decides to stay.* She gulped. *What if he chooses to stay here permanently?*

Another week went by, and with each passing day, Salome became more discontented and depressed. She wanted more than anything to tell Stephen that she yearned to go home, but she didn't think he would understand. Her husband had made it clear that he enjoyed his new job and looked forward to hunting in the fall. He'd made friends with some of the men in the one and only church district here and had commented this morning that he liked log-cabin living.

"Well, I don't!" Salome slammed the cupboard door shut, nearly catching her finger.

She had laundry to do and bread to make but didn't feel like doing either one of those things. *Think I'll walk down to the phone shed and see if there are any messages.*

Salome opened the back door and stepped outside. Although the sun shone brightly, a bit of a chill hung in the air.

Rubbing her arms briskly, she hurried down the path to the phone shed. After stepping inside, Salome noticed the blinking light on the answering machine. She took a seat on the wooden stool, clicked the button, and listened to the first message.

"*Guder mariye*, Salome, it's your *mamm*, just wondering how you're doing. Are you adjusting to life in Montana? I understand that your place is with your husband, but I sure do miss you."

Tears rolled down Salome's cheeks and landed on the writing

tablet next to the phone. "Oh Mama, I miss you too."

She sat several minutes, crying and wishing she could go home. The more Salome thought about being forced to move here, the more upset she became. Anger and resentment toward Stephen welled in her soul. *I never should have agreed to leave Iowa—it's where I belong. Not here in the wilderness with deer and other wild creatures roaming through the yard.*

Salome wanted to call her mother and respond to her message with one of her own, but she couldn't do it right now. *I would probably end up bawling like a newborn calf, and I don't want to upset my mother or make her feel sorry for me.*

Without checking for other messages, Salome left the phone shed and ambled back to the house. Maybe the best thing was to keep busy and try to keep her mind on other things.

"How did your day go?" Stephen asked when they took their seats at the table to eat supper that evening.

Salome's face tightened. "It was *schtump.*"

He squinted. "Why was it dull? Didn't you find enough things to keep you occupied?"

She folded her arms across her chest. "Never mind. I'm sure you're not interested." *All you ever think about is yourself,* she added silently.

"I am interested in hearing about your day, but could it wait until after we pray?"

Salome gave a silent nod and bowed her head. It was difficult to pray when she felt so resentful and agitated toward her husband.

A few minutes later, when Stephen rustled his napkin, she opened her eyes and passed him a plate of meat loaf, followed by boiled potatoes and steamed carrots. When Stephen finished dishing up, she took some for herself.

Stephen cut a piece of meat loaf and forked it into his mouth.

"Yum. . . . This is sure good."

"I used the venison our bishop gave us the other day."

Stephen's eyes sparkled with obvious enthusiasm. "I can hardly wait till I get the opportunity to bag a deer. While I wait for hunting season, I hope to do lots of fishing."

Salome gave no reply. Stephen hadn't even brought up the topic again of how her day had gone. She clenched her fork and stabbed a piece of potato. *I bet he's forgotten all about his question.*

They ate quietly, until Stephen asked Salome a question. "Did you get a chance to visit with any of the neighbor women today?"

She shook her head. "I don't have much in common with any of the women in this community. Most of them are several years older than me."

"Age shouldn't have anything to do with friendships. We can learn from people older than us and glean wisdom from their experiences."

"Well, I'm not interested in establishing any new friends here. I have plenty of friends back home. I can call or write them whenever I want." Salome's tone was harsh, but she couldn't seem to stop from saying more. "And the reason my day was dull is because. . . Oh, never mind." She rose from her seat, picked up her empty dish, glass, and silverware, and hauled them over to the sink.

"You seem kind of testy tonight. Is something wrong?"

"No, everything's fine."

Salome cringed when Stephen put his dishes in the sink, kissed her cheek, and said, "Did you make anything for dessert?"

"I baked some peanut butter *kichlin.*"

"Some cookies sound good to me. Maybe we can have some with a dish of applesauce after I come in from doing a few outside chores." Stephen gave her another kiss and went out the back door.

Salome ran water into the sink and added some detergent. *He has no clue how I'm feeling. I wonder what he'd say if I told him how I really feel about living in this isolated wilderness.*

◆――――◆――――◆

Salome lay in bed that night listening to the hoot of an owl from one of the trees outside their bedroom window. She'd heard that sound back in Iowa many times, but it had never grated on her nerves. Here, nearly everything bothered Salome.

She fluffed her pillow and turned onto her side. It was difficult to find a comfortable position. Salome remained like that for several minutes, but unable to sleep, she crawled out of bed, slipped into her robe, and tiptoed out of the room so she wouldn't wake Stephen.

Upon entering the kitchen, Salome turned on the battery-operated light sitting in the middle of the table. Then she lit the propane-operated stove to heat water for tea. While it was heating, she took out a chamomile tea bag and placed it in her cup. She hoped drinking some herbal tea would make her sleepy so that when she returned to bed she would nod right off.

When the water was ready, she poured some into the cup and let the tea bag steep. They were running low on tea and several other staples, so while she sat there, Salome decided to make out a grocery list. Her tablet sat on the desk across the room, along with an old coffee mug full of pens and pencils. *Since I can't sleep, I might as well accomplish something.*

She swirled the tea bag until the water looked dark enough to taste. Salome cupped her hands around the soothing warmth it gave and took a sip. *Ahh. . .that hits the spot.* She set the cup down and pulled out the spent bag, then rose to throw it in the garbage can.

Afterward, Salome picked up the tablet, pulling a pencil from the holder. She turned back to the table when something moved quickly just out of her line of sight. *Am I seeing things or what?*

Salome took a seat at the table and sipped her tea. *Guess I'd best write down some things we need.*

In moments, her list started to take shape. *I wish Dad and Mom could come visit us. It's not the same here at all.*

Salome looked up from her writing. Again, something caught her attention as it darted and disappeared under the sink, not far from where she sat. *Great, there's a mouse in the kitchen.* She groaned and drank more of her tea. "Well, now I'll add mousetraps to the list."

Salome didn't care for rodents in the house, and she wanted it out as soon as possible. Her immediate thought was to wake Stephen and see if he could do something about the critter. But she calmed down while finishing her tea and changed her mind. Her husband might not appreciate having his sleep disturbed.

Salome surveyed the floor of the room now with heightened awareness. She didn't want that filthy mouse getting at any of their staples. She stood up to check in the pantry and all the cupboards, making sure every bit of open food had been put away in an airtight container. She hoped the rodent would stay away from where they slept tonight. All she needed to top off the night would be to hear that mouse running across the bedroom floor. Tomorrow she would ride her bike down to the Kootenai General Store and get everything she needed.

"I'll be heading for work soon. Is there anything you need me to do before I go?" Stephen smiled at Salome from across the breakfast table.

"*Jah*, I'd like to catch that *maus*. It bothers me to have the creepy thing in our log cabin.

"You told me this while we were eating breakfast, but I can't do anything about it until you purchase some traps." Stephen shifted on his seat. "Is there anything else, besides catching the mouse, that I can do for you this morning?"

She shook her head. "Nothing I can't do for myself." Her tone was sharp, but she didn't care. The bitterness Salome carried grew stronger with each passing day. What really irritated her was that Stephen didn't even seem to notice. Did he really think she was happy here?

He pushed his chair away from the table and stood. "Guess if there's nothing you need done, I'll be on my way." Stephen came around and gave her a kiss on the cheek. "I hope you have a nice day."

All Salome could manage was a brief nod. She couldn't find it within herself to wish him a good day in response.

After Stephen left the cabin, she did the dishes, then slipped her black outer bonnet on her head. Grabbing her list, she went outside to get her bicycle. It was a mountain bike with larger tires, which was what many of the Amish here used for transportation when they didn't have too far to go. One basket was attached to the handlebars, while another one sat on the back of the bike, so there would be enough room to put whatever items she bought at the store.

Salome climbed onto the bike and headed down the road. On the way, she passed the log-cabin schoolhouse. She'd heard that on the second Saturday of June the Rexford area would host the annual West Kootenai Amish Community Auction. The money brought in from the auction would help to fund the local Amish school. No doubt as a member of the Amish church here, Salome and Stephen would be expected to take part in the event.

Soon the store came into view. In addition to a grocery store, the building included a restaurant where the owners served a Friday night and Saturday morning buffet. During the week, hamburgers were served. Salome and Stephen had not eaten in the restaurant yet, but this was her second time in the store.

Salome parked her bike and entered the store, which sold a variety of craft items along with the groceries.

Three Amish women who were also shopping spotted Salome and greeted her with a smile. Two of the women appeared to be in their midsixties, and the third woman was younger and had a small child with her. She believed one of the women was married to Stephen's coworker John. The women said a few words to Salome, speaking in

Pennsylvania Dutch. To be polite, she responded and continued to shop.

I don't fit in, she told herself. *I have nothing in common with the older women, and since I have no* kinner *yet, I would have nothing to talk about with the younger woman either.* She moved along, looking for all the items from her list. The store wasn't busy, and Salome took her time looking at the various things this place of business offered. It wasn't like being back home where there was an abundant array of products to entice a shopper. Salome hunted for the mousetraps. She certainly didn't want to leave without them. Once she found them, she also picked up two boxes of tea bags and put them into her basket. *I just want to go home and be with people I know and love.*

"Hi, Mama. It's so good to hear your voice." Tears welled in Salome's eyes as she held the phone receiver to her ear. When she'd called her parents' number, she'd never expected her mother would answer. Usually all she got was their voice mail.

"It's good to hear your voice too," Mama said. "How are things going? Have you planted a garden yet?"

Salome fiddled with the pen beside the message tablet. "Not yet. There are so many deer and other wild animals running through our yard, I don't see the point in trying to grow a garden."

"Maybe Stephen could build you a small greenhouse. That would keep your plants safe from intruders." Mama's voice sound cheerful and optimistic. It was a far cry from Salome's negative attitude these days.

"I doubt he'd have time for that. Whenever Stephen's not working, he's off fishing. And he's already talking about going deer hunting this fall." Her voice rose until it was almost a shout. "He thinks living in the wilderness is wonderful, but I am not happy here!"

"Calm down, Daughter; you don't have to shout. What's happened to that gentle spirit you've had since you were a child?"

Salome's skin tingled as perspiration formed on her face and neck. "It's hard to have a gentle spirit when you're forced to live somewhere you don't want to be." Salome's fingers curled around the pen and she gripped it with such force, her knuckles turned white.

"But you agreed to go there with Stephen."

"Jah, but I didn't know what it was like or how much I'd dislike it."

"I see." There was a pause, and then her mother spoke again. "Does Stephen know how unhappy you are?"

Salome blinked against salty tears. "I doubt it. All he thinks about is himself and how happy he is living in the wilderness."

"Have you told him how you feel?"

"No—what's the point? He'd probably just remind me that I agreed to move here." Salome nearly choked on the sob rising in her throat. If her mother didn't understand, then who would?

"I'm sorry to have to cut this conversation short," Mama said, "but your *daed* just signaled me that he's got the horse and buggy ready to head for town. We have some shopping to do."

"Okay, I'll let you go then."

"Before we hang up, I want you to know that I'll be praying for you—that you'll find the courage to tell Stephen how you feel about living in Rexford, and that your sweet, gentle spirit returns soon."

After Salome hung up the phone, she remained in the shed for a while with her head down. *Should I take Mama's advice and tell Stephen that I don't like living here and want to move back home? If I do, how will he respond?*

"John King invited me to go fishing with him this Saturday," Stephen said as he and Salome prepared for bed. "His wife, Maryann, will be going along, and John suggested that I invite you too."

Salome dropped her hairbrush on the nightstand and whipped her head around to face him. "So what was it—an afterthought?"

Stephen gave her an incredulous stare. "Now what would make you say something like that?"

"If they really wanted me to go, then shouldn't his wife have asked me personally when I saw her at the general store today?"

"Maybe Maryann didn't know her husband had asked me to go fishing with them." Stephen pulled the covers back and crawled into bed. "What's gotten into you lately, Salome? You speak so harshly sometimes."

She fastened her hands against her hips. "And with good reason."

His forehead wrinkled. "What do you mean?"

"Oh, nothing. You wouldn't understand."

"Try me."

"I'm not happy here." There—it was finally out. She stood waiting for his response.

"Is it because I'm working so much and we don't spend enough time together? Because if it is, then you ought to go fishing with me Saturday. We'll be together the whole day."

"Ha!" Salome lifted both hands. "You'll no doubt be visiting with John most of the time. You'll be so busy sharing your 'big fish' stories, I bet you'll hardly even know I'm there."

"Sure I will, but if you'd rather not go, that's okay too. I just thought it might be a fun day."

"Okay, I'll go, but I'm sure it won't be fun." Salome climbed into bed and closed her eyes. She wanted to tell Stephen that she desired to move back to Iowa but lost her nerve. Even when she'd said she didn't like it here, he hadn't understood and probably never would.

"Good night, Salome," Stephen said, gently patting her back.

She lay there, unresponsive. Maybe if she gave him the silent treatment, he might wake up and realize how unhappy she was.

I can't believe I agreed to go fishing. Salome shifted on the blanket where she sat beside the picnic cooler. Stephen, John, and Maryann had their fishing lines in the water. Salome had been offered a pole but had declined, saying she would rather just watch.

A fly buzzed overhead, and Salome swatted at it. Today was a bit warmer than it had been earlier in the week, so she picked up a paper plate and fanned herself with it.

Bored and in need of something to do, Salome pulled a notepad and pen from her tote bag. She would use this time to write a letter to her sister Elizabeth.

Salome had only written a few lines when Maryann came over and took a seat on the blanket beside her. "Wouldn't you like to do some fishing?"

Salome shook her head. "I'm sure my husband will catch enough fish for both of us."

Maryann glanced at the men. "Stephen seems to be having a pretty good time." She chuckled. "Of course, so is John. Just look at them both laughing and talking up a storm."

Salome didn't care to look at the men, but she made an effort to act interested. "Uh-huh. It sure looks like it."

"I understand you and Stephen are from Kalona, Iowa."

"Jah, and I surely do miss it." Salome heaved a sigh.

"I take it you're not too happy here?" Maryann tipped her head to one side.

"No, I'm not." Salome's posture sagged. "I miss my friends and family back home, and this wilderness is too remote for me."

Maryann gestured to their husbands, who were now walking toward them. "I'd like to talk to you more about this, but as you can see, the men are coming—they probably want to eat lunch. How about meeting me at the restaurant inside the general store on Monday at noon? We can talk about your situation over lunch."

Salome gave an affirmative nod. "Okay." She wasn't sure why she'd agreed to meet Maryann. There really wasn't anything she could say that would change Salome's mind about this isolated Montana Amish settlement.

Half an hour before noon, Salome got on her bike and headed for the general store. She hoped meeting with Maryann wasn't a mistake. After all, they were at least thirty years apart, and Salome felt sure they wouldn't have much in common or find anything interesting to talk about. But she'd promised to meet Maryann at noon, and it wasn't like Salome to go back on a promise.

A short time later, Salome pulled up to the store and parked out front. Upon entering the restaurant part of the building, she spotted Maryann sitting in a booth. Salome took a seat across from her.

"I'm glad you could join me today." Maryann smiled.

"*Danki* for inviting me for lunch." Salome studied the menu in front of her. "I haven't eaten here before. What would you suggest?"

"They make really good burgers." Maryann tapped her menu. "That's what I'm going to have."

"Guess I will too."

After the waitress came and their orders had been placed, Maryann leaned forward. "I invited you here today to share my story."

"Oh?" Salome couldn't imagine what Maryann would have to say, but it wouldn't be polite not to listen.

"When John and I first moved to Rexford fifteen years ago, I was not happy at all."

Salome's mouth opened slightly. "You've been here that long?"

"Jah."

"But if you weren't happy here, why'd you stay so long?"

"In the beginning, I stayed for John. He loves to hunt, fish, and hike. After our move to Rexford, he was the happiest I'd ever seen him." Maryann smiled. "Our kinner enjoyed living here too."

"Did you ever tell your husband that you weren't happy living here?" Salome asked.

"Not in so many words, but I'm sure he knew I was unhappy because I said some unkind things to him."

Salome's face heated. "I'm ashamed to admit it, but I've done the same thing. My mamm always said I had a sweet, gentle spirit, but that's not true anymore." Tears sprang to her eyes. "I don't like living here, and my gentle spirit is gone."

"You can have it back again." Maryann's tone was soft and soothing.

"I. . .I don't see how."

"Would you like to know what I did?"

Salome nodded.

"First of all, I prayed and asked God to take my bitterness and to control my tongue so I wouldn't speak harsh words to John anymore." Maryann paused to drink some water from her glass. "I made up my mind to quit feeling sorry for myself, change my negative attitude, and take an active part in the community. I also went fishing and hiking with John, and in the process, we drew closer in our relationship than ever before."

Salome dabbed at the tears beneath her eyes. "When Stephen first brought up the subject of moving here, I agreed to come even though I didn't really want to."

"You did it because you love your husband, right?'

"Jah, but I didn't realize until I got here that it would be this isolated and I'd be so lonely."

"I felt that way at first too, but later, when I made up my mind to change my attitude, I made friends and began to enjoy our new life in the wilderness."

Salome sat quietly, mulling over everything Maryann had said. Could she set her own needs aside and find contentment living here for Stephen's sake?

"I'd like to mention one more thing." Maryann spoke again. "Some Amish men who come here seeking adventure only stay a few years. John and I are an exception when it comes to how long we've lived here. Many people come and go. So there's always a chance that your husband will tire of it and decide to move back to Iowa."

"True, but then again, he might not."

"Well, if that should be the case, then will you let your gentle spirit return and accept it as God's will?"

Salome wasn't sure she was ready to respond, and she felt relief when the waitress came to the table with their orders. One thing she would do, however, was pray about her situation. It was something she should have been doing all along.

For the rest of the day Salome thought about the things Maryann had said to her during lunch. She also took time to pray about her situation and read some scriptures. One in particular spoke to her, on the topic of grievous words. Salome's words lately were often unkind—especially toward her husband.

My mother was right, she told herself. *I've lost the spirit of gentleness, and I want to get it back. If Maryann could get over her bitterness and be content to live here for fifteen years, then with God's help, I can too. I need to honor my husband and make the best of my situation. Perhaps in time I will come to like this small remote town as much as Stephen does.*

Salome stepped into the kitchen and took out her baking supplies. She placed them on the table and eyed the cabinet doors that opened underneath the sink. Several days had passed since Stephen had caught the mouse in the trap. Salome had peeked inside at various times each day, until it had been caught. She hoped there would be no more mice in the cabin. If any did sneak in, she'd be ready for them though.

Salome smiled and continued with her task of getting the food out to prep for this nice meal. When Stephen got home from work, she would have not only supper waiting for him, but a special dessert surprise.

"What is that yummy smell?" Stephen asked when he entered the cabin a few hours later.

"For supper I made a savory stew with some of that deer meat the bishop gave us. And there's corn bread and coleslaw to go with it." Salome gestured to the kitchen. "But you'll have to wait to see what I made for dessert." She stepped up to Stephen and gave him a kiss.

He grinned at Salome and gave her a squeeze. "Now that's the kind of greeting that can melt a man's heart." He gave her back a few tender pats. "Did you have a good day?"

Still held in his embrace, Salome nodded. "I met Maryann for lunch, and when I came home I read the Bible and did some serious praying."

Stephen smiled. "I had a good day too. You might not understand it, but I really enjoy working at the lumber mill."

"There are a lot of things I don't understand, but I'm trying to." Salome swallowed hard. "I owe you an apology, Husband."

"For what?"

"For the harsh things I've said to you since we moved here." She paused and drew a quick breath. "I admit this is not my favorite place to live, but I've been wrong in trying to punish you for moving here by saying unkind things. Will you accept my apology?"

"Jah, I will." He looked directly into her eyes. "Would you be willing to stay here for a year? Then if you still don't like it, I'd be willing to move back to Iowa."

"You would do that for me?" Tears welled in Salome's eyes.

"Of course I would. Even though I really do like it here, I want my *fraa* to be happy too."

"Well, I'm going to make every effort to be happy." She smiled up at him. "In fact, the next time you decide to go fishing, I'd like to accompany you. Only this time, I'll join you at the lake with a fishing pole instead of sitting on a blanket feeling sorry for myself."

"That sounds great." He leaned toward Salome, and they kissed again. "Now about that special dessert. . . Are you sure you won't tell me what it is?"

She giggled and tickled his ribs. "Okay, you talked me into it. The dessert I made is your favorite cherry pie. I bought a can of cherry filling at the general store today and made some whipped topping to go with it."

He gave a wide grin. "I love you, Salome."

"I love you too." Salome felt good about her change of heart and resolved to be a considerate wife with a gentle spirit. And from now on, if she wasn't happy about something, she would talk to her husband but remember to do so in a gentle, loving tone.

A soft answer turneth away wrath:
but grievous words stir up anger.
PROVERBS 15:1

KARI'S JOY

by Jean Brunstetter

Kari Lambright hollered through cupped hands for the third time: "Anna, where are you?"

Her little sister liked to play, and hiding was at the top of her list of fun things to do. But right now Kari wasn't sharing in her enthusiasm.

Kari's stepdad, Paul, kept pretty busy working at the shop, and her mother worked hard around the house. Grandpa, a widower, lived in the *daadihaus* and often filled in for her folks because he had time on his hands. Like him, she also had to fill in quite a bit because she was the firstborn and much older than her siblings. But her five-year-old brother, Samuel, and her three-year-old sister, Anna, were very energetic and at times like this could overwhelm Kari.

Mom and Grandpa had needed to run to the store and then to the post office. Kari had been asked to watch her siblings and make sure they went down for their naps. First she needed to find them and get lunch.

"Are you two getting hungry?" she called. "Would you like a sandwich for lunch? There's *oi* salad from yesterday."

The two children appeared in the kitchen. Samuel shook his head. "Not egg sandwich."

Little Anna copied her brother's head shaking and made a funny face.

"What are you doing, Anna? You ate up your egg salad for lunch before. You're just being a copycat." Kari looked back at her brother. "Would you be okay with a peanut butter and jelly sandwich instead?

"Yum! That's good," Samuel responded with a grin.

Their sister stood with a blank expression. "Anna, would you like a peanut butter and jelly sandwich?" Kari asked.

She giggled and ran out of the room.

Samuel sat down at the table and quietly waited for his lunch.

Kari started making their food. It wasn't long before little Anna crept back into the kitchen. Samuel snickered as Anna hopped a couple of times and flicked at the leaves on the plant near the doorway, making them move about until she lost her balance and knocked the pot over. Dirt scattered across the floor, and the plant lay on its side.

"Anna!" Kari stopped what she was doing and shook her finger. "We'll need to get this mess cleaned up before Mom comes home."

Her little sister stood with large eyes glistening. "Sorry, Kari."

"It'll be all right. We'll get this swept up and have our lunch." Kari scrambled to retrieve the broom and dustpan. Anna stepped away from the dirt and watched with tears slipping down her face.

Samuel came over and gave his little sister a hug. Soon the floor was clean and the plant back in its place. It didn't look hurt, but soil needed to be added back into the pot.

"Everything is fine. The mess is gone, and I'll take care of the plant later." Kari went back to getting their drinks and food on the table.

She set the last sandwich down in front of her. "Let's take our seats so we can pray."

Kari's siblings climbed up into their chairs. Then they lowered their heads together in prayer. When it was time to eat, Samuel took a big bite of the half he held in his hands. Anna just sat there.

I wonder what's up.

"Sister, why aren't you eating?"

Anna drank half of her beverage first, then lifted the top slice of bread, revealing the inside spreads, and closed it.

Kari took a bite of her sandwich. "This tastes so good, and I like our homemade strawberry jam. We'll have to make more because there's only a couple of jars left in the pantry."

Anna got down from the table and walked up to the fruit basket on the counter. Kari then realized her sister wanted a peanut butter and banana sandwich. She wiped at her mouth with a napkin. "Do you want banana slices on your bread?"

"*Jah.*"

"How about more *schocklaad millich*?"

Their heads bobbed.

"Okay, while you enjoy your chocolate milk, I'll make Anna's sandwich the way she wants it."

Anna climbed up into her chair and knocked the rest of the milk over onto the tablecloth, where it rolled toward Samuel's plate. "Sorry." The little girl frowned.

He stared at the liquid as it came near his plate. "Oh no."

"Not again. I see it, Samuel." Kari grabbed a couple of paper towels and dabbed at the chocolate milk. *I hope that spot will come clean.* "I should have given us plain milk instead." She looked at Anna. "You'll need to be more careful with your drink," she grumbled.

Her little sister sheepishly sat there while Kari mixed up more chocolate milk. When it was ready, she gave the drink to Anna. Kari could see the hurt on her sister's face and felt bad for coming down on her like she had. "Sorry, Anna, I shouldn't let myself get mad."

Samuel started on the second half of his sandwich and had finished with his drink. He held up the cup he used and smiled. "More, please."

"Hang on. Here you go, Anna. Now there's bananas on your sandwich." Kari took the cup from her brother. "Okay, Samuel, I'll get you more to drink."

Kari wasn't getting to enjoy her lunch like she'd hoped today. She filled his cup with milk and added the syrup. "After lunch, you two are supposed to take your naps."

She handed Samuel his cup and took a seat. Kari bit into her sandwich and savored the salty-sweet blend on the soft white bread. She even closed her eyes for a moment to savor the moment, but the silence ended.

"Sister, I want a story," Samuel said as he munched on the

remainder of his sandwich.

"Would you like a story too, Anna?"

She nodded.

"Okay, after we're done and I've gotten the stuff all put away, we'll have story time."

Maybe the worst is over, Kari thought. *Besides, what else could happen?*

After everything had been put away from lunch, Kari got her siblings up in their bedroom for their naps and made sure each had a blanket to lie under.

She stepped over to their books and held up a few titles so Samuel and Anna could see them. "Okay, which one of these would you like me to read to you?"

They both pointed to the book with the chicken on the cover. Kari set the other books aside and began to read to them. Samuel yawned and snuggled into his blanket. Anna seemed to be fighting to stay awake. She shifted under the blanket and played with her stuffed bear.

"Anna, try closing your eyes." Kari waited for her to comply and then continued to read the story.

Her sister still resisted going to sleep, while Samuel's eyes grew droopy. Kari kept reading and hoped Anna would grow tired, but it didn't happen. *She usually takes naps for Mama. This isn't fair. I'll have to read her another book.* Anna wiggled her feet under the blanket.

"Well, this book is finished, but I'll read the other one right here." Kari spoke softly while she picked up the next book about a train. "I think this is your brother's favorite story."

A bit later, Kari was over halfway through the book, and Anna was still wide awake. *I don't get it—she needs to take a nap. I'll finish this story, and then I'll have her stay in bed. She'll get bored and fall asleep.*

Kari read slowly to the end, then closed the story book and whispered, "I'm all done reading and you need a nap, Anna. I want you to stay in bed and close your eyes."

Her sister rolled toward Kari and closed her eyes.

She got up from the bed and left the door ajar so she could hear if either child called to her. Kari headed downstairs and looked at the clock on the kitchen wall. "*Mamm* should be home pretty soon with Grandpa. I'll go find some soil to add to the plant Anna upset earlier."

Kari looked under the sink for a bag of soil. Then she retrieved the plant and filled the pot with more dirt. "That should do it." Kari put the bag of soil back where it belonged. *I should go peek in on Anna upstairs.* First she placed the plant back in its spot and cleaned off the workspace.

When Kari headed upstairs and got to the bedroom door, she saw Anna out of bed. As she entered the room, she discovered her sister was coloring on the wall. In a quiet yet stern voice she said, "Anna, you need to stop that right now. Mama isn't going to be happy about this."

Anna set the crayon down fast, with a wide-eyed look on her face.

"Where are you supposed to be? Remember I told you to stay in bed and close your eyes."

Her sister nodded.

"Please go lie down under your *blaenket*."

Anna ran over and curled up under her blanket.

Kari went to the kitchen to get something to clean the crayon off the wall. When she returned, her sister was lying down. Kari hoped to erase all the marks from the wall.

Slowly the colors came off, but not as quickly as she wanted them to. Kari paused and looked over her shoulder at Anna, who sat up watching. "Sister, you need to lie down and take a nap." Kari waited for her to do what she'd asked.

Not much time passed before she heard a buggy pull in. *That must be them coming home, and I'm still trying to remove these marks.*

Kari heard noises downstairs as her mother and grandfather came in with their purchases, but she kept scrubbing at the crayon marks.

When she heard someone coming up the stairs. Kari turned to see her mama looking into the room. Anna sat up in bed and held her hands out to her.

"You should be sleeping, little one," their mother said.

Kari frowned and spoke in a quiet tone so as not to wake up Samuel. "Anna didn't want to sleep and decided while I was downstairs to mark up the wall here."

"Thank you, Kari, for taking care of your siblings while I was out. We'll work on that spot and get it off. I've got something down in the kitchen that will remove it more easily. Come with me." Mama picked up Anna and carried her out. "I'll try to rock her in the living room, but I'll grab that special sponge first for you to use."

"Okay. Thanks, Mom."

When they reached the kitchen, Grandpa was sitting at the table working on a crossword puzzle. He looked up. "How'd it go, Kari?"

"I was hoping it would've all gone fine, but things didn't go so well."

Mom grabbed the sponge and laid it on the counter. "This little cleaning tool should do the trick when you're ready. Maybe you can let Samuel sleep before going up there to clean. Meanwhile, I'm going to try to get this one down for a nap." Her mother slipped out of the room with Anna.

Kari took a seat next to Grandpa and sighed. "It's not easy taking care of my siblings. I've been losing my self-control around Anna today. She's been hard to deal with, and I've lost my temper a couple of times."

"Your siblings aren't the problem, you know. You've been going through all kinds of changes, and that's hard to adjust to. You've lost your father and brother. Then you gained a new father, as well as a brother and sister. Your parents are asking you to help out more as you get older, and those young ones aren't always interested in doing what they're told."

"When Samuel was born, Mom did a lot of the work. But after Anna arrived, it got more complicated."

"It certainly did, and you're still adjusting to your new situation. But it's important to remember that while we may be tempted to lose our temper, gentleness comes from love, and we all need to be loved." His big, rough hand patted Kari's arm. "We need to be gentle with each other in the good times and the bad. Even with our younger siblings."

"I'll need to think about this."

"Just pray about it, Kari. The Lord will help you."

"I hope so, Grandpa." She looked toward the other room. *Why can't I see things the way* Grossdaadi *does? I will pray for help.*

A few days had passed, and Kari got up to help Mom with breakfast. When she came down to the kitchen, the aroma of pancakes tickled her nose. "It smells like sweet vanilla and is making me hungry."

Anna plodded around the table still in her pajamas, holding on to her stuffed tiger. Samuel trailed into the kitchen next with his floppy blond hair. He took a seat and looked half awake.

"Would you finish getting the table ready and go out to the barn to check on Grandpa?" Mom asked as she poured batter in a skillet.

"I will." Kari got busy setting the table.

Her brother was resting his head on the table. Samuel wasn't a morning person, and sometimes he could be grumpy until he'd been awake for a while.

"Excuse me, Samuel. I need to put a plate by you. Are you about ready for a pancake?"

"Yep." He lifted his head and rubbed his eyes.

Mom looked at Kari. "I think most of us got to sleep in this morning except for *Daed* and me."

"How come?"

"He needed to hurry to the shop to meet a customer. I barely had his pancake off the skillet and plated before he wolfed it down and left."

"Sounds like it will be a busy day for him." Kari set the last cup onto the table.

Mom poured more batter into the pan. "*Jah*, your father works hard to provide for us."

"I'll go check on Grandpa and let him know that it's time to eat." Kari left the kitchen.

When she entered the barn, Kari saw Grandpa over by the bags of feed. He sat on a box holding something small. Kari walked closer to see what it was. "Oh, how cute! Marble has brand-new kittens. Look at all of them."

Grandpa smiled. "She has seven sweet babies, and they all look very healthy."

Kari stood watching him speak softly to the little kitten. His large, calloused hand stroked the soft baby's fur. She was amazed how someone so big could be so gentle. She carefully picked up another baby and joined him. Kari couldn't believe how tiny it was and how adorable too. Marble lay there purring as her young nursed against her.

"We probably need to go get ready for breakfast." He put the kitten gently near its siblings.

Kari did the same. "Yes, Mom had me come out to get you."

Heading to the house, she thought about ways to improve her attitude toward Samuel and Anna. Kari wanted to do better at caring for her brother and sister with gentleness and love. *Thank You, Lord, for showing me kindness in action today.*

After breakfast, Mom let Kari know she'd be running some errands. It was a nice morning, with the sun shining brightly through the living-room window. Kari sat on the couch enjoying the rays of it hitting her shoulders.

"I'm heading back to the shop." Dad stood by the doorway.

Mom got up from the rocker and moved over by him. "You must have taken a break."

He put his hat back on. "I did, but now I'd better get going again."

"I hope your day goes well. I made you a lunch and thought I'd bring it out to you."

"Thank you." He turned. "I'll just take it with me."

"See you later, Daed." Kari smiled and watched them leave the room together.

Samuel came in and climbed up onto the couch. Kari turned and tousled her brother's hair. "You like watching our father go to work."

"Jah." He leaned against the back of the sofa and stared out the window.

"I'll watch with you." Kari sat up.

They both waved and waited until he crossed the yard and went inside the shop.

Anna dashed over to the couch. She climbed up and took a seat.

Samuel pointed toward the shop and looked at his sister. "Daed is working."

Anna smiled and climbed back off the couch.

"Where are you going, Sister?"

She motioned to the toy box and went over to it. Anna removed the lid and took out some of the stuffed animals. Samuel joined her and rummaged through the toys too. Kari saw that about half of the contents were on the floor.

Grandpa meandered in and smiled. "I can see some imaginations are getting to work."

It was true—Samuel had a toy horse out and was shaking the reins behind it. Anna sat next to him holding a baby doll as if they were heading someplace.

"*Mamm* said earlier that she would be leaving. Will you be going with her this morning?" Kari leaned forward.

"No, I'm staying home, but I might go over to your dad's shop later." He lifted his index finger. "I should grab my crossword book and work on the puzzle I'm trying to finish." He got up and left.

Kari went up to her room and sat down on the unmade bed. *I don't want to spend my whole summer taking care of the siblings.* She scowled. *Most of my friends are working and making money, but not me.*

Standing up, Kari made her bed, finishing up by smoothing the coverlet. She sniffed and noticed how stuffy the room seemed, so she opened the window to freshen up the space.

"That's better." She breathed in the fresh morning breeze.

Letting her head relax against the window frame, she could see across the countryside. Fog floated lazily through the valley. Kari noticed how the mist left a heavy coat of water droplets on the plants that sparkled in the sunlight. Kari let out a long, contented breath as she enjoyed the view. Despite this nice quiet moment, uncomfortable questions surfaced. *Why did my father and brother have to be taken? When will I have my own life?*

She heard her door creak open and turned as Anna came in with a stuffed bunny. "Hello, Mrs. Rabbit." Kari gave the bunny's foot a quick shake.

Anna let out a laugh as she made the toy hop around on the bed.

"Kari," Mom called from downstairs.

Oh great. I wonder what she wants now. "Yes, I'm coming."

When she got to the top of the stairs, she saw Mom holding an empty laundry basket. "I've started the *wesch*. When it's done, would you please hang the clothes out on the line?"

"Yes, I'll take of the laundry." Kari looked back toward her room. Anna had rumpled her bedding. She and the bunny lay under the coverlet. "Sister, I just made my bed." She groaned.

Anna held the stuffed toy closer to herself. "My bed." She giggled.

I am not in the mood for this right now. Kari came over and pulled the covers off of her. "I'm going to tickle you, Anna."

"No, my bed."

Kari tickled her tummy. The girl squealed and giggled in delight from the attention. It wasn't long before Samuel arrived and peeked in with a wide smile. Soon he was on Kari's bed getting tickled too. After a bit, she gave her siblings a chance to rest. "Did you both like being tickled?"

"Jah."

Kari rose and motioned to the door. "Let's go see how your beds look."

Anna and Samuel got up and headed for their room. Kari quickly restored her bedcovers and then followed them to their room. "Hmm. . . You two need to try fixing your bedding." She stood there and watched little Anna lay down her toy. Then she tried to pull the sheet up to the headboard.

"Good job, Anna. You'll need help with the rest of it."

Samuel went over to his bed and tugged the sheet and blanket against the headboard. "Look, Sister." He hurried to do the work, and it showed. But he was only five years old, and he thought it looked great.

Anna pulled on the bedding a little more, but Kari followed behind her to do it right. Then she set the pillow on top of the bedcovers as her little sister stood aside with Samuel watching.

Kari went over and fixed Samuel's bedding too. "Okay, now that's done. I think I'll go find Mamm to see what to make us all for lunch."

Kari left her siblings and went downstairs. Grandpa sat in the living room napping with his crossword book lying on his lap. She peeked into the kitchen, but Mom wasn't in there. She listened but didn't hear anything. "Maybe she's outside in the garden," Kari mumbled.

She headed back to the kitchen and went out the door, finding Mama planting a new row of strawberry plants. "I've been wanting to get these put in since yesterday, when our neighbor brought them by, but I got busy."

Kari knelt near her. "We sure don't have a lot of strawberry jam left in the pantry."

"You're right, and that's why I'm adding more plants, hoping to give us extra berries next year." Mom dug out a hole with her spade, then set in a new plant. She was wearing her favorite gardening gloves. "What's Grandpa doing?" she asked Kari.

"He's in the house sleeping—or at least he was."

Mama put soil in around the new plant. "What are your sister and brother up to?"

"I played with them in my room. Then we went into their bedroom to try to learn how to make their beds."

"Thank you for doing that. It never hurts to establish good habits, and making our beds in the morning is a nice one." Mama picked up a large plant and looked it over. "I hope we get a good amount of strawberries this summer and next."

"Me too. Oh, I came out to ask you what you'd like me to fix us for lunch."

Mother dug again at the soil. "There's sliced ham and cheese you can eat."

"Okay. That's Grandpa's favorite." Kari rubbed her thumb over a berry leaf. "I'll go and check on my siblings to see what they're up to." *I hope Anna is better this time with me watching her.* Kari rose to her feet.

It was as though Mom had read her mind when she looked up at Kari with gentleness and commented, "I'll be praying that today goes better than the last time you watched Anna."

Kari nodded.

"Okay, so after I get these planted, I'll be coming in to wash up."

"All right." She turned and headed for the house.

Once inside, Kari stopped and looked in the kitchen cupboard for some chips or crackers. *These cheese crackers will go well with the sandwiches.*

Grandpa still napped in the chair, so Kari crept by him and went upstairs. At the top she could hear Samuel and Anna talking to each other and found them playing with some blocks on the toy table. Kari watched them play and thought about taking them outside to have some fun. It wasn't long before she heard her mama in the house. Kari was sure Mother wouldn't take long to freshen up and be on her way.

She headed back downstairs and found Mama in her room. "If you'd like, I'll go get the buggy out and hook up the horse for you."

"That would be a great help. I should be ready pretty quick." Mom continued fixing her hair.

Kari left for the barn and pulled the buggy out like she'd done plenty of times before. Then she took Millie from the corral and tied the horse up before putting on the harness gear. Kari soon spotted Mom coming from the house. She was in a different blue dress and apron and had put on her white *kapp* instead of the scarf she'd had on in the garden.

Mother thanked Kari and gave her a big hug. "I'm not sure how long I'll be. I'll grab lunch in town first and then take care of the errands I need to do."

"Okay, have a nice time." Kari watched Mama pull out of the yard.

She looked toward the empty clothesline. *Before I go and forget what Mamm asked me to do, I'd better go retrieve the laundry from the washer.*

Kari strode across the yard to the laundry room and grabbed the clothes, putting them into a basket. She took the items out to the line and got them all hung out in the sun. Then she noticed her grandfather outside on the porch and went to him. "How was your nap?"

He smiled and took a seat. "It was good. I thought it would be nice to come outdoors with my Bible and do some reading."

"I'm going to go see if Samuel and Anna would like to come play outside."

"That's a good idea. No sense wasting all this beautiful weather being indoors."

Kari went into the house. Coming through the doorway, she stopped and closed her eyes. *Lord, I'd like things to go better this time watching over my siblings. And please direct my attitude to be more Christlike. Thank You, Jesus. Amen.*

Upstairs Samuel played with his set of cowboys and Indians while Anna named the pictures in a book for her stuffed bear. Kari thought about letting them keep playing but really wanted them to go outside for a while.

"Hey, you two, let's go outside and play instead." Kari watched as they looked up.

Anna hopped up and came right over to her. Samuel started to put some of his figurines back into the bag but then stopped. "I'm ready too."

Her siblings followed her out to the yard. "Doesn't that sunshine feel nice?"

Anna's head bobbed, while Samuel squinted at the light. "The sun is good," he said.

They all stood on the grass in their bare feet. Kari noticed Grandpa sitting and reading his Bible on the shaded porch. "How about if you two race to see who is the fastest."

They both smiled up at her and seemed ready for some friendly competition. Kari marked the starting place and the finish line. "First, let's see which of you walks the fastest."

Her siblings lined up, and Kari told them to start. They looked cute moving through the grass. Her brother won, but he didn't make too much of it.

Kari stood there for a moment. "How about skipping next? I'll show you how to do it first, and you two can try it with me." She started to skip for them, and they followed her around the yard. Kari couldn't help laughing as she thought about how funny they must look. Samuel and Anna joined in the laughter, which made it a lot more fun. After a couple of times around the yard, Kari had the two of them line up to race. "Okay—on your mark, get set, go!"

Samuel had some trouble getting his rhythm together, while Anna took off like a shot. They skipped across the way, laughing more than competing with one another.

Kari looked over at Grandpa, who wore a big smile while watching them play. She liked that they were all outside enjoying the morning and that everything was going so well.

Taking a quick break, Kari strode over to feel one of the towels on the line. It wasn't quite dry yet, but she couldn't help leaning in close to breathe in the fresh scent. Then Kari went back to her siblings to have them do another race.

"How about this time you two run to see who is the fastest." Again, she motioned for them to line up.

Samuel looked over at Grandpa and waved. Anna hopped around, waving in different directions and seeming to enjoy herself.

"Okay, are you both ready to race?" Kari held up her hand.

Her siblings nodded.

"Get ready, get set, go!" Kari put her hand down.

Samuel and Anna ran across the lawn. But this time her brother went a lot farther and slipped on some hose lying in the grass. He fell and scraped his knee on the sidewalk, then began to cry.

Kari dashed over to him and knelt down to check things out. "I'm sorry you got hurt." She began blowing on the wound. "Does that take some of the sting away?"

In tears he nodded. Anna stepped over and watched.

"I'll take you inside so I can take care of your scrape." Kari held his hand as she led him into the house.

In the bathroom, she got out supplies for cleaning and dressing the wound. Kari was gentle to her brother while cleaning up the scrape. She talked calmly to him as she added some antibacterial ointment to his knee. Finally, she dressed his small injury with a bandage. Anna stood by them, watching quietly the whole time.

Kari wiped away his tears with a tissue and smiled. "How's that, Samuel? Does your knee feel better?"

"*Danki*, Sister." He leaned in and hugged her.

Kari returned his embrace. "You're welcome, Samuel."

Anna wriggled in on their hug too. Kari felt warm inside, realizing that by acting with the spirit of gentleness, she had brought love and comfort to ones who needed it most.

Thou hast also given me the shield of thy salvation:
and thy gentleness hath made me great.

2 Samuel 22:36

Goodness

TAUNTED

by Wanda E. Brunstetter

When Alice Lapp entered the Crossroads Farmers' Market with her husband and four children, the first thing she noticed was a sign advertising kettle corn. The delicious treat had been a favorite of hers since she was a young girl. Just the sweet, buttery aroma of it made her mouth water.

"Who wants some kettle corn?" Alice gestured to the tall Amish man who was busy scooping glazed popcorn into a small paper sack for his young English customer.

Alice watched as the boy dove right into the fresh, warm delight. She noticed others chomping on kettle corn as they shopped.

Her husband, Abraham, grinned. "I suppose the *kinner* might enjoy some kettle corn."

She nudged his arm. "I wasn't only talking about the children. The mere smell of it makes me want to try some."

"Okay, okay." Abraham lifted his hands. "We'll stop for some kettle corn, but don't blame me if everyone gets too full for lunch."

"I'm sure we'll have enough room in our tummies." Alice looked at the children. "Am I right about that?"

All heads bobbed.

The family moved over to the popcorn stand, and it wasn't long before everyone had their own bag of the tasty treat. Alice enjoyed the flavor and went for a second handful. She could see that her husband and children liked it too. They were quick to finish each handful and go for the next.

"I'd like to check out some of the fresh produce for sale," Alice said. "Does anyone want to come along with me?"

"I will," twelve-year-old Becky piped up. "Maybe someone has fresh *aebiere* for sale."

"That would be nice," Alice agreed. "Especially since the strawberries in our garden aren't doing so well." She looked down at her six-year-old son, Luke. "I think maybe you ought to come with us."

He shook his blond head. "Can't I go where *Daadi* goes?"

Alice looked at her husband. "Would you mind keeping an eye on our youngest boy?"

" 'Course not." Abraham tousled Luke's hair. "How'd you like to help me pick out some beef sticks and sausage links to take home?"

Luke gave an eager nod before chomping on a handful of kettle corn.

"How about you two?" Abraham pointed to their twin boys, Samuel and Raymond, who had recently turned ten.

Raymond bobbed his head. Samuel did the same.

"Let's meet at the chicken dinner stand in an hour," Abraham told Alice. "That should give us enough time to look around a bit."

Alice smiled. "Sounds good." She looked at Luke. "You be good now, and stay close to your daadi, you hear?"

"Jah." Luke grabbed his father's hand, and the four of them headed off.

Alice gave Becky's arm a little nudge. "All right, Daughter, let's head for the produce stands."

A short time later, while Alice looked at some beautiful ripe tomatoes, she caught sight of her English neighbor Linda Allen talking to another English woman Alice had never seen before. She wished she and her neighbor could be friends, but something was amiss. The neighbor's unfriendly behavior had begun ever since they had moved in next door. Alice couldn't figure out what it was until this moment, when she heard Linda say something about Alice's family to the other woman.

Without looking their way, Alice turned her ear in that direction so she could hear more of the conversation. It wasn't right to eavesdrop, but her curiosity had been piqued when she'd heard her family mentioned.

"Our place is near Abraham Lapp's," Linda said. "Frank and I couldn't believe when we moved into this area two months ago that there were so many Amish families living here."

"Yes, there are quite a few in Dauphin County who have migrated from the Lancaster area. But didn't you realize when you bought your home that your closest neighbors were Amish?"

"Not really. Our home used to belong to my grandparents, and when they died, they willed it to me. I hadn't been to this area since I was a teenager, so I had no idea there were so many Amish people living here now. They really have some strange ways, don't you think?"

"Well, I. . ."

Becky said something to Alice, but Alice put her finger to her lips as she continued to listen to the nearby conversation, all the while keeping her head turned in the opposite direction.

"The reason my husband and I decided to move here instead of selling my grandparents' old house was for our children's sake."

"What do you mean?" the other woman asked.

"Frank and I thought living in the country and close to nature would be good for them. Our oldest, Ricky, wanted a horse, so we bought one for him right away."

"We feel that Dauphin County is a good place to raise our children." The other woman paused and cleared her throat. "There's too much going on in our society today to divert their attention to things that are not good for them."

Alice's fingers curled into fists when Linda spoke again. "I can't believe the Amish folks in the area are still living like our pioneer ancestors did. Wouldn't you think they'd want to modernize and come into the twenty-first century?" Linda's voice grew louder. "There ought to be a law against them driving their buggies on our roads. They slow us down, and the horses leave their droppings wherever they go."

Her neighbor's tone made Alice cringe. *We, as well as all other Plain people, should have the right to live the way we want without being ridiculed. If America is a free country, then why can't other people accept us for the way we are?* She closed her eyes briefly and sucked in some air. *At least I know now why our neighbors have been so unfriendly and why it hasn't gotten better.*

"Mama, we need to get going." Becky tugged on Alice's dress sleeve. "I bet Daddy and the brothers are over at the chicken dinner stand already."

"Huh?" Alice blinked.

"We need to go find Daddy."

"Oh, yes, it might be time for us to meet up with him and the boys." Alice pulled from her purse the old pocket watch her father had given her when she turned sixteen. "You're right, Daughter; it's been over an hour since we began looking at the produce. They're probably wondering where we are." She glanced over her shoulder and was surprised to see that the two English women had moved on. *If we accept them and their modern ways, why can't they accept us and our plain way of living?* Alice wondered as she and Becky walked away.

"Mama, did you hear what that lady said about us and the other Amish people who live in the area?" Becky asked as they headed off to meet the rest of their family.

"I sure did."

"Why doesn't she like us, Mama?"

"I guess because our mode of transportation, lifestyle, and way of dressing are different than hers."

"We don't complain about the way they live."

Alice leaned in close to her daughter, speaking in Pennsylvania Dutch. "And we shouldn't either. But our family can keep trying to set a good example. You and I heard only those two women express their feelings about us Amish. That isn't the way everyone thinks of us, and you should know that, right?"

Becky nodded and gave a brief smile.

Alice clasped her daughter's hand. "We Amish are not perfect, and it's possible that some might not understand the English way of life, but as Christians, we need to accept everyone and be kind." Alice looked up ahead and saw Abraham and the boys waiting for them. After hearing what her neighbor had said about them, Alice realized her appetite was suddenly gone. However, for her family's sake, she would eat what she could and say nothing about what had happened back there in the produce area.

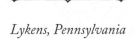

Lykens, Pennsylvania

By the time Alice and her family returned home later that afternoon, she'd developed a headache and felt the need for a nap. Looking at Becky, she asked, "Would you mind keeping an eye on your siblings so I can rest awhile?"

Becky nodded. "Sure, Mama, no problem. We'll all go outside so the house will be nice and quiet for you."

"Actually, I need Samuel and Raymond's help in the barn for a bit," Abraham said. "So Becky can keep Luke entertained until they're free to play outdoors." He placed his hands on Alice's shoulders. "We've had a busy day at the market, and you deserve some rest."

Alice smiled and headed down the hall to their room. When she stepped inside, a cool breeze blowing through the partially open window greeted her. She drew a deep breath and lay down on the bed. Pulling a light covering over her legs, she closed her eyes and tried to relax.

Alice hadn't said anything to Abraham, but she was still upset by what she'd heard their neighbor say at the market today. Alice had hoped that by now the neighbors would be friendly and that there might be times when they would fellowship together. But from the way Linda talked, it didn't seem likely that she would want to be Alice's friend.

I need to stop thinking about this. Alice rolled onto her side, putting a pillow between her knees to take some pressure off her back. *If I keep dwelling on it, I'll only get myself worked up, which will make my headache worse.* Alice couldn't wait to be rid of the throbbing between her temples, and hopefully this time of rest would be just what she needed. She reached down and pulled the blanket up close to her chin. While there was no chill in the room, it felt comforting to be covered. Soon her mind went blank as she relaxed in the splendid quietness.

Alice took a few more deep breaths and finally succumbed to sleep.

Some time later she was jolted awake when Luke ran into the room crying, *"Mammi!* How come that lady don't like me?"

Alice rubbed her eyes and sat up in bed. "What lady are you talking about, Son?"

Luke pointed toward the window. "That mean one who lives over there."

Alice patted the bed beside her. "Climb up here and tell me why you think our neighbor lady is mean." After overhearing her neighbor's conversation today at the market, Alice could only imagine what Linda might have said to her youngest son. The question was why—what had Luke done?

Luke scrambled onto the bed and positioned himself next to Alice. "That boy, Toby, came over to play with me." He sniffed. "Becky was pushin' us both on the swings, and then. . ." He paused to swipe at the tears rolling down his red cheeks.

"What happened?" Alice prompted.

"Toby's *mamm* came into our yard and hollered at him. Said he shouldn't be playin' with an Amish boy and that he should never come over here again."

"Is that so?" Alice's eyes narrowed.

"Jah, and then she grabbed hold of his hand and took him on outa the yard." Luke clasped Alice's hand. "Why'd she do that, Mammi? Did I do somethin' wrong?"

She stroked her son's head. "No, Luke, you didn't do anything wrong. We live differently than they do, and sometimes people run from what they don't understand."

"They didn't run home, Mammi, they walked."

Alice bit back a smile. Her son was too young to understand about prejudices, and for now, she didn't want him to worry about that kind of thing. "Say, I have an idea. Why don't you come out to the kitchen and help me put a little snack together? We'll take it outside to share with the rest of our family. It'll tide us over till it's time to eat supper."

"All right!" Luke jumped off the bed and raced for the door. "I'll meet you in the *kich*, Mammi."

Alice lifted her face toward the ceiling and closed her eyes. *Heavenly Father, please give me the grace to show goodness to others who have been unkind to us. And help our neighbors to realize that although we live a Plain lifestyle, we are really not that different from them.*

Sunday afternoon, as the Lapps were on their way home from church, Alice noticed a group of English teenagers standing alongside the road up ahead. As they drew closer, one of the boys, whom Alice recognized as their neighbors' oldest son, Ricky, picked up a corncob. The next thing she knew, he pitched it at their buggy. The cob missed and hit the horse instead. The gelding whinnied, and as he galloped down the road at rapid speed, the buggy jostled and all the children hollered.

Alice sent up a quick prayer. *Lord, please help my husband get the horse under control.* She glanced over at Abraham. The muscles in his arm quivered beneath his shirtsleeves as he kept a firm hold on the reins.

"Slow down, boy!" Abraham shouted. He looked quickly at Alice, then back at the road. "I hope our horse isn't seriously hurt."

Alice swallowed hard. A corncob could do a lot of damage if it hit a vital spot. She remembered reading an article in *The Budget* a few months ago about a young boy who'd gotten hit in the face with a corncob. He ended up losing his sight in one eye.

After several more tension-filled minutes, the horse finally settled into a slow trot.

Alice breathed a sigh of relief. "Is everyone all right?" She turned to look at the children, huddled in the back of the buggy with wide eyes.

"We're okay, just shook up." Becky's chin trembled.

"How come that boy threw the corncob at our *gaul*?" Samuel asked.

"Don't think Ricky meant to hit the horse," Abraham replied. "Looked like he was aiming for the carriage."

"Why'd he wanna hit the *kutsch*?" Raymond questioned.

"I don't know, Son. Maybe he was trying to impress his friends. Or maybe one of them dared him to do it."

"Wonder how the neighbors would feel if one of us threw something at their car," Samuel said.

"In the Bible we are told to love our neighbors as ourselves and to bless those who persecute us."

"What's *persecute* mean?" Luke asked.

"It's doing mean things to someone."

"We are not supposed to do hurtful or unkind things, not even to those who persecute us," Alice interjected.

Abraham nodded. "Your mamm is right. As Christians, our testimony will be greatly diminished if we fail to live up to the standards God gives us in the Bible. A true believer should never seek revenge."

"But what about the boy who threw the corncob?" Becky asked. "He shouldn't be allowed to get away with it."

"As soon as I check our horse over for any injuries and get him put away, I'll go over to the Allens' house and tell Frank what happened," Abraham said. "He needs to know what his son has been up to."

———◆———◆———◆———

Alice stood at the kitchen window, watching for Abraham. He'd gone over to their neighbors' place twenty minutes ago. Fortunately, their horse had no injuries. But the corncob had frightened him, and it most likely hurt when it hit his side. The whole incident had certainly frightened the children.

I hope everything goes well over there. Alice gripped the edge of the counter. *What if the Allens don't care about what their son did? It's going to be difficult to live here if our neighbors have animosity toward us.*

"Mama, is it okay if me and Samuel go outside to play?" Raymond asked when he entered the kitchen.

Alice turned to face him. "It's fine, but don't go out of the yard."

"We won't." Raymond turned and started out of the room.

"Take your little brother outside with you, please. And make sure you include him in whatever games you and Samuel play," Alice called after him.

Raymond stopped walking and groaned. "Aw, do we have to let Luke play with us? He can be such a *baddere.*"

"Your brother is not a bother. Now, if you won't include him, then you and Samuel can stay inside."

"Okay, I'll tell Luke he can join us." With shoulders slumped, Raymond shuffled out of the room.

Alice turned to look out the window again. She caught sight of Abraham walking toward the house. Eager to hear what he had to say, she hurried out the back door.

"How did it go with the neighbors?" she asked when he stepped onto the porch.

Abraham shook his head. "Not good. The boy's parents were none too friendly, and his dad said, 'Boys will be boys,' and that he was sure his son meant no harm."

"So no apologies or a promise that it won't happen again?"

"Nope." Abraham stepped into the kitchen, and Alice followed.

"Guess we'll just have to keep an eye on things and hope something like that doesn't happen again."

Alice grimaced. "Or something worse could occur."

He placed his hand on the small of her back. "If it does, we'll deal with it. In the meantime, we need to pray."

Tuesday morning of the following week, Alice woke up to a surprising scene in their front yard. After lifting the window shade in their bedroom, she spotted long pieces of toilet paper draped all over the trees in their yard.

"Oh my!" She covered her mouth with her hands.

"What's wrong?" Abraham rolled out of bed. "Is something going on outside?"

"Not right now, but I'm guessing it was done sometime during the night."

Abraham joined Alice at the window. "For goodness' sake! Now, who could have done that to our trees, and what was the reason for this vandalism?"

"I can't say for sure, but if I had to guess, I'd say it was Ricky Allen." Alice looked at Abraham and blinked. "He was probably upset because you told his parents about the corncob hitting our horse. In retaliation, maybe he and his friends decided to decorate our trees in an unattractive fashion."

Abraham frowned deeply. "I can't go talk to the boy's dad, because I have no proof that Ricky did it. And even if I did, his dad would probably make light of it, like he did when I went over there Sunday afternoon."

"You're right. We'll have to take down all the toilet tissue and say nothing to Frank or Linda. Hopefully, if we don't make an issue, it won't happen again."

Abraham's brows furrowed. "I'll head outside now and start on the cleanup. I'd like to get it done before the kinner are awake. If they see the mess, there'll be plenty of questions."

"I'll help you."

Abraham and Alice quickly got dressed and hurried from the room. Alice was relieved to see that none of the children were out of bed.

"Let's see how many streamers we can pull down by standing below the trees," Abraham suggested. "I'll have to get the ladder to reach the higher ones."

"This is the first time anything like this has ever happened to us." Alice grabbed and pulled several strips of toilet paper down, letting them fall to the ground.

"And let's hope it's the last," Abraham muttered. "I don't understand why some folks can't live peacefully with their neighbors and leave well enough alone."

Alice bobbed her head. "We're going through a lot of unnecessary work right now, when we could be doing something important."

"You're absolutely right. Unfortunately, we don't have much choice." Abraham pulled several more streamers down. "I'm going to get the ladder now. I'll be back soon." He strode toward the barn.

When he came back and got the rest of the toilet paper down, Alice gathered up all the pieces they'd pulled out of the trees and put them in the garbage. While Abraham put the ladder away, she went back to the house to start breakfast.

When Alice entered the kitchen, she found Becky setting the table. "How come you and Dad were outside in the yard?" she asked. Before Alice could respond, Becky added, "I looked out the window and saw Dad carrying a ladder, and you were putting something in the garbage."

Alice wouldn't lie to her daughter, so she explained about the toilet paper they'd found in their trees. "But please don't say anything to your brothers about this. I don't want to upset them."

"I won't, Mama." Becky swiped her hand across her forehead. "I bet Ricky Allen did it. I don't think he likes us."

"We suspect that too, but we have no proof, so we won't accuse anyone."

"But Mama, if Ricky did hang the toilet paper in our trees, shouldn't his parents be told about it?"

Alice shook her head. "Even if we knew for sure it was him, it's doubtful that his parents would do anything about it."

"So what are we supposed to do?"

"Nothing, Becky. We need to be kind to our neighbors and set a good example."

The following day, while the boys were outside playing, Alice asked Becky to join her in the kitchen to bake some cookies.

"Sure, Mama." Becky smiled. "What kind are we gonna make?"

Alice tapped her chin. "I don't know. Why don't you choose?"

Becky went to the pantry and took out a jar of peanut butter.

Alice laughed. "I had a feeling you'd want to make peanut butter *kichlin*. It's your favorite kind, jah?"

Becky nodded. "I'll get out the other ingredients."

While her daughter went about doing that, Alice preheated the oven and took out the cookie sheets. After all the ingredients were set out, Alice measured and Becky mixed with a wooden spoon. Soon the first batch of cookies was ready to go into the oven.

Becky had just slid the cookie sheets in when Raymond dashed into the kitchen. "Samuel, Luke, and I were playin' with my kite, and the string snapped right in two." He paused for a breath. "Then the kite landed in our neighbor's yard."

"You mean the Allens' yard?" Alice asked.

"Jah. Is it okay if I go over there and get it?"

Alice was on the verge of saying yes but decided it might be best if she went for the kite. "You stay here with your brothers. I'll go over to the neighbors'." She looked at Becky. "Can you handle baking the cookies while I'm gone?"

"Jah, Mama. I'll make sure to set the timer and take 'em out as soon as they're done."

"*Danki.*" Alice slipped on her outer bonnet and went out the door.

She left the yard and walked swiftly over to the neighbors'. Alice saw the kite in their front yard and was about to go over and pick it up when Linda stepped out of the house. "Is that one of your children's kites?" Her tone was anything but friendly.

"Yes, it is. I came over to get it."

Linda slapped her hands against her hips and gave a huff. "Well, please tell them to keep their things in their own yard from now on."

Alice's whole body tensed. "It was an accident. The string broke and the kite ended up over here." She reached down and picked it up. "We'll try to make sure nothing like this ever happens again. Goodbye, Linda. I hope you have a nice day."

The woman gave no response—just went inside and slammed the door.

Alice turned and headed out of the yard. It grieved her to see this kind of aggravation coming from their neighbors. It looked like she would need to pray harder about this.

A week later, when Alice opened the back door to feed the cats, she was shocked to see garbage strewn all over the grass. Abraham held a garbage sack and was busy picking it up.

"What in the world?" Alice stepped off the porch and hurried up to him. "Did someone do this on purpose to taunt us?"

Abraham shrugged. "I don't know for sure, but I honestly believe our neighbor, or someone else in the area, doesn't like us and hopes we will leave."

"But this is our home. We came here a year ago to enjoy a calmer life, without all the tourism and commercialism we faced in Lancaster."

"I agree." He tossed some more garbage into the sack. "But if this kind of thing keeps going, it may not be calm here either."

"Are you thinking we should move again—find someplace where there aren't so many prejudiced people?"

Abraham shook his head. "I doubt there's anywhere on this earth where there is no prejudice. I've been talking with the Amish man I work with at the bulk food store, and his family had some unkind things done to them when they first moved here. He said things are better now though, and that he's actually become friends with one of the English men who didn't like him at first."

"Maybe it will take some time for our neighbors to accept us and realize we're just people like them," Alice said. "If we are kind and try to be friendly, they might take a different attitude toward us."

Abraham nodded. "I certainly hope that's the case. It's not good for our kinner to be subjected to taunting, but perhaps in the long run, it will make them stronger and more sensitive to others."

The following week, on a Wednesday evening, Alice heard the blare of sirens. When the sound drew closer, she and the rest of the family went to the living-room window to look out.

As two fire trucks and a rescue vehicle approached their property, they slowed down.

"What's going on? Are they coming here?" Luke pulled on Alice's black apron.

Abraham jerked the front door open. "I see smoke! It's coming from the Allens' place. I'm going over to see what happened."

Alice closed her eyes and bowed her head. *Dear Lord, please let everyone be okay.*

Twenty minutes later, Abraham returned. "The Allens' barn is burning at a pretty rapid pace."

"Was anyone hurt?" Alice felt concern.

Abraham shook his head. "And they got all the animals out in time."

"That's good to hear."

"But unfortunately, a large section of their barn is ruined and will need to be rebuilt."

"That's a shame." Alice pursed her lips.

"I'm going to see if any of the men from our church district would be available to help on the rebuild. I told Frank that I would help, and he said he appreciated it."

Alice smiled. "I'm so pleased."

Alice couldn't get over how many Amish men showed up to rebuild the Allens' barn. Many women came as well, offering the men food and drink.

Mr. Allen worked right along with them, and so did his son, Ricky. In fact, the boy even had a smile on his face.

I wonder what brought on his change of attitude. Alice glanced at Linda, who was setting out all the baked goods that had been brought here today. She also wore a smile.

"We can't begin to thank you for all that you and your Amish friends have done for us today," Linda said when Alice approached. "I need to be honest with you."

Alice tipped her head.

"When we first moved in next door and saw that your family wasn't like us, we were concerned."

"About what?"

"We saw how differently your way of living was from ours, and we thought you were a bit strange."

Alice said nothing, just waited for Linda to continue. This wasn't the first time she'd heard someone mention that the Amish and other Plain people were strange.

"It's easy to think stereotypically of any group of humans when you haven't gotten to really know the people and given them a chance." Linda paused for a breath. "I'm really sorry for the way we've been treating your family; it was narrow-minded of us. Most people, when you've treated them badly, will seek revenge and repay with the same or even worse treatment. Yet you've remained kind and looked past our inadequacy. That's a quality that has become rare in this day and age. I'm glad you're our neighbors, and if there's ever anything we can do for you, please let us know."

Alice smiled. "We will."

Linda put her hand on Alice's arm and gave it a squeeze. "I'm sorry for my unfriendly attitude since you and your family moved here. I was wrong about you Amish; you're not a strange people. I see now that you are kind and loving." She paused and glanced toward the barn. "Frank had a long talk with our son too, and from now on, I think he's going to be better behaved."

"We try to make sure our children do as they're told, but no child is perfect and they sometimes make mistakes."

"True." Linda gave an affirmative nod. "I'm seeing things more clearly now, and if you'll have me, I'd like to be your friend."

Alice gave Linda a hug. "I would like that, and I think our children would too." She pointed at Luke and Linda's son Toby. The boys were playing on the swings across the yard, far from the work going on in the barn.

"I believe you're right," Linda said. "We'll have to schedule another play day for them soon."

"Yes, let's do that." Alice gazed at the barn, where men and older boys were hard at work. She hoped the ridiculing and taunting would end now, but even if it should continue, they had done the right thing. As Christians, they had a duty to love their neighbors and treat them as they wanted to be treated, and to overcome evil with goodness.

Be not overcome of evil, but overcome evil with good.
ROMANS 12:21

PAM'S FRIEND

by Jean Brunstetter

Topeka, Indiana

There Pam goes again yelling and slamming anything in reach. She professes to be a Christian, but sometimes she doesn't sound like one. Mary Troyer drummed her fingers against the armrest of the glider out back. *When will my neighbor friend treat people and animals with goodness?*

"Floyd, get that dog out of here. He chewed on my shoes!" Pam's voice rang as she pushed the screen door open and her husband led the animal out. "If that dog keeps this up, we're getting rid of him!" Pam closed the door with a bang.

Mary heard Floyd talking gently to the dog, and a minute afterward, he went back inside. It was obvious Pam was on the warpath. And it wasn't easy to listen to someone get so upset like she did.

Mary had been married to her husband, Timothy, for two years. After moving to the neighborhood, she'd become acquainted with Pam Hayward, an English lady. Mary was bothered to see her neighbor treat others so rudely, and so far there hadn't been any improvement. Pam could often be abrupt and curt. Mary thought it was best not to say anything, but recently she'd begun to wonder if she should talk to Pam about her attitude. She just wasn't sure how to go about it so she wouldn't offend her neighbor.

Two days later, Mary went out to fill the bird feeders around the perimeter of their house. She saw her husband leave in their buggy to go to the feed store. Mary waved at him and continued her task, while the birds overhead in the fir trees chattered. She wondered if it was because they were waiting for the seed to eat. Soon Mary became distracted when the mailman came up the next-door neighbor's sidewalk, delivering a package. She watched him leave a parcel at Pam's door. Before he got back into his vehicle, Pam came out and picked it up. A few seconds later, she plodded down her steps yelling, "Hey, this isn't mine! You've delivered the wrong package. Where's mine instead? Is it still in your delivery rig? I'm expecting something important to be shipped to me through the mail." Pam looked through one of his van windows, and then she gave him back the parcel. "Are you sure my package isn't on your truck?" Pam stood with her hands resting on her hips.

"Yes, ma'am, I don't have anything else for your residence today." He put the box away and climbed in. "Sorry for the mix-up." Then he drove off to continue his route.

She seems pretty upset. I'll go and speak to her. I hope it will help the situation. Mary set the bag of wild bird seed down and walked over to Pam. "Hello. Is everything okay?"

Pam pointed at the retreating vehicle. "That mail person we have is such a scatterbrain. Today he left someone else's package on my porch. Then he acted all nervous about it when I asked if he still had mine in the truck."

"I'm sure he didn't mean to do that." Mary used her apron to wipe away the beads of sweat on her forehead.

Pam continued her rant. "Why can't he do his job right? I mean, is it that difficult to see that the address on the package doesn't match my house numbers?"

Mary's tone carried favor for the postman. "You could be blowing this out of proportion. It's only a package, and he doesn't do this all the time. He was probably upset because you spoke harshly to him."

"I'm not blowing this out of proportion, and I wasn't harsh to him either. I thought you would understand my situation, but I guess I was wrong." Pam frowned. "I think you should go; we're done talking."

Mary's heart clenched as she watched her neighbor go back into her house. *Guess I didn't handle that well. Maybe I shouldn't have said anything at all.*

That evening Mary cleared the table of the dinner dishes. *I want to help Pam, but I'll need some input.* She scraped off the plates and rinsed them. Timothy had gone outside after the meal to feed the horses. He'd mentioned he needed to work on a broken buggy light too.

Mary dabbed at the perspiration on her forehead. The afternoon had been hot and sticky, and the house still held the heat from the day. When she finished her work, Mary figured she'd take a walk outside, hoping the cooler evening air would feel better. She also planned to check on Timothy.

In the meantime, she couldn't help reflecting on her friend's abrupt ways. Mary felt a strong desire to help Pam. As she stood by the open window washing dishes, she heard her neighbor hollering—at their dog, maybe? But the clear view Mary had showed Pam yelling at her husband and then slamming their back door. *If only Pam could see that a lack of goodness toward others can be incredibly hurtful.*

After the dishes were done, Mary decided some iced tea with lemon would be nice and she'd get Timothy a glass too. She grabbed two glasses out of the cupboard and set them on the table. Mary got out some sliced lemon and the tea from the refrigerator, then carried the glasses to the freezer to fill them up with ice cubes. Mary enjoyed standing near the coolness of the icebox and lingered there for a moment. *This feels so nice, but I don't want to chance letting things thaw.* She closed the door and finished preparing the tea. She carried the drinks out the back door and walked straight to the buggy shed. When she stepped in, she didn't see Timothy at first and hesitated. *Maybe he's still with the horses.* Mary looked toward the barn but then heard a noise.

"Hello?" Mary paused.

"Hey, I'm in the *waegli*."

Oh, that's right, Timothy said he'd be in the buggy.

"I've almost got the old one out. It's worn out."

"That's too bad, but it'll be nice to be able to turn on the dome light again so we can see inside the buggy after dark."

"I agree."

"I've brought you some iced tea with lemon." Mary leaned against their rig.

"Thank you for bringing this out." Timothy took a deep sip and set the glass in the cup holder next to him. "That really hits the spot."

She smiled. "I thought it would help cool us off."

"It's refreshing, and it tastes good too."

Mary swirled the ice cubes within her glass and frowned.

"Okay, what's up?"

"I still feel bothered by what happened earlier today with Pam."

"I can understand your mood and how you must feel. Friendships can be tricky, and you've got to know how to deal with certain people."

"You're right about that. I'm concerned about Pam's attitude and sharp tongue. It's not becoming for someone who says they're a Christian. I need to know how to improve and deepen my friendship with Pam." Mary stood by the buggy.

Timothy reached out and touched her hand. "I'll be praying that things will work out for you to speak with Pam again. The Lord can give us the right words if we pray and trust in Him."

"Thank you. And I'll be doing the same this evening before going to bed." Mary drank her tea.

"We have light again." Timothy pointed to the brand-new light. "I'm not an electrician, but at least I got the wiring figured out on this thing."

"I had no doubts that you could fix it, Husband."

He nodded. "Thank you. By the way, do we have any more of those brownies left? I could use a little snack or dessert."

"*Jah*, there are a few left. I can put on some coffee to go with them. Or maybe it's too warm for a hot drink."

"I don't mind having a cup even if it's warm out. And I'm done for the evening." He set aside the screwdriver and finished his iced tea.

"Okay, I'll walk with you back to the house then."

Mary watched Timothy put away the items he'd used and close up the buggy shed. He took hold of her hand as they walked toward the house. Streaks of pink flooded the sky, and they stopped to admire the beautiful sunset. It was a wonderful end to a day that had been marked by some unpleasant moments.

A couple of days had gone by since Mary had gone over to Pam's place. She'd been thinking about her neighbor and felt perplexed about how to fix things. Timothy left for work earlier than usual, and her sister Karen would be coming soon. Mary set out all the supplies they'd be using to can pickled beets. She'd gotten the jars and lids washed. And she'd started cooking up the beets and checked on their tenderness. The aroma was pleasing to Mary; she'd been raised on them and they were always her favorite vegetable. There was a rap on the back door and Karen stepped in. "I'm ready to get started, Sister." She came over and gave Mary a hug.

"If you don't mind, would you make up the vinegar brine we'll need?" Mary went back over to the beets simmering on the stove. "There's a saucepan you can use right there."

Mary watched Karen set down her handbag and wash her hands. *My sister loves to do canning, and her pantry is going to be overfilled again, I'm sure.* Karen looked over the recipe on the counter, getting out some measuring spoons and cups from one of the drawers. It was nice to have the help, and Mary enjoyed being with her.

Karen came over and stood by her. "Okay, this will be good. I'll use some of the beet juice along with some sugar, vinegar, and pickling salt.

Do you have the cloves?"

Mary looked at her spice rack. "We're good; I've got a brand-new container of them." She handed it to her sister. "I'm about ready to drain the beets. I poked them with a fork and they're tender."

"I'll ladle some of the juice now and put it into the saucepan you have ready." Karen hummed quietly while putting the brine together.

Mary toted the pot over to the sink and drained it. "I need to tell you about my neighbor friend."

"Okay, I'm listening." Karen turned on the burner under the sauce pan holding the red, pickling juice.

Mary explained the whole story to her sister while they worked on peeling the beets. It was nice to have her older sister there to listen.

"You know, it wouldn't hurt for you to give your neighbor some beets when they're finished." Karen stuffed a jar with sliced beets and added cloves to it.

"That's a good idea, Sister."

"Also, an apology would be good too. Even though you were trying to help her out."

"I think you're right. Pam was upset and I didn't handle the situation tactfully."

"By setting the example of goodness to her, Pam will hopefully learn to do the same." Karen stopped peeling and went to the stove. She retrieved the steaming deep-red brine and filled the jars with it.

While her sister took care of filling them, Mary stepped over to the stove to heat up the deep canner for processing the glass containers. "I am so blessed to have you to talk to. It has eased my stress, and we're getting something accomplished at the same time."

"I'm glad to have given you some ideas to try with your friend." Karen poked the handle of a wooden spoon into the prepared jars to get rid of some trapped air bubbles. "Be faithful in prayer and things should get better."

"I shall."

Karen tightened the last jar. "These eight are ready. I'll go ahead and set them into the canner."

"Sounds good." Mary waited for all the jars to be placed inside before filling up the deep steamer with water. Once the beets were covered, she turned the burner on high. "What will you be making for supper this evening?"

"I've got plenty of pizza dough in the refrigerator and all the trimmings for two families to enjoy."

"Mmm, that makes me hungry."

"You and Timothy are welcome to join us for supper this evening."

"Are you sure?"

"Absolutely. Also, we could get in a game of Rook after our stomachs rest."

Mary smiled. "You've talked me into it."

"Good. We can probably eat around six this evening."

"That'll be fine. Timothy should be home at five and then we'll come over."

"All right." Karen looked toward the canner. "How's the water?"

"It's heating but not ready quite yet." Mary opened one of the drawers. "I should find the tongs for grabbing the jars from the canner, but I'm not sure where I put them."

"I'll help you find the tongs." Karen stepped over to another drawer and started digging through it.

"They're not in this one." Mary tapped her cheek. *Where are they?*

"I don't see them in this one either."

"Maybe they're in the pantry in the plastic container." Mary closed the drawer and went inside the small closet for a moment. "Found them!"

"That's good. Those tongs make it much easier to handle the hot jars."

"I agree."

Karen looked over at the stove. "The kettle is starting to show some steam."

"Good, we'll be on our way soon. Let's prep some more jars for the next batch."

Together they worked on the second batch to can. This had been a productive day. Mary got to talk to her sister about what to do about Pam, and they both were getting the beets put up for this year.

Mary got more beets ready to cook. *I hope my efforts with Pam won't flop like the last time.*

A day later, Mary stood at the stove heating water for tea. Looking out the kitchen window, she watched a pair of doves eating some seeds under a feeder. *Thank You, Lord, for another beautiful morning.* Mary clicked off the burner under the pot of hot water and poured it over her tea bag inside the mug. *I think I'll go next door and visit with Pam today.*

She went to the pantry and opened the door. Mary stared at the glistening jars of beets all lined up on the shelf. *I know Pam will like these because she's sampled them before and commented on their good flavor.* She picked out a couple of jars and carried them to the kitchen table.

Then Mary went for a couple of cookies from the jar and retrieved her steaming cup of tea. Timothy had left for work already and she'd cleaned up the breakfast dishes. Now it was time to relax. Her sweet snickerdoodles tasted good along with the chai tea she sipped.

Mary's thoughts went to the previous evening, which they'd spent with her sister and her family. The pizzas tasted so good, especially with Karen's homemade dough. She'd made a deep dish–style crust for one of them, and it was delicious. Mary saved a slice to have for her lunch today. Also, the game of Rook was great. She and Karen won a game and then the men did too. Karen had made brownies for dessert and chocolate chip cookies. It was a fun night eating and playing cards.

Mary smiled and sipped her tea. The house was quiet, but outside she heard the neighbor yelling about something again. She rose and looked out the window. A couple of dogs were wandering around in her yard, but when Pam came out on the lawn, they took off.

Great. . .she's already having a bad day, and now I'm feeling hesitant about following through on my plan. This has a bit of a similar feel to the other day, which isn't helping me feel confident right now. Mary continued to sip her tea and tried to stop dwelling on Pam's outburst with the stray dogs. *I want to make things right with my neighbor friend, so I'm going to follow through with it.* She drank the rest of her tea and set the cup in the sink. Mary went to her room to freshen up, then picked up the jars from the table and went out the door.

Mary headed across the lawn and up the steps to her neighbor's home. She gave a few raps on the door and waited. It wasn't long before Pam came out. "Hello."

"Hi, Pam. I want to apologize for the things I said to you the other day, and I've got some freshly canned pickled beets for you too." Mary handed her the jars.

Pam set them down by her feet and gave Mary a hug. "Thank you for apologizing. I'm also sorry for my behavior. Come inside, please."

"Okay." Mary followed Pam into the kitchen.

Pam motioned to a chair. "I have to admit something."

"What is it?"

"I know I need to change my attitude. I'm not happy being so harsh to others. You seem to treat people with patience and love. You're a good person, Mary."

"Thank you. . . . I can say that I am not perfect, and it isn't always easy for me to practice goodness. The Bible teaches us that we should do good to all people, and I want to please God."

"I guess I've been too preoccupied with my own issues to care about others, and that isn't right."

Mary nodded. "It's a simple choice, really, and once you've made that decision, the only work is in keeping it going."

"I would like to change even if it isn't going to be easy."

"It takes time, but you can do it if you pray and ask God to help."

"Thank you, Mary." Pam smiled. "Oh, I noticed your sister was over. Did she help you make up the beets you brought over?"

"Yes."

"It must be nice to have a sister you can do things together with."

"Karen and I usually get along well, but sometimes there can be misunderstandings. We always talk about things and work through problems so there aren't any bad feelings."

"I'd like to have that kind of a relationship with my sister, Shelly. She lives nearby, but we don't get along well."

"I'm sorry to hear that." Mary shifted in her seat.

"I didn't want you to know, but for some reason I felt the need to share that."

Mary clasped Pam's hand. "I'll be praying for you and your sister."

"Thank you." Pam's eyes glistened with tears. "I'm glad you came over today. It's been good for me to open up about things."

"Well, friends should be able to talk to each other and share."

The two women laughed and visited for a while. Mary felt pleased she'd carried through on her decision to mend their relationship. She had gotten to see another side of Pam today that she'd never seen before. Watching her neighbor open up today had been refreshing. Would this time together result in changed behavior for Pam as the days moved on?

Mary waited for Timothy to clean up for their meal that evening. She wanted to share with him about her visit with Pam today. It wasn't long before he came in and took a seat at the table. "I'm sure glad to be home. It was a busy day at the trailer factory."

"You sound tired. Let's pray so we can get started." She closed her eyes.

They prayed silently and then Mary passed the meatballs in sauce to Timothy. Then she dished herself a portion of the noodles and handed the bowl to him.

"I thought about making mashed potatoes, but the pasta sounded better to me." She spooned a few meatballs and some gravy over her noodles. "There are warm rolls wrapped in foil next to you."

"Okay, I'll open them. Would you like one?" he asked, after choosing a couple for himself.

She lifted her plate close to him. "Please."

"Oh good, pickled beets. I've been waiting for you to prepare these."

"I'm happy you like them so much. By the way, I did go over to Pam's with a couple of jars of beets today."

Timothy looked up from his plate. "How did that go?"

Mary shared the whole story with him and her thoughts about it. He seemed positive about what she'd said to Pam and reminded Mary that example and prayer could be two good keys in this situation. Mary agreed and hoped that Pam would try to put kindness into practice.

She set her water glass down. "So far it has been quiet next door. I weeded in the flower beds this afternoon, and there was no yelling."

"Let's hope it can continue." Timothy smiled. "Dinner is very good, *Fraa*."

"Thank you. I've made a blueberry pie for dessert, and there might be some vanilla ice cream to top it off."

"Mmm. . .I can't wait for dessert. Blueberry is one of my favorite pies."

As they finished their meal, Mary and Timothy chatted about his workday and what plans he had for fixing the loose back porch hand rail.

Tomorrow would be an off-Sunday for Mary and Timothy. She thought about visiting another Amish church district, like they sometimes did, but would wait and see what her husband wanted to do.

For now, Mary had some Saturday chores to do, and one was cutting the grass. After checking the fuel level, she rolled the mower out from the shed. Mary had forgotten that she had filled it up after the last time she'd used it, so that was one less thing to do now.

She gave a quick pull and the mower started. Mary pushed it along under the warm sunshine; it felt nice. The birds scattered from their feeders as she came rolling nearby. "Sorry, fellas, but I've got work to do."

Sometimes her husband did this chore, but today Timothy had left to do some work over at his dad's place. He'd mentioned that he would be gone through lunch, since his dad wanted help fixing his tractor.

Mary had some leftovers to heat up and would be dining alone. Which wasn't a big deal for her these days since it was only them at the house. She continued mowing until the back of the yard was completed. *I think it's time for a break; I'll go dump this grass then get a drink of water.*

After unhooking the grass catcher, she headed to where the clippings lay in a pile and shook out the bag. Then she walked back to the mower and attached the thing back into place. While doing that, Mary thought she heard the sound of the mail truck out front. *I'll go see if it is.* Coming around the house, Mary saw the letter carrier's vehicle stop at the neighbors' place. He set a few packages on their front porch and then headed back to his rig.

This mailman wasn't their usual carrier; maybe their postman was out sick today. Mary went to the box and collected their mail, then headed into the house. She wondered if this postman had done okay next door with the mail he'd delivered. So far things were quiet next door, but it had only been a few days since Mary's visit.

In the kitchen, she grabbed a glass and filled it with water, then went back outside to work on the side yard and front.

Once Mary fired up the mower, she was hard at it again. The grass was much thicker on this side of the house, so she'd be working there longer. With each pass she made, the mower became heavier to push, and it wasn't long before the grass catcher needed emptying. *Timothy did a great job feeding this part of the lawn.*

Perspiration beaded on Mary's face, but she worked hard until the side yard was done. The front yard was a lot quicker to do, and there was more to see. Mary liked to see people going by in their buggies and other vehicles. Right away, Mary waved at a couple of buggies that went by. After a few passes with the mower, she noticed Pam come out to get her mail. Mary tried not to stare but snatched glances when possible. Her neighbor picked up each of the packages and looked them over. Also, she grabbed the letters from their mailbox.

Mary couldn't tell if there were any problems just by observing Pam's body language. *Maybe things went okay this time.* She kept moving the machine along the grass. Soon she finished the yard and dumped the last bag of clippings, then put the mower away. She went into the house and had another glass of water. *I think I'll put leftovers from last night in the oven and heat them up for lunch. While they're heating, I'll sit on the front porch and rest.*

Mary took a seat in a wicker chair and sipped her water. She couldn't help admiring her hard work. The yard looked good and the smell of cut grass was wonderful. Mary had in mind another chore to do after lunch, and that was hosing off the house. She could see the cobwebs hanging around and a few spiders' nests too. Mary looked around the eaves then reached over to the railing and tugged on it. *Timothy does need to reinforce this, and the sooner it happens the better.* Mary released it and sat back in her chair. She saw Pam coming outside and heading to her car. The neighbor had a package and placed it inside on the passenger seat. It wasn't long before Pam pulled out of the driveway and her vehicle disappeared.

Mary headed back inside to check on her food. The timer she'd set was about to go off, so she opened the oven. The food looked hot and

Mary gave it a stir to double check. *It's steaming and I'm ready to eat.* Grabbing some oven mitts, she carried the pan to the table and placed it on a potholder. Then she retrieved the pitcher of lemonade from the refrigerator and poured some into her empty water glass. She pulled out the chair where her place setting was, sat down, and prayed silently. The food smelled good, and the taste was even better. Her cold citrus drink was a nice contrast to the hot meal. Mary heard the birds singing from the open kitchen window. She felt relaxed in the quiet room with the fresh air filtering in from outside.

When Mary finished her lunch she took the dishes to the sink and rinsed them off. Her stomach was full and she was tempted to relax in the easy chair. But there were still places on the house that needed to be washed off with the hose. When Mary stepped over to the stove to make sure she'd shut it off, there was a knock at the kitchen door.

"I wonder who it could be," she murmured before opening the door.

"Hello, Mary."

"Hi, Pam, come in."

"I just wanted to return one of your jars."

"Thank you. Did you enjoy the beets?"

"Oh yes, they were delicious. We ate them heated for supper last night, and I had them cold on a salad for lunch today."

"I'm glad you enjoyed them. Would you like to have a seat?"

"Sure, that would be nice." Pam slid out a chair from the table. "I just got back a while ago from delivering a package."

"Hmm. . .like a gift?"

"Nope." She shook her head. "The new mail person messed up and gave me a wrong parcel. So I took it to the right address. The person was happy to receive it; they'd been waiting for it to come."

"That was nice of you."

"Actually, it felt good doing it." She grinned.

Mary joined her at the table. "Which neighbors?"

"It was the Daniels up a block from here. Nice older couple."

"Yes, I know who you're talking about."

"It was mentioned that it was a birthday gift from their daughter for Mr. Daniel, so he was delighted to receive it."

"I'm sure."

"Oh, and I have some good news."

"You do? What is it?"

"Remember when we talked last, and I told you about my sister, Shelly?"

"Yes." Mary leaned in closer.

"Well, we've been talking again and we're getting together for lunch this coming week." Her eyes glistened.

"That is wonderful news. It's good to hear such a nice update."

"Thank you for your prayers. I've been working on changing my ways, and I'm already seeing positive results from it."

"Kindness is a good thing. It can heal ourselves and others too."

"I agree with you. It's not always easy, but it is worth doing." Pam rose from her chair.

"Well, I need to get back home. My husband is getting ready to head downtown."

"I'll walk you out."

They hugged, and Mary followed her neighbor out the door. After watching Pam head back home, Mary closed her eyes. *Thank You, Lord, for helping my friend to understand the importance of goodness and put it into practice. You inspire me to keep my focus on You, for I want my life to be filled with goodness and love toward others.*

For the fruit of the Spirit is in all goodness
and righteousness and truth.
EPHESIANS 5:9

Faith

HIDING PLACE

by Wanda E. Brunstetter

Sarasota, Florida
In the village of Pinecraft

When Sharon Raber stepped off the tourist bus at seven thirty in the morning, she saw a host of Amish and Mennonite people eagerly greeting others who'd also been on the bus. She spotted an older Amish woman whom she recognized from her community back in Nappanee, Indiana, although they weren't in the same church district and she didn't know the woman's name. Her face, arms, and what Sharon could see of the woman's legs were quite tan. It was a good indication that she had been here awhile.

Sharon was aware that many Amish and other Plain people came to Sarasota during the winter months, either for a vacation or to spend the entire winter. She'd come for a different reason though. The next three weeks would not be an actual vacation; it was a chance to leave her painful memories behind and be alone for a while. Six months ago Sharon's husband, Mark, had been killed when his driver's van was hit by a bus. Sharon and Mark had only been married a year, and after the shock of his death wore off, Sharon sank into a state of depression. Even though her parents had tried to dissuade her, she'd made arrangements for this trip, which she hoped might give her a sense of peace, if nothing else. Although she hadn't admitted it out loud, Sharon was angry with God for taking her beloved husband. Perhaps spending time at the beach or doing some other things by herself would help ease her pain. However, she didn't think her faith in God could ever be restored.

Sharon turned back toward the bus and saw that the luggage door had been opened. She waited while several others got theirs, then stepped forward and removed her suitcase. Hoisting her tote bag over one shoulder, she grabbed the suitcase handle and began pulling it across the parking lot. The little house she'd rented was on Kruppa Street, so she didn't have far to go.

Sharon had only taken a few steps when the older woman she'd seen before came alongside her. A younger Amish woman and two small girls were with her, each pulling a suitcase.

"You look familiar," the older woman said. "Where are you from?"

"My name is Sharon Raber, and I'm from Nappanee, Indiana. You look familiar too. Aren't you from there as well?"

"Yes, I am." She held out her hand. "My name is Iva Esh, and this is my daughter, Anna Mae, and her girls, Meredith and Susanne."

"It's nice to meet you." Sharon shook each of their hands.

Wearing big smiles, the girls bobbed their heads and said it was nice to meet her.

"Did you come to Florida alone, or are you with someone?" Iva asked as they all began walking.

"I'm alone." Sharon glanced down at her suitcase, then back at Iva again. "This is only my second time visiting Pinecraft."

"My *mamm* lives here all winter," Anna Mae interjected. "So if we want to see her anytime between the first of December and beginning of April, we have to come down here where it's sunny and warm."

Iva snickered and gave her daughter's arm a squeeze. "You love coming to Sarasota; now just admit it. And I'm sure you come for more than time spent with your old mother."

"You're only sixty, Mamm, and that's not old. And while I'll admit, we do enjoy the sunshine and trips to the beach for shells, we miss you when you're away from home."

"Do you own a place here in Pinecraft?" Sharon directed her question to Iva. "Or do you rent a home like I'm doing?"

"I have my own place, over on Yoder Avenue." Iva smiled. "It's small and nothing fancy, but it's just right for me and a few guests."

"It's nice that you can be here all winter." Sharon sighed. "I'm only staying for three weeks, but hopefully it'll be long enough for me to relax."

"Well, if you're looking to relax, then you've come to the right place." Iva paused and put her hands on her granddaughters' shoulders. "There are also a lot of fun things to do around here. Isn't that right, girls?"

Meredith and Susanne nodded.

"We're catching the city bus and going to the beach tomorrow after breakfast," Iva said. "Would you like to join us, Sharon?"

She hesitated a moment but finally nodded. "I know where the bus stop is. What time should I meet you there?"

"The bus leaves Pinecraft for Siesta Beach at nine."

"All right, I'll see you then." Sharon waved and turned onto Kruppa Street. Although she didn't know Iva, other than their brief meeting today, she felt like she'd made a friend.

When Sharon approached the place where she'd be spending the next three weeks, she became filled with mixed feelings. Was it a mistake to rent the same place she and Mark had shared? Well, she was here now and had paid for the whole three weeks, so she had to go in.

She stepped onto the porch and bent to get the key the owner had told her would be under the mat. After placing the key into the knob and turning it, she entered the house.

Leaving her suitcase and tote bag on the living room floor, Sharon walked into the kitchen where a telephone sat on the counter. She made a call home and left a message for her folks, letting them know she had arrived safely.

Next, Sharon opened the cupboard closest to the sink and took out a glass. Her mouth felt dry and she needed something to drink. After Sharon filled her glass with water and quenched her thirst, she glanced at the calendar on the wall opposite her. It was hard to believe it was the first of February. When Sharon left home, there was snow on the ground. Here the sun shone brightly and warm air blew in through the screen of the partially open window. *No wonder Iva comes here for the winter.*

Sharon returned to the living room. Clasping her suitcase handle, she wheeled it into the bedroom. *I should unpack, but I don't feel like it right now. What I really need is something to eat.*

There were two busy restaurants nearby, but Sharon didn't feel like dealing with the crowds. She opened her tote bag and took out two granola bars and a small plastic container filled with tea bags. This would have to do until she went shopping at the market on Bahia Vista Street. Before she did that, she would need to rent a bike so she wouldn't have to walk or catch a bus everywhere. Sometime, if she felt up to the challenge, she might even ride her bike out to the beach.

Sharon went back to the kitchen and fixed herself a cup of black tea. Then she took a seat at the table and ate her sparse breakfast. She should have prayed before eating, but what was the point? What she wanted most, she couldn't have, so why ask God for anything?

Sharon slumped in her chair and rubbed the heel of her palm against her chest. *Maybe I made a mistake coming here.* Being in this home where she and Mark had come soon after their marriage had opened up all of her wounds.

Maybe if I'm only here for some meals and to sleep it won't be so bad, she told herself. *There are plenty of things to see and do outside, so that's where I need to keep my focus.*

As Sharon approached the bus stop the following morning, she was surprised to see about twenty other Amish people waiting. She spotted Iva and her family and walked up to them.

"*Guder mariye.*" Iva smiled. "So glad you could join us."

"Good morning. *Danki* for inviting me." Sharon shifted her heavy tote bag. In addition to the sandwich and bottle of water she'd packed inside a small lightweight cooler, her bag contained sunscreen, two large plastic sacks for shells, and a small blanket to sit or lay on. She'd also slipped in a pair of sunglasses.

"Did you get settled in yesterday?" Iva asked.

"*Jah.* I unpacked, went grocery shopping, and rented a bicycle from the bike shop down the street from where I'm staying."

"That's good. It's nice to have a bike so you don't have to walk or catch the bus everywhere."

Sharon looked at Iva's granddaughters, each holding a plastic bucket with a small shovel attached. "Are you two excited to go to the beach?"

Their eyes sparkled as they bobbed their heads.

"I'm gonna make a sand castle," Meredith said.

"Me too," her sister agreed. "And I'm gonna look for shells with Mama."

Their mother looked at them and smiled. "I bet when it gets hotter this afternoon, they'll both decide to go wading in the water too."

Sharon glanced down at her flip-flops, remembering how much fun she and Mark had, walking knee-deep in the warm gulf water. She hadn't even cared when her dress got wet; it didn't take long at all to dry.

Her throat thickened, and she swallowed hard. *If all I think about is Mark while I'm here, I'll never relax or feel any peace.*

Even the constant loud chatter from other people waiting for the bus couldn't drown out Sharon's thoughts.

Finally, the bus pulled up and everyone climbed on board. Sharon took a seat beside a young Amish woman she didn't know. As the bus started moving, she closed her eyes. There wouldn't be much to see between here and the beach, except for a lot of traffic.

The moment Sharon stepped foot on the white sandy beach, a sense of nostalgia took over. She paused and looked out at the aqua-blue water where many people swam and played in the waves. *Will everywhere I go and everything I do remind me of time spent with Mark?* She gripped her tote bag tightly and shielded her eyes from the glare of the sun. *Why did I think coming to Florida would offer me peace? If anything, it's made me feel worse.*

The idea of returning to Nappanee flitted through her mind. But if she went home, she'd lose the money she'd paid in advance for the home she had rented. Also, if she went back, she'd have to admit to her folks that they'd been right when they tried to talk her out of making the trip. No, Sharon wasn't about to admit defeat.

"Did you bring a pair of sunglasses?" Iva asked. "The glare of the sun can be quite hard on the eyes."

"Yes, I did. They're in my tote, and I'll put them on when I find a place to lay my blanket."

"How about here?" Anna Mae pointed to a sandy spot where no one else had placed their things. It wasn't even noon yet, and already the beach was crowded with people—English in skimpy attire, and Amish in Plain clothes. Of course, some younger Amish women, with black scarves on their heads, wore full one-piece swimsuits. Sharon, even in her youthful running-around days, would not have worn a swimsuit in public.

"Should we have an early lunch or look for shells first?" Anna Mae looked at her mother.

"I think we should eat first and then look for *seeschaal*." Iva gestured to the sand beneath their feet. "Otherwise our hands will be dirty and we'll likely end up with *sandboddem* in our food."

"Eww. . .nobody likes sandy soil in their food." Meredith wrinkled her freckled nose.

As though not to be outdone, her younger sister made a gagging noise.

The three women spread their blankets on the sand, and then after everyone took a seat, they opened the coolers and sandwiches were handed out. Iva, Anna Mae, and the girls bowed their heads for silent prayer, so Sharon did the same. They would probably be shocked if they knew she hadn't uttered a prayer on her own since Mark died. She might even be in for a lecture.

When Sharon felt sure they'd all finished their prayer, she opened her eyes. Sure enough, the women's and girls' eyes were open now too.

As everyone ate their lunch, the sun grew hotter. When Sharon finished her sandwich and drank most of her water, she took off her flip-flops and slipped them under her tote. Then she put on her sunglasses and grabbed out the two plastic bags. "I brought these to put shells in. I'm only going to need one, so would anyone like the second bag?"

Both girls' hands shot up.

"It's kind of you to share." Iva smiled and pulled her tote bag to the middle of her blanket. "But we brought several plastic sacks as well." She pulled them out and handed one to each of the girls and their mother. "There's even a bag for me."

"Okay, let's go find some shells!" Meredith leaped to her feet. Her sister did the same.

Shortly thereafter, the five of them walked along the water's edge. Sharon was the first to spot a shell. The color was beige and it had an oblong shape.

"Well, look at that. . . . You've found an olive shell." Iva pointed. "Oh, and there's part of an oyster shell." She pointed in another direction.

Meredith scrambled to pick it up, and Susanne started to cry.

"It's okay," Anna Mae said. "There are plenty of shells on the beach. I'm sure you'll find one soon."

An hour later, everyone's sack was nearly full, so Anna Mae put more sunscreen on her daughters. Then, taking hold of each other's hands, Anna Mae and the girls waded knee-deep into the water.

Sharon took a seat on the blanket, and so did Iva. "You might want to put some sunscreen on too," Iva suggested. "You're quite pale, and your skin's likely to burn."

Sharon bristled. "I put some on before I met you at the bus."

"Even so, it's been a few hours since we left Pinecraft, and you probably need more by now."

"I suppose you're right." Sharon dug in her tote bag for the bottle of sunscreen and lathered some on her face, arms, and lower legs. Iva also put more sunscreen on. Sharon supposed even with as tan as Iva was, she could get burned if her body was exposed to the sun too long.

"Tell me a little about yourself." Leaning back on her elbows, Iva looked at Sharon.

"There's not much to tell." Sharon hoped the woman wouldn't ply her with a bunch of questions.

"I assume since you're here by yourself that you're single."

"I'm a widow." Sharon could barely get the words out. "I came down here to get away from things and. . ."

"Hide out?"

"Sort of." Sharon shifted on the blanket. "It's been six months since my husband died, and I've suffered with depression."

"So you were hoping this trip might help you deal with your loss and acquire a sense of peace?"

"Jah."

"I'm sorry for your loss. I am also a widow, so I understand what you're feeling."

Sharon stretched her legs out and wiggled her feet in the warm sand. *Iva is considerably older than I am, and since she has a daughter, and possibly more children, she probably had her husband for a good many years. There's no way she could understand the pain that I feel after losing Mark so soon after our marriage.*

"I'm sorry for your loss, and you're sorry for mine. Life is full of disappointments, right?" Sharon's tone was curt and to the point. "I–I'm sorry, I didn't mean. . ."

Just then, the girls ran up to them. "Mama says we need to lie here on the blanket and dry out so we don't get our seat on the bus wet." Susanne plopped down, and Meredith did the same.

"How come your mamm is still in the water?" Iva looked in that direction.

"She said she wanted a few minutes to herself," Meredith responded.

That's what I need too. Sharon turned onto her side, resting her head on her arm. *If I'd come to the beach alone, I wouldn't have to answer any questions or try to explain myself.*

That evening, Sharon sat at the kitchen table looking over all the shells she'd found today. She'd spread newspaper on the table before placing the shells, in case any of them still had sand inside.

What should I do with all these beautiful shells? she wondered. If Sharon went to the beach again, she would probably find more, so she needed to figure out something useful to do with them. When she and Mark had come to Florida, Sharon had taken the shells they'd found back home and put them in one of the flower beds. But they'd ended up disappearing into the soil or getting broken, and some had been hauled away by animals. One day, Sharon had seen a squirrel in the yard with a piece of a shell in its mouth. She had no idea what the silly critter planned to do with the shell, because it certainly wasn't food.

Sharon picked up one of the olive shells she'd found today and rolled it around in her hand. *Maybe tomorrow I'll ride my bike up to the thrift shop Mark and I went to while we were here and see if they have some plastic jars I could use to display my shells. If I only buy a few, there should be plenty of room to put the package in the basket on my bike.*

Sharon had rented a two-wheel bike rather than a three-wheeler, like so many of the older Amish people rode here in Pinecraft. She was used to riding a two-wheeler at home and could get around much faster on that than a bike with three wheels.

Sharon glanced at the clock on the far wall. It was way past suppertime, but for some reason she didn't feel hungry. Even so, she figured she ought to eat something; otherwise she might wake up in the middle of the night with her stomach growling.

After clearing a spot on one end of the table, Sharon opened the refrigerator and took out the ready-made salad she'd purchased at the store yesterday. She added some ranch-style dressing, took out a fork, and sat down at the end of the table. For one second, she almost bowed her head, but changed her mind. She couldn't think of anything to thank God for at this time. The truth was, rather than telling God she was angry with Him, Sharon had come here to hide from God.

As Sharon browsed around the thrift shop the next day, she noticed that things looked pretty much the same as when she'd been here with Mark. There were several rows of used clothing, including some Plain dresses that had probably been donated by the Amish and Mennonite people who lived in the area full-time. She passed by the racks and walked into the area where household items were sold. On one shelf were several vases and jars. The prices were a bit high for what she wanted to pay, plus they were glass and might break before she could transport them back to Nappanee. What she really wanted were some clear plastic jars, and they didn't need to be fancy. Once she returned home she could transfer the shells to something a little nicer, and a glass container would be fine.

Sharon pushed her way along with the metal cart she'd seen when she first entered the store. Toward the back, she discovered several "As Is" items. On one of the shelves were several plastic jars, just right for what she needed. She was pleased to find a Styrofoam ring as well. She would glue shells to it and make a wreath to give to her niece, Eva, when she got home.

When Sharon heard her name called, she turned around. She was surprised to see Iva, Anna Mae, Meredith, and Susanne.

"Well, this is a nice surprise." Iva grinned. "We wanted to invite you to come here with us today, but when we came by the place you're staying, you weren't there."

"We came to look for something to put the girls' shells in," Anna Mae added.

Sharon reached into her cart and pulled out one of the plastic jars. "I found these on that shelf over there." She pointed. "As you can see, there are plenty more, and they're perfect for storing and displaying our seashells."

"I want that one." Susanna pointed up at a jar.

"How about this one for you, Meredith?" Iva took down two jars and handed them to the girls.

"Danki, Grandma," they said in unison.

"You're welcome."

"We should get a jar too, Mamm," Anna Mae said. "We'll most likely find more shells before the girls and I go home."

Iva nodded and plucked two more jars off the shelf. She looked at Sharon. "From here we're going over to Der Dutchman for lunch. Would you like to join us?"

Sharon was on the verge of saying she planned to make herself a sandwich when she got back, but changed her mind. The buffet at the restaurant had lots of choices, and if she ate enough she might not have to bother fixing anything for supper.

"I'd be pleased to join you."

Iva smiled widely. "Good, then as soon as we pay for our items, we'll be on our way."

"Why don't we stop and drop off our packages first and then head to the restaurant," Anna Mae suggested.

"Good idea," Iva agreed. "Sharon, if it's okay with you, we'll stop at your place after we drop off our things, and we can walk to the restaurant together."

Sharon nodded and gave a brief smile. This would be the first big meal she'd had since arriving in Pinecraft.

◆――――◆――――◆

For the next week, Sharon kept pretty much to herself. As much as she enjoyed Iva's company, she didn't want to cut into the time she had left with her family. So Sharon went for long walks, rode her bike to the beach, and spent time coming up with creative ways to display the shells she'd found.

Today it was raining, so it was a good time to stay indoors and curl up on the couch with a novel. She'd found one that looked interesting on a bookrack in the lobby of Der Dutchman's restaurant. It was about a pioneer family heading west in search of gold. The husband had told his wife that if he found enough gold in California, they'd be wealthy and would never have to worry about a thing.

Eager to know what happened next, Sharon pulled out the bookmark she had inserted at the end of the chapter she'd finished before going to bed last night.

Sharon had only read a few pages when she heard a knock. She closed the book, placed it on the end table, and went to see who was at the front door. She discovered Iva on her porch, holding an umbrella over her head.

"I hope I'm not disturbing you," Iva said.

Sharon shook her head. "I wasn't doing anything important. Please, come in."

Iva shook her umbrella, closed it, and stepped into the house.

When Sharon offered Iva a seat, she put the umbrella on the floor by the door and sat in the rocking chair. "We've missed seeing you this past week, so I decided to stop by and see if you're all right."

"I'm fine." Sharon returned to her seat on the couch. "I thought you needed some time alone with your family and didn't want to intrude."

"You would not be an intrusion. When we all went to the beach and had lunch at Der Dutchman, we enjoyed your company."

"I enjoyed yours as well, but your daughter and the girls will be leaving in a few days, and you should spend that time with them."

Iva got the rocking chair moving and sucked in her lower lip. "Maybe the two of us can do something together after they leave. If you'd like to, that is."

Sharon nodded. "We could make another trip to the beach or ride our bikes to the marina and look at all the boats."

Iva smiled. "Either of those would be fun. It'll give us a chance to get to know each other better."

"That would be nice." Even though Sharon was still hiding from God, what harm would there be in spending time with a new friend?

Sharon stood beside Iva, waving at Anna Mae and the girls as their bus pulled out of the parking lot.

Iva wiped tears from her eyes and sniffed. "I'm sure going to miss them."

Sharon put her hand on Iva's arm and gave it a gentle pat. "They'll miss you too, but you'll be going home in a few months."

"True." Iva's eyes brightened. "And I have many friends here in Pinecraft, so I'll keep busy with plenty to do."

"Do you ever go home before April?"

"Not unless there's something I need to be there for—like a wedding, funeral, or if some family member gets sick. I feel better physically when I'm in the warm sun, so that's why I don't spend my winters in Indiana anymore." Iva grimaced as she lifted one arm. "These old bones of mine can't take the cold anymore."

"It's good you're able to be here then."

Sharon and Iva began walking through the dispersing crowd.

"What are your plans for the rest of the day?" Iva asked.

"I want to buy some fruit and a few other items I need at the store."

"How about this afternoon? Would you like to come over to my house for lunch?"

Sharon figured Iva, having just said goodbye to her family, would feel lonely the rest of the day, so she accepted her invitation. "Is there anything I can bring—maybe some fresh *aebiere* for dessert?"

"That sounds yummy." Iva smiled. "It's wonderful that here in Florida, strawberries are in season right now."

"Jah. I'll see you around noontime then." Sharon turned in the direction of her rental, and Iva turned toward her home.

Sharon was getting ready to leave the fruit stand in Pinecraft when she heard someone mention that a tropical storm in the forecast would be upon them soon and that everyone should be prepared.

Sharon glanced at the darkening sky and shivered when raindrops fell and the wind picked up. *I hope it doesn't become a hurricane.* Although Sharon had never experienced one, she'd heard from others how bad a hurricane could be.

Sharon placed the strawberries and other fruit she had purchased into her basket and climbed onto the bike. By the time she neared her rental, the wind had picked up so much that it was hard to pedal.

When Sharon reached the house, she put the bike in the shed, grabbed her packages, and hurried into the house. *I hope Iva's inside and safe in her house.*

The windows rattled as the wind roared outside, and for the first time in a long while, Sharon uttered a prayer. *Dear God, please end the storm soon and keep everyone safe.*

Sharon had seen a battery-operated radio in the kitchen but had never turned it on. Now, with the storm brewing outside, she felt it was necessary to listen to a weather report.

After she turned the radio on, it didn't take long to find the local weather station. The announcer said it appeared that the tropical storm would continue for a few more hours, but that it shouldn't develop into a hurricane.

Sharon sighed with relief. Nothing catastrophic was likely to happen, and she should be able to go over to Iva's without a problem.

At a quarter to twelve, Sharon gathered up the plastic bowl with the strawberries in it and grabbed her umbrella. She'd only taken a few steps out the door when the wind caught the umbrella and turned it inside out. Sharon opened the door and set it in the house. The rain wasn't coming down too heavily, and because of the wind, she'd be better off without it.

Hurrying along with her head bent against the strong gusts, Sharon stumbled on a branch that had fallen and nearly lost her balance, righting herself just in time. Iva's place was only a block and a half away, but it felt like a mile.

Forging ahead and clinging tightly to her plastic container, she made her way along until she came to Iva's house. With relief, Sharon stepped onto the porch, knocked on the door, and waited.

Within seconds, Iva answered. "Oh, come in out of the storm. I'm so glad you're okay. With the way the wind is blowing, I figured you might have decided to stay home."

Sharon stepped inside. "I wanted to make sure you were all right."

"I'm fine. I was inside when the storm started."

Sharon handed the container to Iva. "I brought the strawberries like I promised."

"Danki. I'll put them on the counter while we eat the shrimp salad I made. When we're ready for dessert, I'll pour the strawberries over the pound cake I baked last evening, and we can add as much whipped cream as we want."

"I prayed for our safety," Sharon said after she'd washed her hands and taken a seat at the table.

Iva smiled. "I did the same. And now we can thank the Lord for keeping us safe." She bowed her head and Sharon did the same.

When they opened their eyes, Iva dished some of the salad into smaller bowls and gave one to Sharon. Then she passed her a plate of rolls and some butter.

"This looks good. Danki for inviting me to eat with you today." Sharon took her first bite of salad. "I was right—it's delicious."

"I'm glad you like it."

They ate silently for a bit, until Iva posed a question. "I haven't said anything before, but I've sensed that you've kept to yourself a good deal of the time because you're struggling with your faith."

Sharon's eyes opened wide, and she blinked a couple of times. "H–how did you know?"

"Because I struggled with my faith after my first husband died just three months after we were married." Iva paused for a drink of water. "I was angry with God and wanted to find someplace to hide."

Sharon's face heated, and tears pricked the backs of her eyes. "That's how I've felt ever since Mark died."

"Would you like to talk about it?"

Sharon nodded, and then she poured out her heart to Iva. "You are right—I came here to hide from God."

Iva reached over and gently patted Sharon's arm. "When Ben was killed in a farming accident, I felt so lost without him. Truth is, I almost gave up on my faith."

"How did you get through it?"

"I stayed busy and kept my focus on everything around me that was positive. I also read my Bible daily and asked God for healing and guidance. Two years later, I met Evan, and a year after that we got married. The following year, we were blessed by the birth of our daughter, Anna Mae. The birth was difficult, and it left me unable to have more children."

"I'm sorry, Iva."

"It's all right; I'm thankful I was able to have one child, and that God gave Evan and me thirty years of marriage before he died of a heart attack."

Sharon drew a deep breath. "So you've lost two husbands but never lost your faith?"

"I almost did when Ben died, but as the years went on, my faith grew." Iva smiled. "I'm thankful for the years I had with both Ben and Evan, and now I focus on spending time with my daughter and her girls, as well as helping others whenever I can." She looked at Sharon with an understanding expression. "Lean on Jesus, and He will help you. If you put your faith and trust in Him, He will guide and direct you in the days ahead."

Sharon picked up her fork for another bite of salad. "Danki, Iva; I will ponder your words."

Sharon headed back to her rental later that afternoon, thankful that the storm had abated. She'd thoroughly enjoyed her time with Iva today, and had left there with much food for thought.

Once inside, Sharon turned her umbrella right side out and put it away. Then she got out the Bible that the owner had left in the house and took a seat on the couch. After reading a few verses of scripture on the topic of faith, Sharon closed her eyes and bowed her head. *Heavenly Father, forgive me for hiding from You and for nearly losing my faith. Please be with me in the days ahead, and give my life a sense of purpose again. Help me to be like Iva and share my faith with others.* Sharon's throat tightened. *I miss my dear husband, and I always will, but I am ready to trust You and move on with my life.*

When Sharon opened her eyes, a sense of peace flooded her soul. No longer did she feel alone. She felt God's presence, and her love for

Him overflowed. She could return to her hometown at the end of next week with a sense of purpose and renewed faith.

Without faith it is impossible to please [God]:
for he that cometh to God must believe that he is,
and that he is a rewarder of them that diligently seek him.
HEBREWS 11:6

BETTY'S DOG

by Jean Brunstetter

Davids came in from outside and pulled off his straw hat. "Our daughter isn't going to be happy this morning."

"What do you mean, David?" Alice's eyebrows came together.

"Well, Alice, Jack's not in his pen. I've looked around the yard and he is not there."

Their ten-year-old daughter, Betty, came into the kitchen. "Who's not there?"

David hesitated for a moment and then looked at Betty. "Your dog is missing."

Betty's eyes filled with tears. "Oh no! Jack can't be gone, Dad!"

Alice watched Betty run upstairs. "I'd better go talk to her." She hurried out of the kitchen and found her daughter lying on her bed, weeping. "I'm sorry, Betty. Somehow Jack got out of his pen, but I'm sure he'll come back."

"I want to get dressed and go around the neighborhood looking for him."

"Are you sure you don't want to wait awhile and see if he comes home?"

Betty shook her head. "I need to go now."

"Okay, I'll go with you after we've had breakfast." Alice left the room and headed downstairs just as the timer went off. She opened the oven and pulled out a golden batch of blueberry scones.

A short time later, Betty came in wearing a simple green dress and a brown scarf covering the bun at the back of her head.

"Would you like a couple of fresh-baked scones?" Alice pointed to the pastries. "They'd sure be good with some butter on them."

"Not right now." Betty sniffed and looked out the kitchen window.

Alice set the tray aside to cool and gently patted her daughter's back. "Your dad wishes he could help you look for Jack, but he needed to get to work this morning. As I said before, I can help you though. We can both look for a while, but then we'll need to go to Grandma's to help, because she isn't feeling well."

"Okay, *Mamm*." Tears pooled in Betty's eyes as she turned toward Alice. "I want to find Jack and have him *heemet* again."

"I know you want him home." She wiped at the tears and gave her daughter a hug. "Are you sure you won't have a warm pastry?"

"I'm not hungry right now."

"Okay, let's go for a walk down the road and look for him."

They headed out the door and had only taken a few steps toward the road before Betty stopped. "I think I'll go double check Jack's pen again; maybe he's back."

"All right, I'll go with you." Alice followed.

Betty ran around the back of the house but returned shortly. "He's not there." Her voice quavered. "I wish Jack was home."

"I'm sorry, Betty. Let's keep looking." Alice headed out of the yard. Betty followed her, calling for the dog. She continued to holler Jack's name, until about halfway down the road something caught Alice's attention. "Hey, is that him?"

Betty looked in the direction Alice pointed, where a dog had run into a nearby yard. "No, Mom, it looks kind of like Jack, but it's not him." Betty's shoulders slumped as tears dribbled down her cheeks. "I really hoped it was my dog."

I wish it was too. "Where else do you want to look?"

Betty looked straight ahead. "Let's cross the road and go farther."

As they walked along the road, Alice noticed how Betty watched for other dogs in their yards. Alice hoped that maybe hers might be there as well. She called Jack's name too, but so far they'd seen no sign of him.

"I'm sorry, dear, but we really should head back now."

"I wish we could keep looking for him." Betty spoke in a shaky voice.

"If Jack hasn't returned home by the time we get back from your *grossmammi*'s house, then we'll try searching for him again." As Alice walked with her daughter back to the house, she wondered what they would do if Jack couldn't be found.

Betty tried calling several more times on their way home, but there was no sign of her golden retriever.

One thing was for sure—Alice would try to keep her eyes peeled while going by buggy to Grandma's place. She looked over at her daughter's pained expression. *If only Jack knew how much Betty misses him. Oh, I hope we find her faithful companion.*

The next morning, when Betty entered the kitchen, Alice noticed her daughter's puffy eyes. *I bet she cried herself to sleep last night.*

"Did you hear a dog barking?" Betty asked, moving over to the window and peering out."

"Sorry, no, I did not." Alice dried off some silverware she'd taken from the dish drainer.

"I thought I heard Jack barking earlier from upstairs, but when I looked out my bedroom window, he wasn't in the yard."

"I'm sorry that it wasn't him."

"Then I came down to look out the living-room window, but he was nowhere to be seen. I really miss him." Betty wiped at a tear and sniffed.

Alice motioned toward the counter. "Last night I found a *haufe* of white papers in one of the desk drawers. You're welcome to use them for the missing dog flyers you want to make."

Betty moved over to the counter. "This pile of papers will work. *Danki*, Mom."

"You're welcome. Are you up to eating some baked oatmeal this morning?"

"I am a little hungry." Betty looked over her shoulder toward the kitchen window again. "Dad's coming up to the house."

"Good morning, Daughter," David said when he stepped inside the kitchen and took off his work shoes. "The meal smells tasty. I worked up an appetite out there in the barn."

Alice smiled. "There's blueberry yogurt on the table to go with the baked oatmeal, and there's also some scrambled eggs in the pan."

"Betty, could you get out the glasses and the apple juice?"

"Sure." She took out three glasses from the cupboard. "Are we going to Grandma's again today?"

"Yes, because Aunt Dorothy left a message and she needs to get into the dentist today for a chipped tooth."

"I'm sure your grandmother appreciates all the help she can get right now." Dad sat in his chair at the table.

Alice brought over the eggs, then set the hot dish of oatmeal by David. "I hope I'm not forgetting anything." She took a seat.

"Looks like everything is here. Let's bow our heads for prayer." He scooted the chair in and closed his eyes.

Alice prayed for her mother, and that Jack would return to Betty. When David cleared his throat, she opened her eyes and dished them each some eggs, while David plopped some yogurt on all the plates. Then Alice sliced and dished them each a sweet square of the steaming baked oatmeal.

"Would you like more *brieh*?" Alice looked over at David.

"Sure, more juice would be good."

"How about you, Betty?"

She nodded and took a bite of the oatmeal.

Alice poured their juice. "I wonder what would make Jack leave like he did. Maybe he got out and kept wandering farther away until he got himself lost. Or maybe, if a critter was in the yard, Jack chased after it and lost his way back home."

David drank half of his juice. "It's hard to say. He's young, not quite a year old yet. I suppose Jack could've done either of the things you mentioned."

Betty nibbled on her breakfast until most of the food was gone. She set her fork aside and looked toward the stack of papers. "I'm done. Breakfast was good. Can I get started on the flyers now?"

"Of course." Dave smiled and took a couple more spoonfuls of the eggs.

"Remember, we'll be going to Grandma's later to help out. So you should have some time to make up a few of those flyers."

"Okay." Betty pushed her chair back and stood. "I've been praying for Jack, and I think the Lord will help us find him." She smiled.

Alice came over and gave Betty a hug. "I'm pleased to see the faith you are showing."

David wiped his mouth with a napkin. "I mentioned to my coworkers about Jack running off. We can let others know that our dog is missing too."

Alice went back to her seat to finish her yogurt. "I agree that we need to spread the word."

"I'm going to get to work on my posters now." Betty took her plate and glass to the sink.

"Okay, but can I get a hug from you before I leave for work?"

"Sure, *Daed*." Betty gave him a big embrace. "Have a good day."

"You too, Daughter."

Betty grabbed the stack of papers and went out to the living room, but she returned to the kitchen a few minutes later. "I'm not sure how to make up the poster. What do you think I should put on it?"

"Well, the breed of your dog is a golden retriever and Jack has short hair. If you write that on the flyer, most people can imagine what your dog would look like. Then you wouldn't have to draw a picture. Would that help?"

"*Jah*, because I'm not that good at drawing animals."

"Sometimes I've seen a poster say at the top of it 'Lost Dog' or 'Missing Dog.' Then there is a description of the animal and a phone number to call. We'll go drive around later and hang up your flyers."

"That sounds good." Betty went back to the living room.

Later, on the way to Alice's mother's, they had a stop to make at the home of one of her friends. Linda had mentioned awhile back that she had skeins of yarn to give to Alice's mother because she knew how much she liked to knit. After securing the horse, they went inside and Alice visited with her friend. Linda mentioned that just yesterday a dog had gotten hit out on the road in front of their place. "The poor thing didn't make it," she added with a slow shake of her head.

Betty's eyes widened and she covered her mouth with her hand.

Alice looked over at her friend. "Do you know what kind of *hund* it was?"

Linda's brows furrowed. "It was a light colored dog."

"Did it have short hair?" Betty squeaked out the words.

"Yes, its coat was short."

"Oh, I hope it wasn't Jack."

"Our dog is missing and has been for a few days now," Alice explained.

"I'm sorry to hear that," Linda replied. "But I've seen your dog enough times to know the poor animal that was hit on the road wasn't your hund."

Betty's eyes brightened. "That means my dog is still out there."

"Yes, and we will get your posters out as soon as you've made up plenty. We should be going now anyway. Thank you for all the yarn." Alice rose from her chair.

"You are welcome, and come by again soon." Linda walked with them out the door.

"We shall." Alice waved before heading to the buggy.

"Bye, Linda." Betty waved too.

Soon they were in the rig and heading to Alice's mom's place. Every time Betty spotted a dog, she asked Alice to slow the horse so she could see if the dog might be playing with Jack.

At her mom's house, Alice got out of the buggy, and Betty did the same. Alice handed her daughter a few things to set up on the porch. Betty carried them over and waited for her to put away their buggy horse.

Opening the door, Alice called into the house, "We're here."

"I'm in the kitchen, Daughter." She waited a few seconds until they entered the kitchen. "I've been feeling a little stronger, so I thought I'd heat up some water for tea." She looked over the rim of her glasses.

"That does sound good. Would you like some help?"

"There's not much to do. I've got a mug out and the tea bag in it. But you could join me though."

"Okay."

"Grandma, I've got something for you to look at for me." Betty gave her a hug and set down the bag of yarn. She handed her the papers she'd worked on.

"Oh yes, these are your ideas for the poster you're making." She studied each one. "I think this one is good, dear. There's plenty of information on it."

Betty reached out and took the one her grandma liked. "This is how I'll make all of my flyers. I can't wait to hang them where people can see them."

"Good. You have a wonderful determination, and I do hope you find Jack. I'm sure he is missing you a lot too."

Betty nodded. "Thank you, Grandma."

"You are welcome." Her eyes twinkled.

"Why don't you work on the posters so that when we leave here we can start placing them on street corners for the public to see?" Alice pointed to one of the bags they'd carried into the house. "I brought the pile of papers from home."

"I can do that now?"

"Jah, I think that would be fine." Alice picked out a mug and a bag of tea to prepare.

Betty looked over at Alice, then back at the flyers she held. "I trust the Lord to bring Jack home, and His grace is sufficient for me."

Alice smiled. *It's good to see my daughter's strong faith, and I hope she will not be disappointed.*

The next morning, Alice worked on cleaning up the kitchen from breakfast. She wiped off the counters and replaced the sponge by the faucet. Looking outside, she saw her daughter standing next to the dog's pen. Alice watched Betty step inside and check the water dish. She then carried it out and refreshed it with new water. *Even though her dog has been missing for days, Betty still holds out hope for Jack's return. I really have doubts that we'll see him again, but maybe my faith is weak.*

David came in from outside and washed up. "I'm ready to take our daughter around and put up more of the missing dog flyers, since some of them have blown off in the wind."

"What will you use to attach the papers?"

He pointed to the brown bag sitting on a chair by the kitchen door. "I've got a stapler and some tape in case the surface we're needing isn't wood."

"That should work." Alice stood next to him.

"Betty was outside with me, but then she took off."

"Actually, I saw our *dochder* through the kitchen window grabbing the dog's water bowl and putting fresh water in it." Alice paused. "I hope we find him."

"It's possible. Our daughter seems to have enough faith for all of us." David patted her arm.

Alice smiled just as Betty walked into the kitchen holding more flyers.

"Are you ready?" David picked up the brown paper sack.

Betty walked toward the door. "Jah, I'm ready to go."

Alice hugged them goodbye. She watched David and her daughter head out to the buggy. She bowed her head and prayed. *Lord, please let us find Jack, and help me to have more faith in You.*

Two more days had passed and still there was no sign of Jack. Every morning Betty went outside and called for Jack. Alice was touched seeing Betty's commitment to finding her dog.

Today, Alice went upstairs to do some sweeping and saw her daughter sitting on the bed. She almost said something but stopped when she realized Betty's eyes were closed tight.

I think she's praying, and I'm sure it's for Jack. Alice moved the broom quietly along the hallway floor, trying not to disturb Betty.

A few minutes went by as she swept the floor in her room. When Alice felt a couple of taps on her back, she turned and saw her daughter there. "Hi, I didn't hear you come up behind me. How's it going?"

"All right." Betty gave Alice solid eye contact. "Do you think Jack will be back with us soon?"

Alice stood there blinking like a deer caught in the headlights. *I think my faith. . .is being tested now. How should I respond to her question?*

Betty tugged on Alice's sleeve. "Mamm? Do you believe the Lord can help?"

"I know He can."

"Please believe too that He will give back my dog."

Alice put the broom aside and gave her daughter a hug. "We'll just keep praying and watching for his return."

Two more days passed, yet Betty kept saying Jack would come home. The other day, while they took some baked goods to Grandma's house, Alice had to pull over to help Betty replace one of the old missing dog posters on a pole. She watched her daughter grab the new paper along with the stapler. "I'll help you with that." Alice set the brake and climbed out with Betty. It wasn't long before they'd replaced the poster and were on their way again.

Betty nudged Alice's arm. "Someone will find Jack, Mom. And when they do, they'll call our number so we can go and get my dog back."

Alice hoped her daughter's faith would remain strong if Jack didn't come home. Sometimes when a person prayed for a certain thing, their prayer wasn't answered in the way they wanted.

When they returned home, Alice worked out in the garden and her daughter sat nearby looking out toward the road. When two of Betty's friends came into the yard, she jumped up and raced over to talk with them.

Alice continued weeding a row of corn. Glancing up, she saw Betty smiling as she visited with her friends.

"Did you have a nice chat with your friends?" Alice asked when Betty came back.

"Yes, Kathy said her family is getting a new puppy."

"Oh, I'm sure she is excited about that."

"Kathy sounded very happy." Betty looked toward Jack's kennel.

"Did they ask if you'd found your dog yet?"

Betty nodded. "I told them not yet, but I'm still waiting and praying."

Betty walked over to the dog's area and stood with her eyes closed. Alice figured she was praying for Jack again. She left her alone and continued to weed the row of corn. *My daughter hasn't given up, but she's probably struggling right now since Jack is still missing.* Alice closed her eyes too. *Lord, please give my family the faith we need to wait for an answer on Jack. Thank You, Lord, for doing all the good things we can't see You do. Amen.*

That night, Alice stood by Betty's partially open door. Her daughter's eyes were closed, so Betty was either sleeping or praying.

When Alice stepped into the room, Betty's eyes opened. "I was going to come in sooner, but you seemed to be praying." She came and sat down on the edge of the bed.

"I like to keep praying and hoping Jack will come home to us."

"Do you want your window closed down some? There's quite a breeze coming in, and I can even smell a little rain too."

"I like it open." Betty sat up. "Actually, I've been listening every night to hear Jack's bark."

"Oh, that's a good idea. We can leave the window alone then." Alice shifted. "Your dad will be in soon to say good night to you."

"What are we doing tomorrow?"

"I think your father has to go to the hardware store. The screens on two of the windows downstairs need to be replaced."

"Oh, is Daed going anywhere else?"

"I don't know, but you can ask him." Alice leaned over and kissed Betty on the forehead. "Good night."

"Good night, Mamm."

David came in just then and sat beside Alice on the bed. "Are you ready for sleep, Betty?"

"I think so." She paused. "Daed, are you going to the hardware store tomorrow?"

"Yes, I am."

"Only there?"

"That's it, just there." He sighed. "Do you want that window shut more? The wind is coming up."

"Nope, because I'm listening to hear Jack."

"Okay, I'll leave it the way it is. Have you said your prayers yet?"

"Yes, but sometimes I forget things so I pray more."

Alice smiled, and David chuckled. "That's all right, because sometimes I do that too. And other times I just like to praise the Lord for all the good things He does for me."

Betty tilted her head. "Oh, like for the bananas on my cereal this morning?"

"Sure, if you think that's a good thing, then yes."

Betty lay there for a moment. "I can think of more things."

"I'm sure you can. Sometimes making a list of things can be helpful."

"Really?"

"Yep. Because you can write stuff down and put them in order."

"Like how?"

"For example, the Lord is first, then family. Friends come next."

"I see—so would Jack be family?"

"I'd say so." David looked down at their daughter and smiled. "Also, depending on what's happening too. Grandma is feeling better, so we should praise the Lord for that. And we're all feeling well here at home, and that is good too. Those are just a couple of reasons we have to be thankful."

"Maybe a list would be good," Alice affirmed. "It can help, and don't be surprised if your list grows."

Betty's eyes grew large. "Really?"

"Yes, but don't worry about that now, because you need to get some sleep." David reached out and gave her a hug. "Good night, Betty."

"Good night, Daed. Good night, Mamm."

The next morning after breakfast, Alice stood by the dish drainer. She'd dried the last of the plates and hung the towel when she finished. She looked over at the plants sitting on the windowsill. *I need to water the flowers; they're looking a bit wilted.* Alice watered each of the plants and shut off the faucet. David came in from being out in the barn. He pulled off his shoes and sat there a moment. "I'll be going soon to get the new screen material. But I'd like to have another cinnamon roll first with one more cup of coffee."

"No problem. Where would you like to have them?"

"I think the living room in my recliner would be great." David gave his suspenders a snap and headed off in that direction.

When Alice brought her husband a cinnamon roll and coffee, she noticed Betty curled up on the couch with a book.

"Can I have another roll too?" Betty asked.

"Sure, we've got plenty to eat. Did you want to pick out your own?"

"Okay, I'll come to the kitchen with you."

Alice lifted the foiled tray that revealed the sweet-smelling delights. "They do look good, don't they?"

"Yes, and I'd like that one." Betty pointed to a roll covered in white frosting.

"Did you want to eat it in the living room? If so, you'll need a napkin."

"I'd like to eat it in there with Dad." Betty reached for a napkin. "Thank you, Mamm."

"You're welcome."

Betty headed back to the living room. Alice couldn't resist having one more either and chose one of the smallest cinnamon rolls on the tray. She joined her family in the living room and sat next to her daughter. "This was your daed's idea to begin with to have another pastry. It sounded so good that I had to have one too."

"I agree." Betty stuffed a good-sized piece into her mouth.

David sipped his coffee. "Yep, those screens will be nice again once I've installed the new material."

"It will be good not to have so many flies getting in. It seems when there's food cooking, they show up and are a nuisance." Alice took another bite of her cinnamon roll. "I could use some assistance outside this morning watering the plants."

"I'll help you." Betty smacked her lips. "I wouldn't mind one more roll."

"Go ahead and pick out the last one, and then we need to do the dishes."

"Okay, Mom."

David got up and took his dishes to the kitchen. He was in there for a little bit, and hearing the water running, Alice figured he was either rinsing off the dishes or washing his hands.

When her husband returned to the living room, he said, "I'm leaving for the hardware store now. Is there anything else there you need me to get, Alice?"

"I can't think of anything right now." She got up and walked with him back to the kitchen.

David put on his shoes and then gave her a kiss goodbye. "I'll be back soon." He hurried out the door.

Alice watched him head to the barn, then she got the sink ready to wash up the last of the morning dishes. She filled the basin with warm, soapy water and placed the items into it. When Betty came in with her dishes, she added them with the others. Alice grabbed the dishcloth and submerged it into the bubbles.

"Is it okay if I go outside now?" Betty asked.

"What are you going to do?"

"I thought I'd start watering the flowers for you."

"Okay, that would be nice." Alice rinsed off a plate she'd cleaned and set it in the drainer.

Betty went outside, and through the window, Alice saw her head for Jack's kennel first. She watched Betty dump out the old water and add new to his dish. Then she stood there a few moments with her eyes closed.

My daughter is praying for Jack again. She has the faith to believe that the Lord will bring her dog home again.

Alice continued to clean the cups and plates. She heard Betty out on the porch. The faucet outside the kitchen door made a metallic noise whenever it was turned on or off. Alice was pleased that her flowers would get a much-needed drink. They were starting to wilt from the heat.

More time went by as she dried and put away the dishes. It wouldn't be long before David would return from the hardware store. Alice thought about what to make for lunch and stepped out the door to ask Betty what she'd like. Alice saw her daughter dragging up some coiled hose to the front porch.

"This thing is caught on the step." Betty yanked on the curled hose.

"Would you like some help?" Alice paused. "Never mind; I see you've got it and you seem to have enough now to reach the other plants. I came out to ask about lunch and what you might like."

"I'd like a wrap."

"Okay, what kind? Ham and cheese, or egg salad?"

"Ham and cheese, please." She'd looked away too long and overfilled the pot of petunias. "Sorry, Mamm, I made a little mess with the water."

"It's okay. In this heat that will dry in no time."

"We sure have a lot of flowers, but I'll get the other pots along the walkway too."

"Thank you. I'll be out here with you now to do some work while you're watering."

Alice moved aside while Betty pulled the green hose down the steps behind her. The porch felt cooler with the pots all watered and the excess water dripping from the plants. The sun gave off an intense warmth this morning.

Alice stepped down from the porch to a flower bed. She worked carefully among her bright-red geraniums in the sun, and began to feel dampness on her forehead as she worked. *I should've worn a lighter scarf—this dark brown wasn't a good color choice.*

"What kind of flowers are these again, Mamm?"

Alice stopped and came over to the pot Betty stood by. "These pink and white flowers are called impatiens, and they like to be in the shade." She folded her arms. "I really like how they brighten up this side of the yard."

"They are pretty." Betty turned on the water and filled the pot.

Alice went back to the flower bed and kept weeding while Betty continued watering the remaining flowers.

Minutes later, the familiar *clip-clop* of their buggy horse could be heard coming down the road. Alice stood up and rubbed her back. "Your daed is here. I'll fix our lunch as soon as he is ready."

Betty reached up high to water a hanging basket and had her back turned away. Alice watched her husband pull up to the hitching post.

He stepped out with a big grin on his face. "Hello! Look what I found at the hardware store." Just then Jack jumped out of the buggy, barking and wagging his tail.

Alice couldn't believe her eyes.

Betty turned from watering and screeched, dropping her hose to the ground. "Jack! Oh Jack—I'm so glad you're home!" She ran to the dog, went down on her knees, and hugged him. "I've missed you so much, and I've been praying that the Lord would bring you back to me."

Alice stepped up to David. "How'd you find Jack?"

"I noticed this panting dog lying out in front by the entrance of the store. It looked like Jack. When I called his name he perked right up and came over to me." David pushed back his straw hat. "So I put Jack in the buggy and grabbed what I needed from inside the store. We had a nice ride home together, and I couldn't wait to show him to you, Betty. What an unexpected surprise."

"It sure is." Alice looked down at her daughter as she continued hugging the dog. After a few minutes, Betty stood and gave her father a big hug. "Thank you for finding Jack and bringing him home."

"You're welcome."

Alice smiled, watching the joy upon her daughter's sweet face. *Thank You, Lord, for returning Betty's dog to our family.* Jack had been gone so long, but Betty never quit praying or believing he would return. Alice's own faith had grown through witnessing her daughter's sincere commitment to faith and prayer.

Now faith is the substance of things hoped for,
the evidence of things not seen.
HEBREWS 11:1

Meekness

RECEIVE WITH MEEKNESS

by Richelle Brunstetter

C an you believe what went on last week?" Alyssa tweezed some fries between her fingernails, painted burgundy-red. "There was a bonfire party planned, and as they were setting it all up, they almost set the house aflame. There was actual fire spreading from the grass to the bushes."

"That's why you don't have fires a couple feet away from a building." Marlene rolled her eyes, slipping her hand into her jeans pocket to pull out her phone. "It's already ten thirty. Where did the time go?"

"You know what they say. Time fries." Jason laughed while stuffing a handful of fries in his mouth.

"Awful. Just awful." Alyssa pushed the basket of fries away from Jason.

Marlene smirked. "They must have fried them too quick. My parents aren't gonna be thrilled if I'm late again."

"Come on. They have to understand it's all a part of the fun when it comes to *rumspringa*." Jason wiped his hands with an already-used napkin. "You'll have plenty of time to attend to important things after joining the church."

"If Marlene *does* join the church," Alyssa said.

"What makes you think I won't?"

"It's a possibility, isn't it?" Alyssa wrinkled her freckled nose, clasping her hands together. "We're not Amish, and you definitely don't come off as such."

"What do you mean?" Marlene picked up her paper cup and sipped from the red straw. Unfortunately, all that was left in the container was melted ice.

Jason rubbed his chin. "How do I describe it? Even when some

Amish dress up in our clothing, they don't always do it right. You can tell by looking at them. Then again, if I tried dressing Amish, I would stick out like a sore thumb."

"So what you're saying is, I have a good sense of style." Marlene ran a hand through her hair and flipped it behind her shoulder.

"More or less." He winked. "Could use some tweaking in your color palette."

Ignoring her friend's comment, she glanced at her phone, noticing there were a couple of notifications on the home screen. "But I'm mostly at home with my parents and sister." Marlene gestured toward herself. "And at work, I don't wear these clothes."

"Amish by day, English by night. Almost like a superhero." Jason puffed out his chest. Marlene could picture a cape tied around his tan neck, flowing in the breeze.

Alyssa shook her head. "That's a terrible superhero."

"Buzzkill."

Marlene restrained her urge to snort at her friends' bickering. While they continued to talk among themselves, her stomach fluttered. She attempted to mask the uneasy feeling by sipping from her straw, which was sucking up air at this point.

After they finished devouring the rest of the french fries, they threw their scraps in the garbage and walked out of the restaurant. The fluorescent parking lot lights glistened in the puddles from the recent rainfall. Marlene was captivated by the sight, tempted to take a photo of it on her phone.

Marlene's prized sedan was only a short distance away, and she always felt relieved seeing the car in one piece. She didn't trust other drivers. The way they cut through parking lots never failed to make her anxious.

Marlene pulled the keys from her pocket and unlocked the car. "Okay, I'd best be on my way."

"Will you be available to hang out with us tomorrow after work?"

Jason patted the roof of the vehicle.

"Most likely. Unless my parents have something to say about it." Marlene opened the car door and stretched like a cat as she placed her bag on the back seat. Then she put her key in the ignition and gave it a twist.

"Honestly, they're a bit too hard on you." Jason laughed, though it came off a bit forced. "It's not like you make poor decisions. You're not much of a party animal."

"We aren't much either," Alyssa responded, texting on her phone with one hand.

"But we could change that." He snickered.

"How about. . .no."

Shaking her head, Marlene plopped into the driver's seat and grabbed the inside of the door. "See you guys later. Text me when you know for sure where we're going tomorrow."

"Bye, Marlene." Alyssa gave a wave with her fingers as Marlene pulled away from the parking space and drove out of the lot.

It's hard to tell that I'm Amish, huh? Marlene gripped the steering wheel. *Maybe Alyssa wasn't joking about that. If that's the case, then. . .*

Marlene Bontrager was in the season of her life when she must decide whether to join the Amish church or not. While she knew in her heart that she wanted to live a humble life, like the way she was raised, the qualities and benefits of the world enticed Marlene to the point where she didn't know how to let go of the English lifestyle.

The bulk food store, where Marlene worked as a cashier most of the time, usually had a plentiful amount of people buying whatever they had available on the shelves. Some were the regulars who lived in the area, and plenty were tourists. Marlene didn't mind, though there were times when the pace became hectic. Not to mention being asked odd-ball questions whenever she had to ring up somebody's items while working at the cash register. She definitely preferred stocking items when those moments occurred during the workday.

"Hey, Marlene." A young Amish woman, who was also an employee, came up to her as she was restocking the shelves. "It's been awhile since you've come to singings with us after church. Have you been doing all right?"

"Yeah, of course. It's just. . ."Twiddling with her *kapp* ties, Marlene cleared her throat. "Conflicting schedules. And I'm not as young as I used to be."

Judy's lips pressed together in a slight grimace. "You're only twenty. You're not that old."

"Okay, Judy, you're right. I'll be there if I have nothing planned this weekend." She slid a box of cereal onto the top shelf.

"Oh, I see. That's fine." Curling her shoulders forward, Judy shuffled her feet. "We really miss having you there."

A wave of dizziness struck Marlene to the point where she could've lost her balance. She was stressed knowing the people she'd grown up with had missed her company. Marlene knew Judy since the beginning of grade school, but they had grown apart ever since she got involved with some of her English friends.

Marlene exhaled, almost finished with stocking the items. "I miss being there too. I will go next time when I can. I promise."

"Glad to hear it." Judy, wearing a pleasant smile, strolled away from Marlene with a wave.

In some ways, Marlene was glad to hear her own promise also. *I guess the old me is still there.*

When it was near the closing hour, Marlene gathered her bag, as well as what was left of her lunch, and hauled everything out of the store and to her car. Alyssa and Jason wanted to go out tonight, and while she looked forward to it, she didn't look forward to asking her parents for permission. Even though Marlene did all of her required chores before leaving, her parents always fabricated reasons for her not to go with her friends. Mom would suggest they come over instead, which didn't exactly pan out the last time. Jason figured it would be hilarious to playfully flirt with her sister. While Marlene was fully aware it was just his way of confidently introducing himself, Krista wasn't having any of it and complained about it to Mom.

Marlene made it home in a short amount of time. It was one of those moments when she was thankful to have the privilege to drive. She couldn't help liking the style of the car along with its color, and it had a lot of bells and whistles to play with. Her dad once said that if they were to drive vehicles instead of getting around in a horse and buggy, then they would no longer be Amish. Marlene understood, but she still wished they were allowed to drive after joining the church. Taking control of a vehicle was exhilarating, and it was something Marlene would miss.

When she opened the front door, Krista, who was a couple years younger, walked into the main part of the house. Marlene smiled, slipping off her sandals and picking them up. *"Guder owed, mei schweschder."*

"Good evening to you too." Krista worked through her long, strawberry-blond hair with a comb. It appeared damp in the dimly lit room, the only light source being the sunset peeking through the blinds. "I just got cleaned up."

"I may do the same in a bit." Marlene peered into the living room. "Where are our parents?"

"They're over at our brother and sister-in-law's house. Why do you ask?"

"Because I was gonna head out tonight." Marlene scurried to the kitchen and placed her bag on the floor near the lazy Susan. Her sister followed, watching as she put her leftovers into the fridge.

Krista had a blank stare, but then her brow arched as she placed her comb on the counter. "Don't tell me you're going out with your English friends again."

"You say that as if it's a bad thing." Marlene grabbed the orange juice container and pushed against the fridge door to get it to fasten shut.

"Kind of. I mean, I'm not saying that exactly." Krista nibbled her lip. "Though, don't you think you hang out with them a little too often?"

Marlene would be lying to herself if she said she never thought of the possibility. When she'd been approached by Judy at work today, it especially made Marlee think about it. But she intentionally pushed those thoughts aside. She felt as if her family was being overly critical when it came to her friends and didn't really see them for who they were. However, Marlene would also be lying to herself if she didn't admit her friends influenced her phone addiction.

Marlene crouched to search for a paper cup in the lower cabinet. "Look, my friends may be odd at times. I get that. But they're not bad people."

"I know. I can't help but worry though. You've said you plan to join the church, right?"

"I do at some point." Setting the cup down, Marlene unscrewed the cap on the juice and poured the pulped liquid until it was filled to the top. "It's tough, you know? Having a vehicle is more convenient because of time. The phone makes communication much easier too." Seating herself in the dining room, Marlene warily sipped her orange juice.

Krista pulled out a chair and sat across from her. "But there's more to it than that."

"I can't seem to let go. Even if I may know that I don't need any of it."

Swigging the rest of her orange juice, Marlene stared intently at the cup. Her palms felt warm and damp, and while she was relieved to confess things to her sister, Marlene still didn't know what to do. She scooted back her chair and stood. "Could you let *Mamm und Daed* know I'll be back later?"

"Unless they get back before you're finished getting ready."

"I'm pretty quick. More so than most people." Marlene lowered her eyelids and gave her sister the smuggest look she could give.

Krista sucked in her cheeks. "Hey, you know how long it takes to pin this length of hair in a bun."

"My hair's nearly the same length, so explain how I beat you out the door this morning." Strolling into the kitchen, Marlene disposed of the paper cup. "And yesterday. And the day before that—"

"All right, fine. I'm slow. I have no excuse."

Marlene patted her sister's shoulder. "*Danki.* I owe you one."

"No problem." Krista rubbed the tip of her rosy nose. "Just tell Jason to straighten himself out."

"And change his wonderful sense of humor?"

"I mean it, Marlene. It isn't funny at all."

Sunday afternoon, Marlene headed back home in her family's buggy after the church service. Poking her head out the back window, she propped it with her hand while observing the passing scenery. The grassland was vibrant, the vegetation in their community thriving this year.

When she pulled her head back into the buggy, Marlene looked over at Krista, leaning against the side of the buggy with drool trailing from her mouth. Marlene hummed, tapping her knuckle on the seat. "Krista fell asleep again."

"Can't blame her," her father responded. "Buggy rides are fairly relaxing."

Mom nodded, leaning against Dad's shoulder. "Especially when you're with people you love."

Her parents had a point. In some ways, riding in a buggy through the countryside felt therapeutic. The scenery was pleasant, there was no traffic, and the rocking of the buggy as the horses rolled it along made Marlene drowsy as well. The cushion squeaked as she leaned back and fluttered her eyes shut. *I think I'll relax today. I could take a nap before going to the young people's group with my sister.*

Marlene awoke to the vibration in her bag, which lay on the lap of her olive-green dress. She dug through her purse and pulled out the phone. Pressing the home button, she saw a couple of messages from a mutual friend of Alyssa's. *It's Claire,* she thought. *I wonder why she's wanting to get ahold of me.* As she checked the messages from Claire, Marlene's eyes widened. *She's inviting me to a party?*

Before Marlene could process this, they had pulled into the driveway and were approaching the hitching post. Marlene wobbled her sister awake.

"Where am I?" Krista mumbled.

"Home. We're home." Chuckling, Marlene did her best to ignore the jitters she felt from the messages.

"Oh, ick! I drooled again." Krista wiped her face and groaned.

"Really?" Marlene climbed out of the buggy. "I didn't notice."

Marlene went straight to her room. Dropping her bag on the bed, Marlene pulled out her phone and browsed the messages again. "Why would Claire invite me to a party when she avoids me?"

Maybe this is my chance to get Claire to like me. If I go to this party and socialize with other people, then she might become a good friend.

Marlene wasn't oblivious to the things that happened at those parties. Not everyone was obnoxious, but some people were, and they would certainly be at a party like that.

Wait a minute. If Alyssa was there with me, maybe it wouldn't be so bad. We could have each other's back if something went wrong.

While Marlene waited for a reply from Alyssa, she plopped onto the mattress, bouncing momentarily until she lay motionless on her bed. *Regardless of what happens tonight, I want to take a nap.* Marlene rested her eyes and allowed the sound of a bird chirping from outside to lull her to sleep.

Waking up after a couple of hours, she checked her phone,

receiving confirmation from her friend that she was indeed going. Marlene got ready for the party, then looked at herself in the mirror, looping her thumbs around the belt loops of her jeans and admiring how her bomber jacket looked on her.

She came out of the bedroom with her bag hanging off her shoulder. *It'll be fine. I'm responsible enough.*

"Where are you heading, Marlene?"

She stopped dead in her tracks right as her hand grazed the doorknob. *Caught red-handed.* "*Hallo*, Mamm." She rubbed her arm, turning to face her mother.

"I thought you were going with your sister to the young people's group tonight."

"I was, but then. . ." Marlene trailed off, growing flustered. This was the first time Marlene hadn't let anyone know she was leaving.

"Marlene, I know you're a responsible adult." Mom approached, glancing down at her above the frames of her reading glasses. "You know the difference between right and wrong, and although we're all concerned about your addiction to the mobile phone and all, you know how to avoid trouble and follow what's right."

Her mother's words reverberated in her head, causing Marlene to shake away a cold chill. Her mother, while getting on Marlene's case a lot for leaving the house all the time, had a good reason to be concerned for her.

"So what do you believe to be the best choice?"

Marlene peered up at her mother. "I'll go back to my room and get changed."

Nodding, Mom gave Marlene a hug. "Let me know how things go tonight with your sister."

"I will, Mamm." Marlene wrapped her arms around her mother.

When they parted ways, Marlene headed back to her room and dropped the bag on the floor. Prying the Converse sneakers off her feet, she kicked them underneath the bed. In a way, Marlene felt relief, knowing that Mom confirmed her concerns about the party. She knew it wasn't a right-minded idea yet had continued to justify it.

Marlene went over to the closet and plucked out the first dress she saw. *I'll have to text Alyssa and let her know I won't be going.* Laying the dress on the chair near her desk, Marlene leaned over and grabbed her cell phone. *This is a good thing. Even if I may be a little disappointed, at least I have no terrible feelings about attending a singing.*

———◆———

Krista insisted that Marlene take the two of them in her buggy that evening. Although they did go back and forth with it, Marlene finally gave in and agreed. Driving a buggy was somewhat basic, considering she'd prefer to drive her vehicle to work and other places. But having the reins wrapped around her hands was familiar territory. She felt an exhilarating flutter in her stomach, not in the same way as driving a car, though it was still a satisfying sensation.

They arrived at a reasonable time. A crowd of young people were in the yard, taking in the tenuous breeze of a temperate September evening. Some were just climbing out of their buggies and rushing over to play games on the lawn.

As soon as she found a place to park, Marlene hopped out of the buggy and secured the horse while Krista waited for her to finish.

"Marlene!" Judy yelled from a distance. She came over in a fast-paced strut. "You showed up here after all."

Swallowing, Marlene attempted to give an enthused grin. "I sure did."

"Where's your sister?"

Krista emerged from the other side of the buggy. "I'm right here, Judy."

All three of them headed to the yard and decided to play volleyball before it was time for the meal. While they were playing, Marlene couldn't help but notice someone she had known in the community for a while. A young man named Levi Zook stood with a couple of his friends, talking and laughing and nudging arms from time to time.

The interesting thing about Levi was that, although he was only a year younger than Marlene, he never involved himself with anything that had to do with the English lifestyle. Ever since he began rumspringa, Levi continued with his usual routine. Sometimes when she would pass by his home, she'd see him plowing his family's fields or hopping on the trampoline with his younger siblings. It didn't seem that owning a cell phone or dressing in jeans and a T-shirt was enticing to him. She found herself wishing to be the same way.

Marlene found Levi to be attractive, especially when his hazel eyes glimmered when he laughed. She'd considered being open with him about how she felt, but after being on rumspringa for so long, Marlene ignored those feelings. *There's no possibility it would work out anyway.* She tugged at her sleeve, gazing back at him. *I wonder if he knows anything I've been up to since we last talked.*

The rest of the evening went by too quickly; she was having fun attending a singing after so many weeks away. Marlene immersed herself in the moving sounds of voices singing in the barn, as well as the mouthwatering meal beforehand that tasted amazing. It made her question why she so often chose fast food over homemade food.

Krista chatted with Judy and a few other girls, and Marlene was tempted to text Alyssa and see how the party was going. She twisted her torso to reach into her handbag for her phone, but then she heard the gravel behind her shift. Marlene peered over her shoulder, and when she saw who was there, she dropped her hands to her sides.

"Guder owed, Marlene." Levi tipped his hat. A piece of straw was caught in a couple of strands of his light-brown hair.

"Evening to you too." She felt sweat beads forming on her forehead.

"Haven't seen you attend a singing for quite a while. How long has it been?"

"I–I would say about a month." Marlene didn't know what to fidget with, so she brought her hands together behind her back.

"To be honest, I was looking forward to having the opportunity to see you again. Was thinking about approaching you after church sometime. Though you and your family always seem to leave before I get the chance."

"I'm surprised you haven't come by where I work. It's where Judy works also."

"*Jah*, I know. Would've been too embarrassing for what I want to ask you."

Marlene broke eye contact with him briefly to check on her sister, who was still talking with Judy behind Levi. Probably talking about them. "What did you want to ask me?"

"I–I was hoping, if you're all right with it. . ." He fumbled with the top button of his shirt. "If we could do something? Together?"

"Are you asking me out?"

He gave an incredulous stare, and then his face flushed. "That's a blunt way of saying it. But yes." Levi's mouth stretched tentatively. "Would you go on a date with me? We could get something to eat, whenever you're available."

Glancing about, Marlene felt a sweep of adrenaline rush through her body. *No, this is a horrible idea. If you let him court you, and if he finds out about your car, he's gonna break your heart in an instant.* "J–jah. That sounds fun." *What did I just say?*

"Good. That's, um. . .I'm looking forward to seeing you."

After they planned where they'd be having supper and what time, Levi said his goodbyes. Although Marlene was excited to go on a date with Levi, she was now caught in a predicament. She had to decide whether to tell Levi the truth or pretend she was as invested in being Amish as he was.

—◆——◆——◆—

Two weeks had passed, and Marlene had been hiding from Levi her obsession with the English life. She kept the cell phone at home whenever they went out and parked the car out of sight before he arrived to pick her up. Marlene also did her best not to talk about hanging out with her English friends. She knew being dishonest with Levi wasn't the solution but figured she'd keep up the charade until she fell out of the English way of life.

"Oh no." She held her phone up to check the time while coming out the front door. "I'm gonna be running a tad bit late."

Marlene had planned to go shopping with Alyssa and Jason today since it was her day off. She hadn't said anything to Levi about not having to work, so Marlene figured she'd planned everything out discreetly. That is, until she saw Levi's buggy when she opened the car door.

"Marlene?"

"Levi?" Covering her face with the sleeves of her jean jacket, Marlene's first inclination was to hurry back to the house. However, rather than following through with that plan, she uncovered her face and accepted her fate. " I didn't know you were gonna stop by."

"I'm sorry. I went by your workplace and Judy told me you had the day off. Just wasn't expecting you to be driving. Or, you know. . ."

"Please, let me explain."

Gesturing to the steps, Marlene went over and seated herself, and Levi did the same. Marlene came clean to him, refusing to leave out any detail as she went over all of it. She was filled with unbearable guilt for lying to him, to the point where she wanted to hide away in her room for weeks.

"So this whole time you were hiding all of this from me?"

Marlene nodded. "I didn't want you to know because I figured I'd be able to resolve this problem on my own." She pressed her palm against the wooden step. "It's not that I don't want to join the church.

Going on dates with you, and attending the singings with you, it made me appreciate everything before rumspringa." Marlene dipped her chin. "And like an idiot, I still can't seem to let go."

"I see." Levi brought his feet up to the next step.

"If you no longer want to be with me, then I understand. You deserve someone who's actually humble. Not someone who's pretending like they are."

"I still want to see you, Marlene."

Lifting her chin, she glanced at Levi. "Wh–what?"

"I understand what you're saying to me, so I have no reason to stop seeing you."

Marlene's chest caved in. She couldn't ignore the twinge in her throat. "But I was dishonest."

"I understand why you weren't honest with me" Moving his hand, Levi placed it on top of hers, giving a reassuring smile. "And I forgive you."

Marlene closed her eyes. She almost felt as if she were about to hyperventilate. *I can't believe he wants to continue seeing me after I almost hopped into my car. I want to stop being obsessed, Lord. How can I become content with the life I had before?*

Levi and Marlene continued to go on dates. Now, since Marlene had nothing to hide, she talked about her English friends with him, explaining some of their moments together.

But one crucial thing remained in Marlene's mind. If she depicted no signs of wanting to join the church, other than her words, why would Levi be set on courting her still? It was something she questioned fairly often, and it overwhelmed her. Marlene felt as if he was wasting his valuable time on her.

Marlene sat in the dining room with a glass that no longer had orange juice in it.

"Are you finished with your drink?" Dad asked when he came into the room with a mug in his grasp.

"Yeah, I suppose." Before she picked up the glass, Marlene retracted her hand and watched her father sit at the table. "Hey, Daed? Can I ask you something?"

Her father lifted his mug. "Ask away." He brought the mug's rim to his lips.

"What would you suggest that I do? I know I've been invested with my English friends and have a car and a phone. But if I don't need those things, then why am I so hooked on them?"

"It's important to stay humble. Otherwise you won't be fully content with the things God provides for you. I myself had a difficult time letting go of my desires before joining the church. Sure, we didn't have smartphones in our day, but I paid for my own vehicle like you did." He chuckled, rubbing his bearded chin. "It was a 1982 Chevrolet Camaro. I really loved that car, and I had friends who encouraged my habits." Dad sipped from his mug again. His eyes narrowed in concentration. "But then I met your mother. While we were courting, she encouraged me to become more humble. I had a hard time letting go of my car, as well as the English way of life." His features softened. "Your mother waited patiently for me to decide whether I wanted to join the church or not."

It was then that the match ignited from friction. Marlene realized Levi was waiting for her to change in much the same way her mother had waited for Dad to change. The only reason she did that for him was because Mom cared for Dad. So that meant Levi cared for Marlene, which was why he continued to be patient with her.

"I need to go see Levi." Marlene's muscles tightened as she gave her father a nod. "Thank you, Dad."

"You're welcome." He grinned. "Now, go to him."

Marlene rushed out the door. She didn't pull out her car keys this time. Instead, she ran to her buggy and led her horse over. *Putting my car up for sale will be difficult, but I've gotta do it.*

When she drove her car past Levi's home, getting there took only a few minutes. But Marlene didn't mind the longer trip in her buggy. Having patience and enjoying life were good things.

When Marlene arrived at Levi's house, he was outside with his younger siblings at the pond. But his attention was directed to her as soon as the horse pulled into the driveway. Levi hurried over to her, helping guide the horse to the hitching post. Once she got out of the buggy, Marlene went to him and embraced him.

"I'm surprised you came all this way in your buggy." Levi wrapped his arms around her.

"I don't need my car anymore." Nuzzling his shoulder, Marlene gently squeezed Levi before letting go of him. "I'm ready, Levi. I want to give up my worldly desires and be committed to our relationship."

Levi appeared bewildered as he stood there. But not a moment too soon, a grin stretched across his face. "In a humble way of living?" he asked.

"In a humble way of living." Then Marlene placed a hand on his shoulder; rising on her toes. She leaned forward and brought her lips to the side of Levi's face. She whispered, "Thank you for having faith in me, Levi."

Wherever lay apart all filthiness and superfluity of naughtiness,
and receive with meekness the engrafted word,
which is able to save your souls.
JAMES 1:21

THE BEAUTIFUL QUILT

by Wanda E. Brunstetter

LaGrange, Indiana

Nora Bontrager smiled as she gazed at the beautiful quilt she'd finished yesterday. She had placed it on a rack against her favorite wall in the shop—the one that received the most light. Even though the shop had battery-operated illumination, the natural light against the particular wall where her quilt hung was the brightest.

Nora fancied her quilts, and she felt they expressed the creativity that seemed to churn within her. This quilt had been made in the Tumbling Block pattern, and the colors were rust, green, and gold. The intricate stitches she'd sewn by hand were almost indistinguishable. This was one of her finest creations. Of course, Nora had felt that way about nearly every item she'd quilted.

Nora was pleased that her husband, Aaron, had built a small shop on their property where she could sell her quilted items. Sometimes, especially when she was low on stock, Nora took in on consignment some items from other quilters in the area. However, none of those seemed to sell as quickly as hers did.

Nora had learned to quilt at a young age, beginning with the simple Nine Patch pattern. As she grew older and more experienced, she began making quilts with more difficult patterns, like the one she'd just put on display. Even during her youth, she'd dreamed about owning her own shop and thought it would be a perfect way to make a living. Nora's desire to make quilted items had grown over the years, and now with the shop Aaron had built, she was able to add to their income. As time went on, Nora couldn't help noticing that her skills had improved. In fact, she'd surpassed all of her friends' efforts as well.

"I'll bet this one will sell quickly." Nora spoke out loud as she admired her work.

The little bell above the shop door jingled, drawing Nora's thoughts aside. She went to see who had come in and was pleased to see her friend Helen standing next to the counter with a cardboard box.

"Did you bring something to sell?" Nora asked, joining her friend.

"*Jah*. I have a queen-size quilt in the Weaver Fever pattern, and also a few table runners." Helen set the box on the counter. "Do you have enough room in the shop to take them in on consignment?"

"I believe so. Why don't you go ahead and take them out of the box?"

Nora's friend did as she asked. "What do you think? Do you like the colors of the quilt?"

Nora gazed at the pink, rose, and brown hues. It was a lovely quilt, but not nearly as nice as the one Nora had recently finished. Of course, she wasn't about to tell her friend that. It might hurt her feelings.

Nora smiled and said, "It's very nice, and I'm sure someone will buy it."

"I hope so, because I could use some extra money right now. Devon's birthday is coming up in a few months and I'd like to buy him something nice." Helen sighed. "I hope the quilt sells in time."

"If not, someone might buy the quilted table runners."

"Maybe so, but I wouldn't get as much for them as I would for the queen-size quilt." Helen moved over to where Nora's new quilt hung. "That is beautiful. Is it one of yours?"

Nora nodded. "I finished the quilt yesterday and brought it here this morning. I'm sure it is one of my best yet. At least that's what my sister Carrie said to me."

"I bet it will sell way before mine does." Helen studied the quilt. "You're an expert quilter, there's no doubt about it."

"*Danki*." Nora had been taught from an early age not to become prideful, but with Helen's compliments, Nora couldn't help feeling a bit proud of herself.

Nora took advantage of a small window of time and walked about the displays in the shop, tidying the various items to show off their colors and patterns. She thought about the different types of shoppers who came into her store. Some customers would be neat and thumb through carefully while they searched for whatever they wanted. Occasionally people scattered the various items about, looking for a certain color or theme. Others would leave small piles in the different sections featuring potholders, table runners, wall hangings, and quilts. But even working alone, Nora didn't mind having to reorganize, because she enjoyed being in her shop.

A feeling of contentment came over her and she released a lingering sigh. *The pace this morning has been steady, and I believe it may turn even busier this afternoon.*

Nora had several more customers stop by her shop that day. Most of them were English who either lived in the area or were tourists from out of town. One woman bought two full-sized quilts; both were ones Nora had made, but so far no one had taken an interest in her new Tumbling Blocks quilt. It was so beautiful, she felt sure it was only a matter of time before someone bought it.

She glanced over at Helen's Weaver Fever–patterned quilt. No interest had been shown in it either. *I'm sure it will sell; Helen has sold one in my shop before, but it has been awhile. At least some of her smaller items have sold.*

I'm pleased that I made some money today. Nora smiled to herself as she closed up the shop and headed for the house. The children would be home from school soon, and she wanted to have a snack waiting for them.

Remembering that she had a stack of potholders and some table runners she'd forgotten to price, Nora went back inside and put the items in a small cardboard box. Then, turning toward the house that sat behind the quilt shop, she headed in that direction. Nora would get the snacks ready first; then, while waiting for the children to get home, she would price the quilted items.

When Nora entered the house, she set the box down on a table in the laundry room and went straight to the kitchen. She got out three paper plates and napkins and placed them on the table. Then she cut some cheese and apple slices. She'd just taken out a jug of apple cider from the refrigerator when three excited voices could be heard. A few minutes later, Harley, age six; Irene, age eight; and Vonda, who was ten, entered the room.

"How was your day at school?" Nora asked.

"It was great." Vonda smiled. "I got a good grade on my English assignment."

Nora smiled. "I'm glad to hear it." She looked at Irene. "How was your day? Did you have a good one too?"

Nora's freckle-faced daughter shrugged her shoulders. "Sort of."

"What does that mean?" Nora asked.

"It means she got in trouble with the *schulme* for talking during class," Vonda interjected.

Nora's brows furrowed as she looked at Irene. "Why did the teacher have to get after you for talking? Can you not remember the rules?"

Irene dropped her gaze to the floor. "I just wanted to tell my friend Miriam something."

"I'm sure it was something that could have waited." Nora pointed a finger at her youngest daughter. "Talking in class disrupts everyone. It had better not happen again, you hear?"

Irene nodded. "The teacher made me write fifty times on the board today, 'I will not talk in class.' "

"I hope you learned your lesson."

"Jah, Mama."

Nora turned to look at Harley. "How was your day at *schul*?"

"Es gut." His blue eyes brightened when he spotted the snacks on the table. *"Eppel un kaes."*

Nora nodded. "Jah, and you can have your apples and cheese as soon as you all wash your hands."

The children darted out of the room, chattering like magpies as they went down the hall.

Nora chuckled. She remembered how happy she'd been as a girl when she arrived home from school to a special treat.

She got out three glasses and poured cold cider into each. Shortly after she'd set them on the table, the children came back in.

"Okay now, you three enjoy your snack, and after you're finished you can change your clothes and go play outside for a while," Nora instructed.

"What about you, *Mamm*?" Irene asked. "Aren't you gonna sit at the table with us and have a snack?"

"I might eat an apple later, but right now I have some quilted items to price. I'll be at the table in the dining room if you need me."

None of the children said anything, but Nora could see the look of disappointment on their young faces. "Maybe tomorrow I'll join you for an after-school snack."

Looking at her, all three children nodded.

Nora left the room and went to get the box she'd left in the utility room. As she took it out to the dining room, her thoughts went to the next quilt she would be starting soon. This one would be in the Lone Star pattern. The material would be in several shades of blue. She felt thankful for her quilting talent. Not all Amish women were into quilting. In fact, some actually came into Nora's shop to buy quilted items. Just the other day two Plain women from a different state came in, saying they were visiting family in the area. They were busy looking through the different items, and each woman came up to Nora's counter to purchase something. They'd both made positive comments about Nora's quilt that hung on the wall, and one of them even asked her what the name of the pattern was. Unfortunately, she'd left the store without buying the quilt.

Saturday morning, Nora hung some of her quilts on the line near her shop. She hoped they would be seen from the road and draw in more customers. Once the quilts had been hung, Nora stepped inside her shop and put the OPEN sign in the window. She felt thankful that her husband, Aaron, had taken the children over to his mother's house. He told Nora before they'd left this morning that after he dropped off the kids, he'd have several errands to run and might not be home until late afternoon—about the time she closed her quilt shop for the day.

Nora made sure everything was in place, and then she stepped up to her newest quilt and studied the three-dimensional tumbling blocks. The pattern had been a challenge, but she was pleased with how it had turned out. Hopefully, today a tourist or one of her regular customers would think so too.

Nora was busy with customers all morning, and at noon a tour bus pulled in. This was a good thing, because it meant possible sales. However, Nora felt a bit overwhelmed having to answer questions and wait on customers with no help. Most Saturdays Aaron was available if she needed him. If she'd had any idea the quilt shop would be so busy, she would have asked him to stay home and run his errands another day.

The bell above the door jingled and ten people came through single file. A few minutes later, five more followed. Nora's shop wasn't very large, and she hoped these folks wouldn't bump into each other trying to see what all she had for sale.

Nora glanced out the front window and saw several people milling around the yard. Some had cameras and were taking pictures of the quilts on her line. She smiled. *Those folks are obviously impressed with my handiwork.*

Nora turned away from the window when someone spoke to her. "May I help you?" she asked the young woman who stood by the counter.

"Yes, I was wondering if you have any baby quilts." The woman placed both hands on her stomach. "I'm expecting a baby in a few months, and I'd like a quilted covering for her crib."

"I have one in the back of the shop. Would you like me to show it to you?"

"Yes, please."

One again, Nora wished Aaron was here to help out. She hurried to the back of the shop, found the quilt, and made her way up front, where she found two more people waiting at the counter.

"I'll be with you in a minute." Nora smiled at the two older women. Both gave a nod in response.

Nora showed the baby quilt to the expectant mother. "This is the only one I have in stock right now. What do you think of it?"

The young woman, as well as the other two women at the counter, raved about the pattern, and also the soft yellow and green colors. After Nora quoted the price, the young woman said she would take it.

Nora rang up the purchase on the battery-operated cash register and placed the small quilt in a box with tissue paper.

Tears welled in the young woman's eyes. "Thank you so much. I can hardly wait until my little one is here and I can put the beautiful quilt to good use." She turned and went out the door.

Nora waited on the other two women and then answered questions from several others. A few customers went out the door, and some more came in.

By the time everyone had purchased what they wanted and gotten back on the bus, Nora's head was swimming. She collapsed on the stool behind the counter and drew a deep breath. It felt good to receive so many compliments, but boy, was she tired. From now on, she'd make sure to have somebody here to help out on Saturdays. For that matter, if business picked up during the week, Nora might hire someone full-time.

She reached for her lunch inside the small cooler by her feet. Nora looked at the clock on the wall near the entrance. "No wonder I'm so hungry and thirsty—it's going on one thirty." Nora took out her cold cider and drank half of it before stopping to take a breath. "Ahh. . .that's just what I needed." She took out her peanut butter and apple butter sandwich. Nora's mouth watered in anticipation of eating it, and it wasn't long before she'd consumed the whole thing. *I've really worked up an appetite.* She felt around for the apple she'd packed inside the cooler too. *When I finish this, I'll feel nice and full.*

Nora looked out the window at the parking lot. So far nobody was out there. Seeing the empty lot allowed her to relax and enjoy the peace and quiet—not that she didn't like having customers come in and check things out. Nora just wanted to rest on the stool, and for added comfort, she decided to lean her back against some piled-up fabric behind her.

After sitting awhile, she glanced at her prized quilt and frowned. Several people had looked at it today and even commented on how lovely it was, but no one seemed interested in buying the quilt.

Nora bit down on her lower lip. *Maybe the price is too high. Perhaps I should lower it a bit.*

Monday of the following week, Nora's friend Helen stopped by the quilt shop again. She came in and placed a cardboard box on the counter. "It looks like you've been sprucing up the area outside your shop. The flowers in the hanging basket look pretty, Nora, and the wind chimes are a nice addition."

"Well, you know, I have to think of things that might appeal to my customers." Nora smiled.

"Those are cute." Helen pointed to a stack of key rings with little quilt patches attached. "Did you make them?"

"Jah. I used leftover scraps of material. I thought it was a good idea rather than throwing them away."

Helen gave an exaggerated eye roll. "My word, Nora, you think of the cleverest things. I can't believe how talented you are."

Nora shrugged her shoulders and grinned. "What can I say—new ideas keep popping into my head."

"I brought some more potholders and table runners." Helen gestured to the cardboard box.

Nora opened the lid and pulled out several potholders. "These are nice. I'm sure they will sell. A lot of people come in here looking for potholders."

"I am glad to hear that. Oh, and I was also wondering if any of my quilted items I brought in before have sold." She clasped her hands under her chin as she looked at Nora with a questioning gaze.

"All your potholders are gone, and two of the table runners, so I'm glad you brought more." Nora smiled. "I can pay you today for everything that has sold."

"What about my quilt? Has there been any interest in that?"

Nora shook her head. "Saturday a tour bus came in, and I sold a few quilts that were displayed outside on the line, but your quilt wasn't among them."

Helen sagged against the counter. "That's too bad. I was really hoping. . ."

Nora put down the potholders and patted her friend's arm. "Don't worry. Summer's almost here, and as the tourist season goes into full swing, things will get busy here in the shop. I'm sure when the right person comes in, your quilt, as well as my newest one, will sell. You know, anyone with a good eye can see how much work goes into the pieces we make."

"That is true, and your hard work especially shows. In fact, I'm surprised your lovely Tumbling Blocks quilt hasn't already sold." Helen's lips parted slightly as she looked at Nora's special quilt on the wall. "It's so beautiful, and you have a special knack for quilting. I can't help but envy you."

Nora gave a satisfied smile. "Danki. It's just a matter of practice and doing what you love." Once more, a feeling of pride set in. How nice it was to receive praise for her work.

The following day, soon after the children left for school, Nora went outside to get the mail. After breakfast, she'd asked Aaron to help her hang two quilts on the line, hoping to draw customers into her shop. These would probably be more attention-getting than the flowers and wind chimes on the porch. One of the quilts was the newest one she'd made in the Tumbling Blocks pattern, and the other belonged to Helen. Perhaps by the end of the day they would both be sold.

Nora had only taken a few steps across the yard when she spotted their goat, Frisky, under the clothesline. She froze, wondering why he was out of his pen and what he was up to. Nora was about to shout at him when he leaped up and pulled one of the quilts off the line. Nora gasped when she realized it was her beautiful Tumbling Blocks quilt.

Shaking her fists, Nora raced across the yard, shouting for the goat to drop the quilt. By the time she got there, Frisky had one end of the covering in his mouth and was pulling it across the yard. Heat radiated throughout Nora's body as she hollered, "Stop, you crazy goat! Let go of my quilt!"

The goat stopped running and let go of the quilt, but then he began pawing at the material with his dirty cloven hooves. He paused once and looked in her direction, then started tugging and shaking the fabric so hard Nora feared he might tear it in two.

About that time, their other goat, Wendy, showed up on the scene.

Before Nora could do anything to stop her, the female goat grabbed the other end of the quilt and a tug-of-war ensued.

Nora screamed and swatted at the goats, but it was futile. In the end, her once-beautiful quilt ended up in several mangled pieces. At this point, Nora realized even if she could rescue the quilt from the goats, there wouldn't be much, if anything, left to work with. All she could do was drop to her knees and weep.

◆———◆———◆

"Those horrible goats we own got out today and ruined my quilt." These were the first words out of Nora's mouth when Aaron arrived home from work. "Didn't you make sure the goats' pen was locked this morning?"

He combed his fingers through his thick brown hair. "Of course I did. Now calm down, Nora, and tell me what happened."

She proceeded to explain what had occurred and ended by saying, "All that hard work I put into the quilt is for nothing now; it's ruined beyond repair!" Tears welled in Nora's eyes as she collapsed into a seat at the kitchen table.

"I'm sorry it happened, and I'll try to figure out how the goats got out so something like that won't happen again." He placed his hands on her shoulders. "You can make another one, Nora. It's not like you lost something that can't be replaced."

She sniffed deeply and swiped a hand across her cheeks. "You don't understand. This was the most beautiful quilt I've ever made. I got so many compliments on it. You even said it was beautiful."

Aaron took a seat next to her. "I did say that, but while compliments are nice, we shouldn't put too much importance on them. If our emphasis is on receiving praise, then we quickly become full of *hochmut*."

Nora's spine stiffened. "I am not full of pride. I work very hard on all my sewing projects and give a great deal of consideration to how

I'm crafting each one."

"I realize that, but to me it seems like pride when you feed on compliments. I'm wondering whatever happened to that young woman I married who was so meek and humble." He paused, looking right into her eyes. "Pride is a spiritual disease that can drive a person away from God. As followers of Jesus we should be looking to do good things that help others in their struggles, rather than gloating over our own success."

"What do you mean, Aaron? I just spent money on trying to get the outside of my shop to look nice in order to attract more customers. It's not only for my benefit either. More customers would also benefit the women who have their quilted items on consignment in my shop. Isn't that helping others?"

"You've misunderstood what I said." He leaned closer to her. "As Christians, we should resist the temptation to impress others with our accomplishments. A follower of Christ should let their good deeds speak for themselves and not go out of the way to draw attention to things they have done well."

Nora sniffed. She was hurt by her husband's admonition, but she would not say so, nor was she willing to admit that she'd done anything wrong. All she could think about right now was the special quilt that she'd had to throw out—except for a few pieces of salvaged material that she would use to make more key rings.

"Mama, how come you're not talkin' much?" Irene asked as the family sat at the supper table that evening.

"I don't have a lot to say." Nora forked a piece of meat loaf into her mouth. Even though her appetite was diminished, she forced herself to eat in order to set an example for the children.

"I heard what happened to your pretty quilt," Vonda spoke up. "I'm sorry, Mama." She reached over and patted Nora's arm.

"What's done is done." Nora could barely get the words out. "I'd rather not talk about it, okay?"

Vonda nodded, and so did the other two children. Aaron offered a brief smile, but Nora looked away. After the lecture he'd given her today, she doubted he felt any pity at all for her having lost the cherished quilt. Was it so wrong to care about something she'd worked really hard to create? As far as Nora was concerned, she had every right to be upset with those crazy, unmannered goats. If it was left up to her, she'd get rid of them. And she still didn't know how they'd gotten out of their pen. Aaron claimed he'd locked the gate, but they'd obviously managed to get it open.

Nora was in no mood to make another quilt—at least not anytime soon. There were so many other things that needed to be done around here, and she also had the quilt shop to run. So for now, at least, she would concentrate on other things and try not to dwell on the loss of her beautiful quilt. After all, pining for the bed covering certainly wouldn't bring it back.

The following Saturday, a few minutes after Nora opened her shop, Vonda came in and stepped up to Nora. "Can I help ya with anything today, Mama?"

"Do you mean here or in the house?" Nora asked.

"Here. I like being around the quilts and spending time with you."

Nora patted her oldest daughter's hand. "I appreciate that, but wouldn't you rather be outside playing with your brother and sister today?"

Vonda shook her head. "They're playin' with the kittens in the barn while Daddy grooms the buggy horses." She smiled up at Nora. "I wanna be here."

"Okay, I'll find something for you to do." Nora looked around the room. "Why don't you make sure all the smaller quilted items are stacked neatly and that nothing has been scattered around? I didn't take the time yesterday when I closed the shop to take care of it all."

"Sure, Mama, I can do that." Vonda looked up at the wall where Nora's beautiful quilt used to hang. It had been replaced with another quilt Nora had previously made but didn't cherish nearly as much. "What's that quilt called?"

"Mariner's Compass. The black and beige colors aren't as beautiful as my Tumbling Blocks quilt, but the pattern is a bit unusual. I'm hoping someone will buy it."

"I bet they will. Nobody makes quilts as nice as yours."

Nora's first inclination was to smile, say thank you, and let pride set in. But she remembered the things her husband had said to her after the beautiful quilt had been ruined. So instead of soaking up the compliment, Nora smiled and said, "I enjoy my work and do the best I can, but I'm sure there are other quilters who do equally well or even better than me." She leaned down and gave her daughter a hug. "You'd best get to work now, all right? It probably won't be long before we see customers showing up."

"Okay." With a cheery smile, Vonda headed toward the middle of the store where the potholders and table runners were displayed.

Nora smoothed the front of her dress and gave a gratified sigh. It felt right to know she'd responded correctly to a compliment this time. Boasting and feeling puffed up about herself had become a habit for Nora. And as with any habit that needed to be broken, she would have to remind herself many times to keep a meek and humble spirit.

As Nora sat in church on Sunday morning, listening to the bishop's sermon, she reflected on the scriptures he'd quoted, found in Proverbs. They all pointed to the importance of having a humble spirit and not allowing pride to set in. Nora felt shame for the times she'd bragged about her handiwork, and especially for the way she'd carried on when the goats tore up her beautiful quilt. She'd been wrong to lash out at Aaron too, and had since apologized to him.

Yesterday, when she'd been between customers, Nora had made a sign on poster board and hung it in the shop. It read: WORK HARD AND STAY HUMBLE. It was good to have that reminder.

Nora returned her focus to the ending of the sermon, and when church was over, she followed the others outside where lunch would soon be served.

As Nora sat beside Helen during the light meal, she brought up the topic of the sermon. "It was a message I needed today, as I have recently realized the importance of being meek and humble."

Helen nodded. "We all need that reminder. It's too easy to let our pride take over—especially when we receive a compliment."

Some of the other women sitting at the table bobbed their heads in agreement.

"We need to use our talents for the Lord by serving others," the bishop's wife, Linda, put in.

"One way we can do that is by giving of our time and talents." Helen turned her head in Nora's direction. "In fact, I've decided to donate the quilt I left in your shop that still hasn't sold to the Haiti Benefit auction."

Nora smiled. "That's not possible, because your quilt sold yesterday, to an English tourist."

Helen's brows lifted. "Then I'll donate the quilt I'm currently working on. I should have it done in time for the event."

Several of the other women talked about what they planned to do to help with the auction. Some would offer items they'd sewn or crafted in some other way. Some said they planned to make baked goods.

"I put another one of my quilts on display yesterday, and even though it's not as beautiful as the one our goats destroyed, I'm going to donate it to the auction."

"I bet it will go right away," Helen said. "Anything made by you is bound to draw attention."

Nora paused to take a drink of water before she spoke. "If it does bring a good price, then any credit goes to the Lord, for He gave me the ability to sew and make quilts. I'm merely His servant."

Every lady at the table agreed, and then the conversation changed to other things.

When Nora finished her meal, she bowed her head for silent prayer just as the others did. *Heavenly Father, thank You for convicting me about my prideful attitude. Please remind me daily that I can do nothing without You.*

> *Better it is to be of an humble spirit with the lowly,*
> *than to divide the spoil with the proud.*
> PROVERBS 16:19

Temperance

BREAKING DOWN

by Richelle Brunstetter

H ave you finished feeding hay to the horses? You're looking a little *schruwwlicher* this morning."

"I know I'm a little disheveled this morning." Aaron turned to his coworker Thomas, squinting his eyes. "I forgot to set my alarm last night and woke up late."

"Well, no wonder you are behind in taking care of the animals."

"I'm getting all of that done right now."

"I could help you out if you need it. It's not a very difficult task."

"I don't need help. I know what I'm doing. I'll get myself caught up when you leave me alone."

"Okay." Thomas stepped back with his palms raised. "Our boss expected you to get that done sooner."

Aaron shook his head and gathered some more hay for the horses. Under his breath, he grumbled, "I'd like to see him get it done so quick."

Aaron Yoder tended to have a short fuse at times. He had been hired by a family friend to train horses. As it turned out though, he spent more time tending to the animals rather than training them. He'd been put to the task of exercising them today.

Something simple hadn't started out so well for Aaron this morning. A new horse came in last night after he'd gone home. Aaron noticed him but went about his routine to exercise the other horses. After he put one of the horses away, he paused and looked at the new animal's nameplate: Buzz. The horse was a young gelding and a nice-looking bay. Aaron let him out in the arena to run around while he went to fetch the next horse. However, Buzz somehow loosened the latch and got back into the barn. The other horses carried on with nickers and stomping in their stalls, while Buzz stopped in short bursts to visit with a few of his new buddies. Aaron turned with widening eyes as the free menace made his social calls and then trotted toward him. Aaron quickly closed and secured the entrance gate just in time before Buzz got past him.

Thomas arrived on the opposite side of the gate. "I was out by the waste pile unloading a wheelbarrow full when I heard a commotion in the barn. What's going on in here?"

Aaron grabbed Buzz's halter abruptly, causing the horse to rear its head. Then he kicked the gate with his boot, making it hit the wall with a *thwack*. "It's this crazy escape artist." He huffed. "Buzz got out."

"It's a good thing that horse didn't leave the premises and end up on the road. Otherwise you'd be in a world of trouble." Thomas went up to the horse and tapped Buzz's saddle. "You're gonna have to keep your eyes on this one."

Aaron eyed the beast. "I don't need this right now, you goofy horse." *I should put you right back in your stall.*

"Is everything okay?"

Oh, great, now the boss is here. Aaron turned to Pete when he came around the corner. He was a stocky fellow and towered over the two of them like a streetlight. "This horse tried to escape, but I stopped him in time before he made it out of the stable."

Thomas nodded. "He's right."

"It's a good thing he didn't. No telling what could've happened." Pete folded his arms over his plaid flannel shirt. "We're responsible for each of these animals, and their owners are depending on us to give them good care."

Aaron gritted his teeth and marched away from Thomas and his boss, guiding Buzz along with him. *It's not my fault this animal is a knucklehead.*

"I'm giving the credit to the Lord for your quick reaction to keep Buzz from getting loose."

If he wasn't leading Buzz away, Aaron would've put his hands over his ears to drown out his boss's words. *Why am I having to hear this? I got the horse back in myself. I'm able to do things without help.*

After many times of getting impatient and nearly losing his temper at work, Aaron was thankful he hadn't lost his job. Sometimes he was tempted to throw around some of the equipment, but fortunately didn't do it. Perhaps Aaron wouldn't have gotten fired for it, but he could've been stuck with just basic feeding and grooming of the horses. Regardless, he didn't want to risk it.

Aaron had a habit of allowing his insecurities to get the best of him. He wasn't always the best at being productive. Even when he did apply a great amount of effort to what he did, Aaron became anxious whenever someone critiqued him on his mistakes.

Aaron tried his best to keep from becoming stressed and overwhelmed. However, he still tended to lash out at the horses when they didn't follow his commands. Aaron was aghast at his own outbursts at times, since the horses were only animals who didn't know better.

He wasn't always extreme when it came to being defensive. In fact, Aaron used to be more willing to listen and be reasonable about the things people said to him. His recent belligerence wasn't right; he was aware of that. But with what had been going on at home with his father, how else could he deal with the intensity of his circumstances?

Aaron headed straight home at the end of the workday. It was early November, and although the weather had been cold some days prior, the last few days had been fairly warm. The pleasant temperatures made buggy drives more enjoyable, for sure.

As he trundled past his family's property, Aaron looked out in the field. His brother Mark caught sight of him and waved. He was out there plowing, which irritated Aaron.

I was supposed to finish that. Aaron stabbed his thumb into the fabric of his pant leg. *I told Mark that too. Now he's messing everything up.*

He drove along the gravel path and up the mound to the hitching post. Springing from the seat and landing heels first on the gravel,

Aaron hooked up his horse and stroked his hand through the animal's short mane, similar to a freshly cut lawn. "I trained you right. That other horse was the problem."

Aaron hurried to the other side of the property and went out to the field where his brother was working.

"Hey, Brother." Mark lifted his straw hat and brushed long fingers through his blond hair. "What's up?"

"I believe you know 'what's up,' Mark." Aaron crossed his arms. "Plowing the field wasn't your responsibility. I told you I was gonna get it done today."

"I'm sorry, but I talked with *Daed* when you left for work, and he said he wanted me to finish the rest of the plowing. There was nothing I could do about it. I didn't want to upset him."

"Well, now he will be upset with me because of you."

"If you would've gotten it done yesterday—"

"Plowing takes time and precision. And your method is mediocre at best."

Mark's mouth straightened. "Thanks for that."

Aaron turned away from Mark and headed back to the hitching post. He wanted to get started with his chores right away, but he needed to unhook his horse and take him to the corral first.

Once the chore was done, Aaron put the buggy in the shed. What a day he'd had at work, but at least he was home, and Aaron wanted to get into the house to see the rest of his family.

"Evening, *Mamm*," Aaron said when he entered the kitchen.

"Evening to you too. How was work today?" she asked.

"Same old, same old. How's Daed doing?"

"He's relaxing. I told him to stay in the bedroom until supper was ready."

"Oh, what are we having for—"

"Aaron! You're back!"

Aaron looked over his shoulder, listening to his two youngest siblings, Andrew and Mary, snickering while trotting down the stairs. The *pitter-patter* of their bare feet against the wooden floors sped up, and the next thing Aaron knew, both of them clung around his waist.

"Hey, calm down, you two." Mom leaned over to ruffle Andrew's hair.

Mary detached from Aaron; however, Andrew still hung on to Aaron's waist, swaying back and forth like a rocking chair.

Aaron's veins throbbed under the collar of his shirt. "Let go of me already!"

"Andrew, please give your brother some space."

Giggling, he let go of Aaron and ran out of the kitchen.

"As for you, no need to raise your voice. He was only hugging you," Mom scolded.

"More like cutting off my circulation from the waist down." Cupping his elbow, Aaron tapped the tip of his shoe against the floor. "What are we having?"

"Something *wunderbaar*. It's a surprise." She playfully pinched the side of Aaron's face. "Your brother has been outside working."

"Something wonderful, huh?" Aaron turned in the direction of his parents' room. "And *jah*, I noticed. I'll be out there with Mark once I check on Daed."

"Check on Dad? But he's sleeping."

"He'll wake up."

Mom made a *hmm* noise, but that was her only response.

Aaron went out of the kitchen. The clunking of his footsteps resounded through the hallway as he approached his parents' bedroom. He turned the doorknob and pressed against the center of the door with his other hand.

"Daed? You awake?"

"Now I am," he grumbled. Rotating on the mattress toward Aaron, his father winced.

"Your back is still hurting, huh?"

"All because I needed to clean out the gutter." Dad sat up with a frown. "I can't believe I lost my balance. Now I'm stuck in bed until I can move without unbearable pain."

Aaron fiddled with the doorknob. "I'm gonna be heading outside with Mark. A lot needs to be done around here before the sun sets."

"I know, Aaron." Dad's shoulders slumped, and he tugged at his light-brown beard. "I'm envious of you and Mark. You two are able to work, and you aren't having to stay in the house all day. I was hoping to get our barn built finally so we could tear down the other one."

Aaron's body temperature elevated as he wondered if Dad would bring up how he hadn't finished plowing the fields. He hoped it had slipped his father's mind.

"As for the fields," Dad said, "I thought. . ."

Aaron rubbed at his wrist. "I was going to plow the rest of the field after work."

Dad shook his head. "You can't do everything by yourself."

"So you're saying I'm not responsible?"

"That isn't what I'm saying at all." His father twisted the top of his nightshirt. "All I'm saying is, if you want to do all of that work, then you need to follow through with it."

"Just because it isn't at your desired pace doesn't mean I'm not following through with it." His body trembled, feeling the urge to slam the door to close off communication between him and his father. Instead, Aaron said goodbye to Dad and headed out of the room, shutting the door with a tad more force than necessary.

In some ways, Aaron wished it was frigid outside, because being in direct sunlight did nothing to calm him. At least Aaron could've buried himself in the snow like he did when he was younger. That would've helped cool him down. *Whatever. I'll just try to simmer down by tending to the animals.*

As Aaron crossed the gravel path of the driveway, he found Mark coming in from the field. Because of his conversation with Dad, he was still fuming. Aaron wanted to have control over something, so he headed over to Mark.

"Daed was set on getting the barn raised this year," Aaron said.

"In his condition, that ain't happening anytime soon."

Aaron walked with his brother as he put the plow away. "I think we should take matters into our own hands and tackle this project."

"You think so?"

"Jah. I know Daed will appreciate it. We'll need some help from friends and family to get this done of course. Every little bit helps." Aaron shoved Mark's arm. "And tomorrow, you'll be observing me as I plow the rest of the field. I need to show you how to do it right." *I may be only eighteen, but I'm the oldest child in this family. Whether I like it or not, this is all on me. And I'm going to prove to Daed how responsible I really am.*

At the beginning of the week, Aaron made the arrangements for raising a new barn on their property. He began by getting the lumber needed, and he tried to conduct himself properly during the preparations.

Things were getting better at work. He was having fewer mishaps and the training was progressing. A few of the horses would be able to go back to their owners, ready for pulling a buggy. But one thing that bothered Aaron, besides his continual efforts to keep his temper under control, was Aaron's boss. He kept making remarks about how important it was to thank the Lord for His grace, or how Aaron should be praying for the things he needed help with. Aaron would shrug off the comments. He wanted to have control and make do with things good or bad.

Today at work, his boss told him they'd be getting six more horses in for training as soon as tomorrow and he needed Aaron for more hours of the day. He couldn't believe what he'd heard. Now he worried about juggling his schedule to do the horse training as well as help out with his father's barn raising. He would have to take time off the day of the barn raising, but his boss stressed to him that he needed to be there to carry the workload.

That evening and the days prior to the barn raising, some people approached Aaron, concerned about the weather. A couple of his friends, Daniel and Jacob, warned about the possibility of a storm brewing over the valley during the upcoming week.

"Come on, now. We've only had sun-shining days throughout this entire season. I'm sure those are nothing but rumors."

"I dunno. It is tornado season after all." Daniel took off his beat-up straw hat and swayed it in the breezeless air.

"Doesn't mean there will be any touching ground around here. We haven't had even a mild tornado for several years."

"Heavy winds could still happen, Aaron," Jacob said. "We could always wait to build a few weeks from now."

Aaron's throat felt as if hot coals rested within his esophagus. "It's my decision, and we're going to do it."

"Okay, whatever you say, Aaron." Daniel threw his hat in the air and let it land on the lawn.

Shaking his head, Jacob finally agreed.

Aaron felt somewhat proud of himself. He wasn't going to allow anyone to talk him out of getting the barn raised as planned.

A day had passed, and Aaron finished up with work for the evening. He was beat from the long day of training, yet relieved that it had gone well. So far he was managing to control his temper, but he almost slipped with a client earlier that day. Fortunately, his coworker came in on the conversation and lightened the mood, which helped immensely.

Working the longer hours gave Aaron extra money in the pocketbook, but it was wearing him down. He hadn't even asked yet for the time off he needed to be at home for the barn raising, and he'd just confided in his helper at the barn about his predicament. He felt hard pressed in his situation.

He went to get his horse and had finished hooking him up when his boss came out from the barn.

"You are making some progress on that young team just brought in."

"Jah. It'll take some time, but they'll come around."

"I hear ya. However, their owner is pressing for you to work with them daily. He wants his horses trained and back to him as soon as possible."

Aaron's throat tightened. "I'm sure he does, but we've got other clients too. And they want us to take care of theirs as well."

"This man is paying extra for you to train them."

"Oh, I didn't know that."

"Yep."

"I'll be here on time tomorrow morning." Aaron guided his rig out of the parking lot.

He rode home, feeling overwhelmed. It seemed like he was carrying the world on his shoulders. Aaron couldn't wait to arrive home, eat, and throw himself into bed—though his dad still needed help around the place since he wasn't back to his old self yet. The ride home gave Aaron some time to think, but he couldn't come up with a solution. The day of the barn raising was coming up fast, and he didn't know what to do. His grip slipped off the reins with perspiration as he guided his horse along. *How long can I manage this stress I'm under?*

Minutes later, the farmhouse came into view and he felt better. Mark was outside putting something away in the barn when Aaron pulled up by the building.

"Hey, Aaron," Mark greeted cheerfully while approaching Aaron. "How was your day at work?"

"It went fine. How's Daed doing?"

"The same. He's lying in bed, probably resting."

Aaron lowered his chin into the collar of his coat. "Have you been making progress out in the field?"

"Yes, things are coming along."

"That's good. I wish I could be here earlier to help."

"I know. But your workload has increased." Mark's smile wavered. "What are you going to do about the barn raising?"

"Good question, Mark. I'm still thinking that through."

"Seriously? We are only days away from it."

"I know, I know. I'm under a lot of stress right now, and this isn't helping."

"Sorry, Aaron, but you haven't shared this with me. Have you told Dad or Mom how you're feeling?"

"No, I'm trying to deal with this on my own. I am the oldest, you know."

"Yes, that's true, but we all can use some help sometimes."

"I'll take care of things. And please, don't say anything to the folks."

"Okay, whatever you say."

Aaron put his horse in the stall and brushed him down. "I've got more chores to do but I'm ready to crash in bed," he mumbled.

His younger siblings came into the barn and began playing with one of the cats. It was an older feline, with woolly gray-and-white fur.

"Look, Aaron," Andrew shouted. "I'm making Patches walk! See?"

He turned from grooming his horse and saw Andrew walking the cat along on the straw. "Don't do that. Quit teasing the poor animal!"

Andrew and Mary giggled at the feline a little more and finally let the cat go.

"I can't wait for us to have a new barn." His sister's pigtails bounced as she came and stood by the stall.

"I can't wait either." Sighing, Aaron moved from his horse and closed the door. "I wonder what's for supper."

"Mom mentioned stew and biscuits." Andrew came over and looked out the doorway of the barn.

"I suppose I'll go in now. Are you guys coming?"

They both shook their heads.

"Okay, but don't bug the cat."

"We won't." His brother laughed, and he and Mary went back into the barn.

Aaron entered the house and went to wash up in the bathroom. When he'd finished, he saw his mom in the kitchen. He could smell the aroma of beef simmering with vegetables on the burner. *I'm hungry, and Mom's cooking is making my mouth water.*

Aaron shoved his hands into his pockets while strolling into the kitchen. "Supper smells good."

"Danki." Mom brushed flour off her hands onto her apron. "Just getting the biscuits ready for the oven. I've got some more to roll out yet."

Aaron took his coat off and hung it on the wooden rack. "I can't wait to eat."

"Looks like another late work evening for you."

"Yep, I'm busy, but that's okay."

"How busy? I hope you're not overdoing things."

"I'll be all right. I'm going to go see Dad before we eat."

She nodded.

Aaron found his father lying there awake. He had a container of pain medicine in his hand and was sipping water from a glass, but set them both on his nightstand when Aaron entered the room. "Hello, Aaron. You're getting in later again. You must be pretty busy."

"Jah, it's getting busier and my workload is growing, but so far I'm managing."

Dad's head tilted to one side. "I detect there's something you're not telling me."

"It's nothing, really." Aaron didn't want his dad to lose trust in his plan to get the barn built. Tomorrow he'd have to tell his boss he needed Friday off.

Rays of sunlight pierced through the blinds, their intensity forcing Aaron's eyes open. Finally, he rose from the mattress and got dressed.

He was still buttoning his shirt when he headed out of his room.

Aaron went into the kitchen and started frying some eggs for breakfast. He then quickly sat at the dining room table and wolfed down his food.

His mother had made him a lunch and he found it in the refrigerator. Aaron was thankful he didn't have to make it, because there wasn't enough time this morning. After grabbing the container from the fridge, Aaron said goodbye to his father, who had sat at the table with a cup of tea, and made his way out the door. He hardly thought about what he was doing, his mind was in such a fog.

Aaron got his rig ready and hooked up the horse. He felt like he was sweating through his shirt even in the crisp cold air. *I've got to do this. I need to ask for the day off.* His knuckles lacked color as he held on to the reins. Aaron wished he didn't have to ask, but he had no other choice.

As Aaron drove along, he caught himself drifting off here and there, and his horse had slowed way down. *If I keep this up, I'll make myself late again.* Aaron cleared his throat. "Come on, boy." He moved along, still thinking through how he'd ask his boss. *I wish this day was already over.*

Soon the arena came into view, but he didn't see the helper's buggy there yet. *Maybe I'm doing better on time getting here than I thought.*

Aaron entered the barn and saw his boss over by one of the stalls.

"Morning." His boss moved a wheelbarrow aside.

"Good morning."

"You're kinda late, Aaron."

"L–late?" He shuffled back a step. "I didn't see the helper's rig outside."

"That's because he called in sick early this morning."

"Oh. . ." *That's going to make things a lot tougher.* "I'm sorry to ask you this. . ." Aaron hesitated.

"What's up?" His boss frowned.

"Well. . .I need Friday off for a barn raising at my place." He explained the whole thing, like he'd done the other day with his helper there at work.

Sighing, his boss pressed a finger against one of the stalls. "This isn't a good time, Aaron. With how swamped we are, I need you to be here right now. I'm not sure if that'll work, but I'll pray about my decision. Maybe you should too, so then you won't have to postpone your big project."

Aaron just stood there blinking.

"I'm going to have to get these stalls cleaned while you're working with our clients' animals."

"Okay, Boss. I'll get right to it." Aaron felt his stomach acid boiling like water in a saucepan while walking away from his boss. *Pray about it? But do I really need to? Isn't it best to take matters into my own hands rather than sitting on them?*

Two days passed, and when Aaron arrived at work, Thomas's buggy was there and he was getting food for the horses. "*Guder mariye*, Aaron."

"Good morning. How are you feeling?"

"My cough is gone and I've got more energy, but I'm still taking it easy."

"That's good to hear. We missed you here at the barn. The boss was busy doing your jobs."

"I'm sure he was."

Aaron hauled some hay into one of the stalls and closed the door.

About then, Pete strolled down the walkway. "Good morning, Aaron. I just wanted to let you know that I've been praying about you taking Friday off. And I'm letting you know that you can have it off."

Aaron couldn't help smiling. "Th–thank you, sir. Well, I'd best get busy; I've got a lot to do." He hurried off to put his lunch away. *I could've gotten my answer ahead of time if he would've said yes to begin with. But that doesn't matter now. All that matters is that I get the new barn built.*

Early Friday morning, Aaron ran around getting things set up for the barn raising. The whole family got up early, and an abundance of energy filled the house. It wouldn't be long before everyone would start showing up for work outside.

Aaron wondered how the new barn would look. He still felt relieved his boss gave him today off so he could be here for this important day. He didn't want anything to keep this project from happening. He wanted his dad to have his new barn built today.

As the morning wore on, the sun came up and folks arrived with their tool belts and extra supplies that would be useful. Aaron unstrapped some of the lumber, and one of the men came over to Aaron.

"We should wait a few more weeks and see what the weather is like."

"I'm not waiting." Heat formed within Aaron's throat. "We're doing it. And we're getting most of it done today."

He brushed aside the concerns. Although the wind had started howling this morning and the sun was now masked by inky clouds, there was no way he was going to call everything off at this point. Not when his boss had given him the day off, and certainly not when his family and friends had already agreed to go through with constructing the new barn.

Everything went well for the most part. The men put in six hours of manual labor, constructing the bulk of the barn's structure, and then called it a day. Aaron's father was pleased with his efforts in leading everyone and providing his own physical strength to help build the new barn.

That evening, vigorous winds blustered through the area. The winds gradually increased to the point where it was no longer safe to be outdoors. The family sat around the supper table as the wind howled outside. Aaron heard tree branches snapping.

"It doesn't sound good out there." Dad's voice deepened.

Aaron cringed. *I hope all the hard work we did today wasn't in vain.* He couldn't help jumping to his feet and moving over to the window to look outside. Aaron raised the blinds, and his jaw dropped as he watched the newly raised barn become dismantled right before his eyes. "No! No! Parts of the barn are blowing away!"

Aaron ran out the door and hastened to the barn. There he was, in the midst of the storm, shouting to the point where he felt the strain on his vocal cords.

"Aaron!" Mark called to him from the house. "Get back inside!"

But he didn't turn back to his brother. Instead, Aaron sank to his knees in defeat. "Why? Why did this happen?"

Leaves and twigs swiveled on by, along with bits of lumber that fortunately weren't larger pieces.

Aaron came back in the house, dismissing himself from supper and refusing to speak with anyone. He stalked into his room and slammed his back against the wall. He slid down until he was sitting on the floor, filled with nothing but grim thoughts in solitude.

The day after the storm tore the barn apart, Mark and some of the others went out to clean up the mess in the yard.

Aaron sat outside on the porch. Anguish loomed over him as he looked at the barn's remains. All that was left were fragments of lumber in a pile. *I wish I had work today. Then I wouldn't have to sit here and look at this mess.*

Hearing the front door creak behind him, Aaron saw Mom closing the screen portion of the door. "I'm making your father some tea. Would you like some when the water's ready?"

Aaron's toes curled up in his shoes. "You know I don't like tea, Mamm."

"Doesn't hurt to ask." His mother sat down with him. "That's a big mess out there, isn't it?"

"I don't need a reminder when it's right out there in front of me." Aaron sat quietly for a moment, bringing his left ankle to his right knee and resting his foot. "I can't help but blame myself for what happened to the barn. It wouldn't have gotten blown down if I'd have listened to what everyone told me." Aaron slapped the arm of his chair. "I hoped to prove to everyone I was capable. I let Daed and everyone else down."

"There's an importance to self-control. There are some things that we as people are not always capable of controlling. That's why we should be asking God for guidance. Otherwise, we may end up making the wrong choice in those uncontrollable situations." Mom patted his arm. "It's okay to be angry, but be careful how you handle your anger. That's what makes the difference."

Soaking in his mother's words while staring at the wreckage in front of him became a moment of true clarity for Aaron. These events that took place would be a lesson he carried with him throughout the rest of his days. Aaron realized that temperance was what he needed in his life to control his outbursts of anger. And the Lord was his source of guidance.

He that hath no rule over his own spirit is like a city
that is broken down, and without walls.
PROVERBS 25:28

TEMPTED

by Wanda E. Brunstetter

Sugarcreek, Ohio

Martha Yoder sat in the front seat of her driver's van, staring out the window at the passing scenery as they headed to her home. Her mood was less happy than when she'd left home. Martha had been to see her doctor today, to get the results of the blood test she'd had done a week ago. The news wasn't good—she was pre-diabetic, and the doctor warned if she didn't change her eating habits and exercise regularly, she would end up with full-blown diabetes. "Give up refined sugar and lower your carbs," the doctor had told Martha. "Twenty to thirty minutes of exercise at least five days a week will also be helpful."

Martha grimaced. She'd hoped the findings would be better than they'd turned out to be. She dreaded the thought of revamping her diet. She loved eating sweets, and giving them up would be hard to do. An exercise program, with the exception of basic household chores and some gardening, had never been on her priority list either. Her life as she knew it was now turned over on its ear. Things would have to change, and Martha wasn't sure how well she would fare through it.

I don't understand any of this. Can I manage a brand-new way of living? I wish there was someone like myself who has been through the same thing and I could talk to them about it. Martha's long sigh was noisy, and she covered her mouth. *Even a friend to talk to about this would help so much.* Martha needed some support, that was for sure.

"You've been quiet since you got in the van." Martha's driver, Dottie, broke into her thoughts. "Did everything go okay at your doctor's appointment?"

"It went fine." Despite her troubled soul, Martha didn't want to talk to Dottie about it. The first person to know what the doctor said should be her husband, Daniel. He'd probably be upset too when he heard the news.

She turned toward the window again. *If I have to give up sugar, then I may as well quit baking sweet snacks and desserts. I bet that won't go over well with Daniel either. He likes sweets almost as much as I do.*

That evening when Daniel came home from his job at Keim Lumber in Charm, Martha greeted him at the door. Even though she dreaded sharing her unsettling news, Martha tried to remain composed as she wiped her clammy hands on her apron. *Sure wish things would've been normal with my blood work.*

"How was your doctor's appointment?" Daniel asked after giving her a hug. "Did you get the results of your blood test?"

"*Jah*, and they weren't good."

His eyes widened. "What's wrong?"

"Come inside and I'll tell you about it."

Daniel stepped in, and Martha shut the door. After he hung up his straw hat and jacket, he followed her into the living room and took a seat in his favorite overstuffed chair.

Martha seated herself on the couch. "My blood work shows that I'm pre-diabetic. The doctor said if I don't eat right and exercise, I could end up with diabetes." Her chin quivered. "I'll have to give up sugar and go on a low-carb diet."

"That shouldn't be so hard. It's not like he said you'd have to stop eating."

Martha's face tightened and she crossed her arms. "But I can't have refined *siesses* anymore, and you know how much I like sugar."

He nodded. "As do I. However, your health comes first, and if it means giving up sweets, then so be it."

She sat quietly staring at the floor.

"Did ya hear what I said, Martha?"

"Jah, I did."

"Then why the long face?"

"Besides changing my diet, the doctor wants me to get more exercise." She grimaced. "You know I'm not good about sticking to an exercise plan." Martha thumped her plump stomach. "Guess that's why I never seem to lose any weight."

"Well, if you eat right and exercise, then I'll bet you will lose some weight and you'll no doubt feel better."

"You're right, but I don't know if I'll have the willpower to do it." She sighed deeply. "I've never had much self-control when it comes to desserts. Even if I don't bake any sweets here, whenever we go out to supper or eat at one of our friends' houses, or at some of the local functions, I'll be tempted. I may not be able to resist the temptation."

"If you want your blood sugar to go down, then you'll have no choice but to practice self-control." Daniel's forehead wrinkled as he stared hard at her. "I'm sure our grown children would agree with me on this."

Martha realized her husband wouldn't back down. He expected her to do as the doctor said, and most likely would remind her of it. Daniel might even enlist the help of their three daughters. Martha didn't like the thought of being lectured or reminded about her health condition. What she desired most right now was empathy from Daniel. *If only he could say to me, "You poor thing. I'm so sorry that you're going through all of this. If I could,* Fraa, *I'd take the whole situation away from you."* But that wasn't her husband's way of expressing himself. Martha would need to find another source to soothe her unease. Although Daniel loved her and did many good deeds on her behalf, he didn't always react to things the way she would like.

Martha smoothed her apron down over her plain blue dress and stood. "I'd best check on supper." With her head down, she shuffled out of the room.

That evening after supper, Martha took out the chocolate cake she'd made yesterday. The mocha icing looked so good it was almost impossible to resist eating a piece. She cut one for Daniel and placed it on a plate, along with a fork. *This is so unfair. My husband can continue eating the way he likes, but not me.* Her jaw clenched. *I don't like giving up my old lifestyle and not getting to eat and live the way I'm used to doing.*

Martha drew a deep breath, savoring the mingled aromas of the cholate cake with its flavorful frosting. Her mouth watered as she eyed the dessert sitting there looking so inviting. *What would it hurt if I had a small slice?*

She got out another plate as quietly as possible. *I'll eat it here in the kitchen so Daniel doesn't see, and then I'll take his piece of cake out to him.* With haste, Martha cut a thin slice and plated it. She had to admit, her plan was working so far. In seconds, she'd be enjoying this yummy delight.

Martha forked a piece of cake and was on the verge of putting it in her mouth when Daniel came into the kitchen. "What are you doing?" He pointed at her.

Martha's face warmed. "I—I was only going to have a small piece. Surely that won't hurt."

"It's made with sugar, right?"

She gave a slow nod.

"Didn't the doctor say sugar has no place in your diet?"

"Well, yes, but I'm only pre-diabetic. If I had actually been diagnosed as diabetic, then I'd be more careful."

Daniel tapped his foot. "You're not off to a very good start, Fraa. If you keep eating things you're not supposed to, eventually your blood sugar will soar out of control."

"Karen Miller's a diabetic, and she eats sweets. I've seen her do it at some of our community functions."

"So if your neighbor gets up on the roof and jumps off, does that mean you should do it too?"

She touched the base of her throat. "What does that have to do with anything?"

"You know perfectly well what I meant."

"Jah." Martha dropped her gaze to the floor. "I guess giving up sweets is going to be harder than I thought."

Daniel slipped his arm around her. "I will pray for you and ask God to help you use self-control."

"It won't be easy, that's for sure." Martha handed Daniel his piece of cake and hers too. "While you're eating both pieces of *kuche* with a cup of coffee, I'll fix myself some herbal tea." She poked her stomach. "Truth is, I'm still really full from supper."

He smiled and gestured to the remainder of the cake sitting on the counter. "How about if I take the rest of the kuche to work with me tomorrow and share it with my coworkers? That way it won't be here to tempt you."

She gave a silent nod. Daniel might be saving her from eating more of the cake, but there were still some peanut butter cookies in the cookie jar he didn't know about.

The following day, while Martha was washing the breakfast dishes, she looked out the kitchen window and saw a horse and buggy coming up the lane. After it stopped at the hitching rail, she saw her friend Regina get out of the buggy. *I'm not in good spirits this morning, but I sure could use a friend to talk to right now.*

Martha waited until Regina's horse had been secured, and then she went out the back door and waited on the porch until her friend joined her there.

"*Guder mariye.*" Regina smiled. "I came by to see how your doctor's appointment went yesterday."

Martha sank into one of the chairs on the porch. "Not well. The doctor informed me that I'm pre-diabetic, and I guess it's the reason I've been feeling so poorly lately." She went on to explain what he thought she should do in order to bring her blood sugar down.

"I'm sorry to hear this, but it's a good thing you're catching it now and will have a chance to do something about the problem before it gets any worse."

Martha's shoulders moved up and down as she sucked in air and blew it out in a rush. "I don't enjoy riding my bike that much, and walking alone holds no appeal."

Regina placed her hand on Martha's arm. "I'd be happy to walk with you if that would help."

"Oh, I couldn't ask you to take time out of your busy days."

"It's not a problem. I can come over three days a week for walks, and then maybe you can either walk by yourself on the other two days or take out your bike."

Martha smiled. "That's very kind of you. It will be more fun to walk with someone than all by myself."

"Sounds good. We can start tomorrow. I'll be over soon after breakfast." Regina looked over at Martha. "In the meantime, I hope you will do as the doctor said and watch what you eat."

"I'll try, but it won't be easy."

" 'Whether therefore ye eat, or drink, or whatsoever ye do, do all to the glory of God.' " Regina bobbed her head. "That's found in 1 Corinthians 10:31."

"I'll try to remember that." Martha squeezed her friend's hand. "*Danki* for coming over today."

"You're welcome. I want to be here for you."

"I appreciate that, because I'm sure I can't do this alone."

The following morning, Regina showed up a few minutes after Martha had finished cleaning the kitchen.

Martha went to the back door and opened it when her friend stepped onto the porch.

"Ready for our walk?" Wearing a bright-eyed smile, Regina rubbed her hands together and spoke in a bubbly tone.

Martha's hands and arms went limp as she gave a slow nod of her head. "Not really, but I guess I have no choice."

Regina tipped her head. "Well, you could ignore what your doctor said and sit here on your porch all day."

"No, I can't do that." Martha reached for her black outer bonnet and slipped it on over her white covering. "Okay, let's go."

The walk down the lane was no problem at all; Martha did it every day when she went to get the mail. It wasn't until they'd walked along the shoulder of the road a ways that she became winded, and it didn't help that Regina was walking so fast she could barely keep up.

Martha paused and took a few deep breaths. "Whew! I'm not used to this type of exercise. Could you please slow down?"

"Oh, sorry. I do a lot of walking, and I usually do it at full speed." Regina slowed her stride.

Martha couldn't believe what good shape her friend was in. Regina had turned sixty-two last month. Martha was a year behind her, but there was no way she could keep up with her enthusiastic friend. It was no wonder Regina was so thin—the woman was full of energy.

"I didn't tell Daniel this, but the doctor told me that I need to lose twenty-five pounds," Martha said as they continued walking.

"Why didn't you tell your husband?"

"I didn't want him to remind me about it every day." Martha frowned. "I don't like being pressured."

"Of course not, but if Daniel knew about your need to lose that weight, I'm certain he would offer his support."

Martha shrugged and forced herself to keep walking. *Regina doesn't know Daniel as well as I do. If she did, she might understand why I don't want him to know. Daniel might think he's offering support, but it would most likely turn into nagging.*

When the women returned from their walk, Martha invited Regina to stay for lunch.

"I'd like to, but I have several errands to run, so maybe some other time."

"Okay. When did you want to go out walking again?"

"How about next Monday? We can go in the morning like we did today, if that will work for you."

"That should be fine." Martha placed her hand on Regina's shoulder and gave it a tender squeeze. "Danki for taking time to walk with me. I doubt I would have had the incentive to do it on my own."

"You're welcome. It was good exercise for both of us, and a nice chance to visit while we walked."

They hugged each other, and then after Regina untied her horse, Martha held it until her friend was in the buggy and ready to go.

As the horse and buggy headed down the lane, Martha turned toward the house. *Hopefully the walking did me some good. I didn't realize how out of shape I've allowed myself to get. Wish I'd taken the time to exercise more. Now I'm paying the price for neglecting good eating habits and not getting proper exercise.*

It was hard not to feel sorry for herself, but Martha knew people would likely be watching her. They'd notice how she handled this new challenge that had crept unexpectedly into her life. She needed to choose the right way of dealing with the problem, but first Martha had to address something else. Her stomach had begun to growl, reminding her that it was time to fix lunch. Thankfully, Daniel had taken that chocolate cake when he'd left for work this morning; otherwise Martha might have been tempted to sneak a piece. Eating right and getting enough exercise were most certainly going to be a challenge.

A week later, after walking with Regina three more times and doing some walking by herself, Martha felt discouraged. She hadn't lost a single pound. In addition to that, she sometimes became weak and shaky.

Maybe it's because I've been eating more than usual, Martha told herself when she entered the kitchen Friday evening to fix supper. Although she'd been getting the exercise she needed, Martha often felt hungry and snacked a lot. She tried to avoid anything with sugar, but sometimes, like this afternoon when she had spotted a candy bar in the pantry, she slipped up. Of course, guilt took over when it happened, making her feel even worse.

Today when Martha said goodbye to her friend, she'd come inside and fixed herself two ham and cheese sandwiches, plus she'd eaten half a bag of potato chips. Although the meal wasn't full of sugar, it did contain a lot of carbs, which could contribute to weight gain.

Now, as she stood in front of the kitchen sink peeling carrots, tears dribbled down her cheeks. *Why can't I control my desire to eat too much and gobble down things that aren't good for me? What is making me unable to practice self-control?*

"I'm home," Daniel called as he stepped in the door. "What's that good smell in my fraa's kitchen?"

Martha turned to face him. "It's the chicken and potatoes baking in the oven. I also have peas cooking on the stove, and I'm getting ready to cut up some fresh carrots as a side dish."

"Sounds like a tasty meal awaiting us."

"Jah, but there won't be any dessert. By the time I woke up from my afternoon nap, there was no time for me to bake a cake, pie, or cookies."

"It's okay; I don't need dessert, and neither do you." Daniel hung his straw hat on a wall peg. When he turned to look at her again, his lips formed a frown. "You look a bit heavier than you did a week ago. I figured since you've been walking three days a week with Regina, and the other two days on your own, you would have lost some weight, not gained."

Heat flooded Martha's face as she glared at him. "So you think

I look fat, huh?"

"I didn't say that. Just said it looked like you've gained some weight. Specifically around the middle," he added. "I hope you haven't been eating things you shouldn't."

Martha's spine grew rigid, and she turned quickly to resume peeling the carrots.

Daniel moved closer to her. "Didn't mean to accuse you. I just thought. . ."

"I know what you thought," she mumbled. Her conscience pricked. "I may have eaten a few things that aren't good for me, but with all the exercise I've been getting, I should be losing weight, not gaining."

"But if you're eating wrong. . ."

"I'd rather not talk about this right now. Can we please change the subject?"

"Sure, but right now I'm going to get washed up for supper."

"Okay. Everything should be ready in about ten minutes."

When Daniel left the room, Martha opened the oven door and checked the chicken and potatoes. Both were done, so she turned the oven off and set the table. It wasn't right to get so upset over her husband's words, but he had no idea what she was going through. She'd been eating sweets since she was a young girl, and it was hard to give them up and eat only healthy things now. Martha wasn't sure she would ever lose weight or lower her blood sugar. She could only imagine what the doctor would say when she went back after more blood work had been done and it showed she had gotten worse.

The following Sunday during church, Martha's ears perked up when the minister who was speaking brought up the topic of temperance, along with the mention of temptation.

"Not everyone's temptation is the same," the elderly minister said. "We all have different weaknesses. We need to figure out what our temptations are and then avoid situations where we might be tempted."

Martha thought about the last time she'd gone to the grocery store, and she'd lingered in the candy aisle so long that she'd finally weakened and bought a candy bar.

Then there was the day she'd stopped for lunch at a restaurant not far from home and had ended up eating a small dish of ice cream.

"When we allow ourselves to be in situations that are tempting, we set ourselves up for failure. Our human nature is weak, and we too often yield to temptation. Of course, God can help us, but we need to help ourselves too." The minister's booming voice pulled Martha's thoughts aside.

"In Matthew chapter 4, Jesus overcame temptation," the man continued. "If we lean on the Lord and claim His strength, not our own, He will help us. It will get easier with each step we take away from temptation and help us resist the next time it comes our way. In order to have temperance, which we often refer to as 'self-control,' we must call upon God for strength."

Martha squirmed on the backless wooden bench. *Does the minister know about my problem with a lack of self-control? Did he preach that message specifically for me?*

That afternoon, when Martha and Daniel arrived home from church, she turned to him and said, "I'm tired. Think I'll go to our room and take a nap."

"If a nap is what you need, that's fine by me. I'm going to head outside and sit on the porch for a while." He grinned. "Maybe I'll practice my birdcalls while I enjoy the pleasant spring weather."

"Good idea. You're good at bird calling, and I wouldn't be surprised if some of the birds answer you back."

"I hope so." Daniel stood up from his chair. "Well, you have a good nap."

Martha smiled and headed down the hall to their bedroom. Once inside, she closed the door and took off her shoes, as well as her head covering. When she stretched out on the bed and closed her eyes, her whole body relaxed.

Although she felt tired, sleep wouldn't come. Martha's thoughts were filled with the message she'd heard this morning on temperance and temptation. *Sugary foods are my weakness, and I need to stop buying and baking things made with sugar and find some substitute sweeteners that won't spike my blood sugar.*

Martha thought about their bishop's wife, Elaine, who had type 2 diabetes and was very strict about her diet, unlike Karen Miller. *Perhaps I can get some recipes from her. I need to do my part in staying away from temptation. From now on, I will be more self-controlled, because I'm going to rely on God's promise that He will provide a way of escape.*

Monday morning, with new determination, Martha headed out the door for her walk with Regina.

"There's a spring in your step this morning that I haven't seen before," her friend commented as they walked down the lane. "Did you have an extra cup of *kaffi* to give you more energy?"

"I didn't have any coffee at breakfast, and I don't have much energy. What I do have is a hope that I can do this with God's help." Martha swung her arms as she trudged on. "Yesterday's sermon on temperance and temptation spoke to my heart."

Regina nodded. "I think it spoke to most of us in attendance. At some time or another we all have to deal with things that involve self-control."

"Giving up sugar and high-carb meals has been a real struggle for me," Martha admitted. "I've weakened several times and had to start over. But our minister's message made me realize I can't do this in my own strength. So I'm going to begin each morning with prayer, asking

God to give me strength to resist temptation every day."

"Good for you." Regina gave Martha a pat on the back. "I have a feeling that in no time at all, you'll be feeling much better and your blood sugar will drop to where it should be."

Martha walked an extra mile that day, and when she returned home, she stumbled into the kitchen, exhausted and hungry. It wasn't quite lunchtime, so she cut up an apple and ate that.

Martha felt good about her choice for a snack, and also about the good walk she'd had with Regina. She enjoyed being with her friend, and the time went by quicker than when she walked alone.

After Martha finished the apple and drank some water, she went outside to see if the clothes on the line were dry enough to bring in. She was pleased to discover that the light wind had blown them all dry.

As Martha pulled towels off the line, a horse and buggy entered the yard. She was surprised when Elaine got out of the buggy.

"I left a message on your voice mail this morning," Martha said as Elaine approached.

The older woman smiled. "I know, and that's the reason I'm here." She handed Martha a manila envelope. "Here are several copies of some of the recipes I use with sugar substitutes. There are pies, cakes, cookies, and even a sugar-free candy. All of them are low on the glycemic index."

Martha smiled and took the envelope. "Thank you so much. I'm eager to give some of them a try. Maybe I'll surprise Daniel and fix a special dessert this evening."

Elaine chuckled. "I bet he won't even be able to taste the difference."

"I hope that's the case." Martha squinted against the sunlight. "He enjoys desserts, as do I, and it will be nice to have some once in a while."

"Jah, but here's a little warning." Elaine placed her hand on Martha's shoulder. "If you eat too many desserts—even the sugar-free kind—you could gain weight and or you might fall into the trap of eating the wrong kind of sweets when you're away from home. The need for sweets can become an addiction."

"I am well aware." Martha's forehead wrinkled. "I think I had already reached that point before I found out I was pre-diabetic."

"Please keep me posted on how you're doing, and if you need more encouragement or have any questions, just let me know."

"Danki, I will." Martha was pleased that she had someone else's support now too. It helped to know that others cared and she could talk to them about her problem.

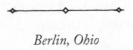

Berlin, Ohio

For the next two weeks Martha kept walking and watching her diet. On Friday evening, Martha knew her self-control would be put to the test. She and Daniel had gone to the Farmstead restaurant for supper, along with their daughter, Irene, and her husband, Richard. Due to Richard's work schedule and other obligations, they hadn't seen them for almost two weeks. Martha looked forward to catching up with her daughter's and son-in-law's lives, but being here, with so many tempting foods on the menu and buffet, gave her cause for concern. It would have been easier if she'd invited Irene and Richard to eat supper at her and Daniel's house, but Richard worked in Berlin, so meeting at the restaurant was convenient for him.

Martha studied the menu, looking for something that went with her new diet. Daniel, Irene, and Richard said they were going to choose from the buffet.

"Come on, Mom, you should have the buffet too. There are lots of food choices, so there's bound to be something you can eat," Irene said.

"Okay, I'll see what I can find." Martha and the others left their table and got in line for the buffet. Friday nights were always busy at the restaurant, and tonight was no exception.

When it was Martha's turn to get a plate and begin choosing what food to put on it, doubts filled her mind again. While there were several items she could have, like those on the salad bar, along with baked chicken and two kinds of cooked vegetables, there were also some foods she would have to bypass.

If only I didn't have to follow a strict diet. Martha clenched her plate tightly as she passed by several foods she used to eat and enjoy. *It's not fair that others can eat these good-tasting things and I'm deprived, although it's for my own good.*

She added an extra piece of chicken to her plate and moved on. *At least I won't go hungry.*

When their plates were full and they'd returned to the table, everyone bowed their heads for silent prayer. *Heavenly Father,* Martha prayed, *please help me not to be tempted to eat any of the dessert items on the buffet, and help me not to envy those who can eat whatever they want.*

When their prayers ended, Daniel leaned close to Martha and whispered, "You did well on your food choices. I'm pleased to see that you're sticking with your diet."

Her husband's encouragement put a smile on her face. "Danki. I'm relying on the Lord to help with my self-control."

"How about dessert, Mom?" Irene asked. "Will it upset you if we have any?"

Martha shook her head. "Feel free to do whatever you want." She gestured to her plate. "What I have here is plenty to eat, and I am not even going to look at the dessert bar."

"I'm not either." Daniel gave Martha's arm a light tap. "Your new eating habits have set a good example for me, and I'm content to eat the tasty sugar-free treats you've baked for us a few times." He gave his belly a thump. "In fact, since we've been eating differently, I've noticed that we've both lost a bit of weight, which is a good thing, jah?"

She nodded and offered him another meaningful smile. *Daniel is more thoughtful and nurturing than I thought him to be. I am fortunate to have such a good husband.*

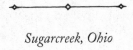

Sugarcreek, Ohio

"You're all smiles today," Martha's driver commented as they headed for Martha's home. "Did your doctor's appointment go well?"

"Yes, it sure did." Martha clasped her hands to her chest. "Not only have I lost ten pounds, but my blood sugar level has dropped into a normal range." She pointed to the new green dress she wore today. "After my weight began coming off, I had to make a few new dresses like this one I'm wearing. Now I just have to keep exercising and eating right so it stays that way, because I still need to lose another ten or fifteen pounds."

"Good for you, Martha. I'm glad your appointment went so well."

"Me too, but I couldn't have done it without the Lord's help."

"In what way?" Dottie asked.

"I've been standing on the promise of God's strength to help me with self-control, and with His help, I will continue to choose the right foods." A sense of joy radiated in Martha's chest. Taking care of her earthly temple would bring glory to God, and perhaps she could be an inspiration to someone else to make changes in their life that involved temperance. Martha could hardly wait to get home and share her good news with Daniel.

There hath no temptation taken you but such as is common to man:
but God is faithful, who will not suffer you to be tempted
above that ye are able; but will with the temptation also
make a way to escape, that ye may be able to bear it.

1 Corinthians 10:13

Wanda E. Brunstetter

New York Times bestselling and award-winning author Wanda E. Brunstetter is one of the founders of the Amish fiction genre. She has written more than 100 books translated in four languages. With over 11 million copies sold, Wanda's stories consistently earn spots on the nation's most prestigious bestseller lists and have received numerous awards.

Wanda's ancestors were part of the Anabaptist faith, and her novels are based on personal research intended to accurately portray the Amish way of life. Her books are well-read and trusted by many Amish, who credit her for giving readers a deeper understanding of the Amish people and their customs.

When Wanda visits her Amish friends, she finds herself drawn to their peaceful lifestyle, sincerity, and close family ties. Wanda enjoys photography, ventriloquism, gardening, bird-watching, beachcombing, and time spent with her family. She and her husband, Richard, have been blessed with two grown children, six grandchildren, and two great-grandchildren.

To learn more about Wanda, visit her website at www.wanda brunstetter.com.

Jean Brunstetter

Jean Brunstetter became fascinated with the Amish when she first went to Pennsylvania to visit her father-in-law's family. Since that time, Jean has become friends with several Amish families and enjoys writing about their way of life. She also likes to put some of the simple practices followed by the Amish into her daily routine. Jean lives in Washington State with her husband, Richard Jr., and their three children, but takes every opportunity to visit Amish communities in several states. In addition to writing, Jean enjoys boating, gardening, and spending time on the beach. Visit Jean's website at www.jeanbrunstetter.com.

Richelle Brunstetter

Richelle Brunstetter lives in the Pacific Northwest and developed a desire to write when she took creative writing in high school. After she enrolled in college classes, her overall experience enticed her to become a writer, and she wants to incorporate what she's learned into her stories. Her first published story appears in *The Beloved Christmas Quilt* beside stories by her grandmother, Wanda E. Brunstetter, and her mother, Jean Brunstetter. Richelle enjoys traveling to different places, her favorite being Kauai, Hawaii.

MORE FROM THE BRUNSTETTERS!

The Brides of the Big Valley

3 Short Stories of Love in a Unique Amish Community—Now a #1 *Publishers Weekly* Bestseller!

In an area of Pennsylvania called The Big Valley, a uniquely blended Amish community thrives in which three distinct groups of Amish identify themselves by the colors of their buggy's top—white, black, or yellow.

Join *New York Times* bestselling author Wanda E. Brunstetter, her daughter-in-law, and granddaughter in experiencing the stories of three young women who search for faith and love within this special place. Deanna is a widow who sees her second chance of love slipping away. Rose Mary is at a point in life where she must choose the path of her faith and the right man to walk with her on it. Leila is burdened with family responsibilities and wonders when she will ever start a family of her own.

Paperback / 978-1-68322-886-8 / $15.99